DEADLY PRIMROSE

Suzette A. Hill

severn House

This first world edition published 2020
in Great Britain and the USA by
SEVERN HOUSE PUBLISHERS LTD of
Eardley House, 4 Uxbridge Street, London W8 7SY.
Trade paperback edition first published
in Great Britain and the USA 2020 by
SEVERN HOUSE PUBLISHERS LTD.

British Library Cataloguing in Publication Data
A CIP catalogue record for this title is available from the British Library.

ISBN-13: 978-0-7278-9041-2 (cased)
ISBN-13: 978-1-78029-687-6 (trade paper)
ISBN-13: 978-1-4483-0412-7 (e-book)

Typeset by Palimpsest Book Production Ltd.,
Falkirk, Stirlingshire, Scotland.

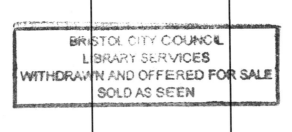
Please return/renew this item by the last date shown
on this label, or on your self-service receipt.

To renew this item, visit **www.librarieswest.org.uk**
or contact your library

Your borrower number and PIN are required.

Libraries**West**

ONE

1958. Charles Penlow's account

' I see Mrs Travers is dead,' I said to Primrose, passing her the evening paper as we sat in the lounge of the White Hart. 'Drink?'

'No, not as such, but you're pretty close,' I replied.

'How close?' she asked.

'By a number of waves, I should say.'

Primrose said that she had no idea what I was talking about and that given the lady's liberal consumption of vodka she was surprised she had been spared for so long.

'Oh no,' I explained, 'she didn't die *of* drink, she was *in* it; drowned in the sea while bathing at Birling Gap. It can get awfully rough there.'

Primrose set down her own glass and stared. 'You have obviously got it wrong, Charles; that can't be the same Travers woman who lives here in Lewes. I know for a fact she hates the sea. One only has to mention the word and she starts to go all green and peculiar.'

Primrose knows a lot of things for a fact but this was clearly not one of them. 'It's definitely the same,' I said. 'You can see for yourself.' And I pointed to the newspaper and its brief account of a Mrs Elspeth Travers of Needham Court, Lewes, having the misfortune to be found washed up on the beach a week previously. She was reported to have been wearing a black ruched swimming costume and pink floral cap.

My companion scanned the report with a sceptical frown. She sniffed. 'Well, all I can say is that she has been keeping that pretty quiet; always swore she couldn't swim a stroke and thought the seaside was greatly overrated. It is extraordinary the lengths some people will go to conceal their hidden vices.'

I remarked mildly that I couldn't quite see why sea bathing should be thought a vice; to which Primrose replied that presumably Mrs Travers considered it so, otherwise why should she have put up such a smokescreen? She also observed rather tartly that for one with such pasty features the choice of a pink swimming cap was clearly a mistake.

Not being au fait with these sartorial niceties and not wishing to sound contentious, I nodded and said that all the same it was rather bad luck and that I feared her twin sister, Alice, would feel the loss.

'I shouldn't think so,' Primrose said. 'Shock perhaps but not much loss; they were never especially close. Besides, they weren't real twins, I mean not the identical sort; just the same age and a passing resemblance, that's all – except that Elspeth was much slimmer and with better hair. They had little in common, neither character nor tastes.'

I was surprised at this, having always assumed the two had enjoyed a moderate sisterly affection and that like many twins shared some special bond. But Primrose informed me otherwise and said that this was yet another smokescreen. 'Oh yes,' she insisted darkly, 'reading between the lines you could see there was a fair bit of sibling rivalry going on there. One can always tell.'

I told Primrose that I bowed to her superior judgement in such matters; and then turning the conversation, enquired how she had got on in her recent visit to Baden-Baden.

'Baden-Baden?' she asked vaguely.

'Yes – where you were going to take the waters for your lumbago. How long were you there – a month or more? I hope it's done the trick.'

'Ah yes, absolutely,' she assured me. 'A *complete* cure.' She drained her glass and bent to disentangle Bouncer's lead from the table leg.

I congratulated her on the speed of her recovery but also expressed surprise at the problem's rapid onset: 'In my experience lumbago is one of those dreary pains that operate stealthily; it sort of creeps up on you slowly.'

She replied firmly that there are several varieties and that hers was not of the creeping kind; it had been the type to suddenly flare without hint or warning. She did not enlarge, and sensing this to be the end of the topic I took my cue and escorted her and the dog to the foyer whence we went our separate ways.

In the car driving home to Podmore Place (the ruined ancestral manor which Agnes and I are foolishly trying to renovate) I reflected on our conversation.

Two things puzzled me: firstly Primrose's obvious reluctance to elaborate either on her sojourn in Baden-Baden or indeed the lumbago attack which had prompted her visit there. Most people seem to take a sadistic relish in apprising one of the finer details of their back troubles, but in this respect Primrose had been mercifully reticent. But I could have done with less reticence about the charming German spa town that I had known before the war, and would have been intrigued to hear if it was still as I remembered. Yet she had been resolutely quiet on both topics. Strange really, as Primrose is a good raconteur and one might have expected more.

I was also curious about her assertion that poor Elspeth Travers had hated swimming. If that really were the case it did seem rather odd that the lady should have donned costume and cap (flattering or not) to sport among pounding breakers. As I had observed to Primrose, Birling Gap is not the safest of bathing places; and while dogs and wayward children may relish flinging themselves into the churning waters, it is not something one would have expected of a staid adult female – unless she happened to be a strong swimmer.

When I mentioned this to Agnes during supper, she immediately mooted the idea of suicide. (My wife has a lurid imagination which, linked to a ready tongue, can sometimes embarrass.) I objected that if that had been her intention she would hardly have needed the headgear. Agnes retorted that old habits die hard, and that anyway if I knew anything about women I would realize that whatever the occasion they like to be properly attired. And after all, she added, Mrs Travers might have changed her mind *in media res*, in which case she would have been only too glad to be thus equipped as it would save a visit to the hairdresser to rescue the perm.

Other than making some fatuous comment about such foresight being a credit to the Girl Guide movement, I said nothing. Alas,

there were more testing matters to confront than the sad fate of
Mrs Travers or her regard for contingency: the cistern in the
downstairs lavatory had collapsed, more woodworm had been
found in the east wing and the workmen had announced they
were taking yet another of their several holidays. Thus I drowned
my sorrows in coffee and in taking Duster for his evening scamper
. . . Actually this is not quite accurate, for the cairn was not in
scampering mood and wore the pinched expression of one baulked
of a more urgent pursuit: sleep. However, he deigned to clamp a
small stick between his jaws and we set off at a somnolent pace.

TWO

The Primrose version

Chatting with Charles Penlow in the White Hart had been
most pleasant and I like to think I had concealed from him
the fact that my four-week absence from Lewes had been
spent *not* in Baden-Baden, but in the south of France. It is true
that earlier I had intimated my intention of visiting that spa to
recuperate from spinal problems. But that had been a mere ploy
to cover my actual reason for rather hastily quitting the area: fear
of police harassment.

In the circumstances 'back trouble' had seemed as good an
excuse as any, and thus the German spa had been the obvious
place to which I might ostensibly de-camp. But given the strain
of my recent imbroglio with that evil little Latin master from
Erasmus House, the local prep school, and my abortive attempt
with aide-de-camp Nicholas Ingaza, (my late brother's erstwhile
friend/accomplice), to tip his corpse over Beachy Head, I felt
that a more lavish context was called for. Thus I had opted
for the fragrant warmth of the French Riviera – Nice to be precise.
This had proved an ideal choice. And many happy days were
spent at its lucrative casino, basking on the warm pebbled beaches
of La Grande Plage and recuperating with fearsome Sidecars in
the lounge bar of the Negresco. Yes, it had all been extremely

soothing and a splendid means of ridding my mind of the Lewes murders and my erstwhile fiendish adversary Hubert Topping . . . and my own (*entirely* innocent) part in the affair.[1]

It also took me far away from the officious attentions of Chief Superintendent MacManus, who, having failed to crack the case, was lugubriously sniffing at anything that came his way. And thus given my own inadvertent involvement and not wishing to be further disturbed, I had put away my paints, closed up the house and discreetly withdrawn the hem of my smock. With luck, I persuaded myself, by my return the fuss would have largely abated. Wisely, Nicholas Ingaza had also withdrawn – though in his case it had been to Tangier, a place rather more suited to his particular tastes than to mine.

Thus, holiday over and well refreshed, I returned to Lewes and carefully resumed my role of gracious lady-artist, being charming to all and sundry while daubing canvases with scenes of Southdown sheep and ancient rustic churches. 'Daubing' is perhaps an unduly modest term, for I have to admit that actually I do the job pretty well – or at least so the punters seem to think, especially the summer visitors. It is amazing the prices people will pay for what they fondly imagine to be local colour. My late lamented brother, the Reverend Francis Oughterard of Molehill, Surrey, once asked why my themes were so repetitive. I told him that if you had hit upon something that worked and from which money accrued, it was idle to waste time on experiments whose returns might be less solid. He had muttered something about the shadow of Mammon – which, given his own preoccupation with eluding the shadow of Mr Pierrepoint and his ready noose, I thought a trifle cheeky. (Fortunately dear Francis *did* elude the hangman and died heroically . . . but that, as they say, is another story.)[2]

Anyway, my two charges inherited from Francis – the cat Maurice and dog Bouncer – seemed moderately pleased to see my return, and for a day and-a-half I was accorded devoted attention. From the dog that is; the cat is devoted to no one. Still, even Maurice was minded to be polite for a while, a rare event.

[1] See *The Primrose Pursuit*

[2] See *A Bedlam of Bones*

Emily Bartlett, school secretary at Erasmus House, also gave me an unusually intelligent reception and supplied titbits of local gossip.

When in the course of her narrative I asked casually how the chief superintendent was progressing with the hideous dew-pond drama and the subsequent incident at the foot of the Downs[3], she said that as far as she was aware he wasn't. Apparently the press was silent, and he and his cohorts stonily unforthcoming. I have to say that was a great relief for, as earlier indicated, I was none too keen on being dragged into that particular scenario again! Of course, *should* the worst occur and MacManus become overly tiresome in his investigations I do have something nestling up my sleeve which might just inhibit further enquiry, or at least enquiry as affecting me. But that is for another day and with luck the day may never come.

Meanwhile, I am intrigued with Charles Penlow's news about Elspeth Travers and her chilly demise amid the swirling waters of Birling Gap. This strikes me as distinctly peculiar; for as I explained to Charles, she used always to declare how much she disliked the sea and was forever issuing dire warnings to those contemplating the pleasures of an ocean cruise. Indeed, I recall poor Peggy Mountjoy complaining bitterly that Elspeth's gloomy predictions had cast a pall of fear over the whole of her maiden voyage.

Naturally Charles paid no heed to my scepticism and instead muttered something about the sister's sad loss. Well, the sister may have sustained a loss but whether she finds it sad I rather doubt. As I observed to Charles, anyone could see the signs of their mutual antipathy (or at least *I* could; others are often less observant, especially Charles whose principal concern these days seems to be the renovation of Podmore Place, that dreary ruin he inherited). But as to the cause of the rift – well, it could be anything; although I suspect it stemmed from Elspeth being so much prettier than the sister and the latter being so much richer. Some sibling rivalries are of course inexplicable, just bred in the bone or fostered by a distasteful event in the cradle. Had perhaps

[3] See *The Primrose Pursuit*

one sleeping twin rolled on the other and never been forgiven? Or been beastly with its nappy? These days it seems fashionable to regard such trivia as being responsible for all manner of adult neuroses.

Fortunately, being five years apart, Francis and I had avoided such hostility – which isn't to say that the wretched boy couldn't be utterly maddening. I mean, fancy joining the Church and then being fool enough to erase one of his parishioners, that tiresome Fotherington woman! The consequences were most distasteful and caused mammoth inconvenience. It was just as well that Ma and Pa were no longer with us – they would have taken a very dim view and probably caved in under the strain. When I asked him why he had done it, he explained that she had been on his wick for some time and he had just wanted some peace and quiet. Well, I must say, that idea backfired all right! Still, it's all water under the bridge now and mercifully he has his peace . . . while I have the dubious legacy of his domestic pets – and the even more dubious friendship of his erstwhile goad and ally Nicholas Ingaza (*when* he elects to return from Tangier).

As to Mrs Travers, yes, it is indeed all very unfortunate. But I have to say that the *manner* of her passing still strikes me as odd, and I may make a few discreet enquiries in that direction. With so much incompetence about one feels compelled to take the initiative occasionally.

Rather to my surprise, incompetence is not something that can be ascribed to Eric Tredwell, Nicholas Ingaza's loud and louche companion. As with my late brother, periodically when trying to contact Ingaza in Brighton I have been forced to encounter this person via the telephone, and know the voice well though not the face. It is a voice of guttural timbre, grating vowels and unremitting good cheer. Indeed, it is good cheer of such relentless jollity that, with contact over, one is moved to seek respite in images of death or the more disheartening passages of the Bible.

Nevertheless, I have to admit gratitude to Eric, for it was his resolute good humour that enabled me to slip away to Nice free from concern for Bouncer and Maurice. Other than darts, beer and abetting Ingaza in the latter's more opaque transactions, Eric's particular passion is our four-footed friends. And it was this passion which prompted him to offer his services as their nursemaid while I was away. 'They'll be safe wiv me,' he had bawled, 'and what wiv His Nibs swanning off to Tangier, or gawd knows where, they'll 'ave the run of the house. It'll be Liberty Hall 'ere!'

The arrangement had worked surprisingly well, and prior to his own decampment Nicholas had been unusually cooperative in collecting not only the animals and their bedding, but even deigning to pack up their toys. And on my return from 'Baden-Baden' Eric had assured me that the three of them had spent a 'luvverly' time (although with Maurice as part of the trio I found that a slightly startling claim). When I suggested I should drive over to Brighton to retrieve the guests, he explained that owing to a vital darts match he could not be there but that he would get Phyllis to bring them to me the next day. When I asked who Phyllis was, he explained that she was his niece – ever so nice and that *everyone* knew her.

Thus, the following morning, I awaited with some curiosity the advent of the nice niece whom everyone knew. Eric had not said how she would arrive. By car or bus? Taxi from Lewes station? Not that it mattered really so long as she was punctual and delivered the creatures safely. Still, it's as well to know these things.

I soon did. For at precisely eleven o'clock there came the whine of an acerbic engine, and from around the bend in the drive appeared a motorbike – plus sidecar. Its rider, swathed in leathers, scarf, gauntlets and goggles, was unrecognizable; the occupants of the sidecar only too familiar. The dog sat erect, its snout in Pointer mode, while the cat clung perilously to its neck, tail wafting in the slipstream. From the hall window I watched with some alarm as the bike seemed to gather speed, and then with a screaming of brakes and tyres come to a spectacular halt a few yards from the front door.

Cautiously I opened the door and gave a tentative wave of welcome. This was reciprocated by a curt salute and a muffled voice shouting, 'Cor, that was a good 'un. A nice bit of drive you've got there, missus!' Phyllis sounded uncannily like her uncle.

'Er, yes,' I agreed politely, 'the gravel has only just been re-laid.'

I glanced at the now displaced pebbles and mangled border. However, the freight was delivered and the girl on time, thus who was I to cavil about a bulldozed terrain?

As the passengers hurled themselves from their carriage I enquired if she would like some refreshment – coffee perhaps or a dry sherry.

'Nah, never touch the stuff,' she said, unwinding her muffler, 'but I wouldn't say no to some pop.'

'Pop?'

'Yeah, soda pop – anything'll do but I like that new Pepsi best.'

I explained that Pepsi was rather too exotic for me but that I did have some orange Kia-Ora.

'That'll fit,' she said graciously, 'but I don't s'pose you've got some ice cream to shove in it? That'd be really good!'

As it happens, stuffed into the refrigerator's cramped icebox was a block of vanilla Lyon's Maid (a frozen offering from my friend Emily) and thus I was able to accommodate her request. It struck me as a peculiar mixture but it seemed to meet with her approval, and pushing up her goggles but remaining in the saddle, she demolished it with gusto.

'You are one of those artists, aren't you?' she asked. 'I quite like pictures, the bright ones I mean – can't stand that dismal stuff. Hey, just think, you could paint one of my Uncle Eric warts an' all.' She emitted a shout of mirth, a sound not dissimilar to those produced by her relative.

I explained that I didn't do portraits, tending to specialize in churches and South Down sheep.

'That's all right,' was the cheerful reply, 'he can dress up as a woolly ram. He'd like that, it would suit him no end!' There was a further guffaw followed by some violent revving. But before finally zooming off, she yelled, 'Your dog and cat, they aren't half cards . . . off their chumps if you ask me!' With a wave and deafening blast of the horn she thrust her steed back up the new-laid drive, and I was left morosely contemplating the ravaged gravel.

Back in the house I encountered the pair of 'cards' sitting quietly by the hall table. They looked sinisterly docile. 'Off your chumps, you are,' I said. Bouncer wagged his tail, while Maurice emitted an almost courteous mew.

THREE

Emily Bartlett to her sister

My dear Hilda,

Naturally one doesn't wish to sound uncharitable, especially as dear Primrose has only been back in Lewes for a week, but I have to admit that accompanying her and Bouncer to Birling Gap the other day was not one of life's better experiences. Far from it!

Until then everything had gone very well. She had returned from Baden-Baden in fine fettle and looking really sunburnt (suspiciously so, now I come to think of it . . . I didn't realize the German spa caught that amount of sun. Perhaps they use tanning machines there – or had she perhaps been further afield? If so, she certainly hasn't mentioned it). I also note that her back, which she had said was causing such trouble, seems in impeccable order and she has been striding about on those long legs fit as a fiddle. Presumably Baden, or wherever else she may have been, has done its work.

In her absence we had the unfortunate drowning of Elspeth Travers, which is very sad and very shocking. But on hearing of this Primrose was less than sympathetic. Admittedly she did say something like 'Oh dear what a shame,' but I don't think her heart was in it. And her mind certainly wasn't, for at the next moment she declared she didn't believe a word about its being an accident as the woman had hated swimming and that in any case had always expressed a particular dislike of that bit of the coast. When Primrose makes assertions of that kind I know better than to argue, so I said nothing and instead asked after the wretched Bouncer.

An unfortunate mistake, for this unleashed a spate of lavish narrative about the welcome the creature had given her and the seemingly good time it had spent in Brighton being looked after by some crony of that Ingaza man the picture dealer

– Eric, I think the name was. Frankly, I have never taken to Mr Ingaza, nor his pictures; and from what I hear, this Eric person sounds even more suspect. But then I cannot say that I am particularly taken with Bouncer either. There is something not quite right about that hound . . . However, the point is that Primrose insisted I went with her and the dog for a 'nice constitutional' at Birling Gap – which of course is where poor Mrs Travers met her death. Not having anything else to do that afternoon (the headmaster being busy administering copious sherry to the auditors) and glad to see our friend safely back from the Continent, I agreed.

Things began very cheerily. I was able to fill her in about the latest doings at Erasmus House – including Mr Winchbrooke's second contretemps with the police on the A27 and Bertha Twigg's unfortunate fall in the gym when attached to the high ropes. Primrose enjoyed that, saying that if Mr Winchbrooke insisted on zooming about like some ancient demon what else could he expect; and that she had always felt the gym mistress bore a striking resemblance to an orang-utan and did I know the old joke about brass monkeys? Naturally I said I didn't. Another mistake. Primrose thus insisted on recounting it at full volume and with wild gestures – a performance which nearly brought us off the road. The dog then bellowed its pennyworth from the back seat and I was practically deafened.

Fortunately the noise abated and we reached our destination in one piece. Once there we alighted to admire the view from the cliff and to let the dog run about. Run about? It promptly hurled itself over the edge like a Gadarene swine while simultaneously roaring like the Minator. Primrose meanwhile started to talk animatedly about her conviction that Mrs Travers' death at that spot was most strange if not downright suspicious. When I said mildly that I was sure the police would be looking into the matter and that Chief Superintendent MacManus was bound to have it in hand, she said darkly that in her view his eyes and hands were likely to be engaged elsewhere. I have no idea what she meant by that, but from the leer on her face I suspect it was something not quite nice.

Then just as I was about to draw her attention to the charming light over the Downs, she grabbed my arm and insisted that we follow the dog on to the shingle below as she wanted to inspect the site more closely. I can assure you, this did not appeal! That tiny cove offers nothing but rocks and fearsome breakers; and apart from the danger of twisting an ankle in the descent I had no intention of having my new suede shoes ruined. (They had been bought at nice Mr Riley's on the High Street and he had advised me most firmly against going near water.) Thus, disengaging my arm, I remarked that not having the agility of a mountain goat I was quite happy to remain where I was. Primrose pulled a face and clambered on down after the dog. The wind and waves were dreadful, so when I was hailed to join her I immediately averted my face and pretended to be absorbed in the scudding clouds.

Eventually she and the dog reappeared, each looking wild and sodden. We returned to the car, where the dog mercifully slept and Primrose again gave tongue about poor Elspeth Travers. 'There is something distinctly fishy about all this, Emily,' she declared. 'That woman was far too weedy to go anywhere near those waves let alone take a hearty dip. It just doesn't make sense.' Whether Elspeth's weediness was meant to include me as well I can't be sure, but the next moment she had uttered the dread words: 'I intend pursuing this.'

I say 'dread' because the last time Primrose went in pursuit of something (nice Mr Topping, the Latin master who suffered that unfortunate fate I told you about) it had all been rather trying – or at least her incessant questioning and suspicions had certainly tried me! Thus I gave a soothing smile and said brightly that I was sure it would all come out in the wash . . . Although actually I don't think she heard that, for in the next instant the car gave a stupendous lurch forward, and with a screech of tyres we had set off at an alarming rate. Mercifully, as we approached the main road the speed subsided, and I can thus report that passenger (and shoes) arrived home unscathed.

Your devoted sister,
Emily

FOUR

The cat's memoir

'She has bought me a new toy,' the dog said smugly. 'I expect it's a thank-you present for duffing up that Topping person – you know, her ENEMY who was nasty to her before she went away. I settled his hash, didn't I, Maurice!'

I regarded him in silence considering how best to reply. Finally I said, 'Yes, you did, Bouncer. We both did – for, as you may remember, it was my remarkable strategy that facilitated your assault.'

He leered. 'Ah, what you mean is that you made the bullets and I fired the buggers . . . you behind and ME in front!'

I must have looked doubtful, for he then said quickly, 'Anyway that's all over a long time ago' – six weeks actually, but unlike mine the dog's memory is frail – 'and now I want to show you my present.' He lunged off into the kitchen and returned with his trophy. It was, as I feared, *another* wretched toy rabbit.

'But you have several of those already,' I objected.

'Not like this,' he growled. 'If you knew anything about fake rabbits, Maurice, you would know that this one is very special.'

I asked him in what way special, remarking that except for the garish ribbon round its neck and pink fluorescent glow, it looked much the same as the others.

'Oh, I'll soon rip the ribbon off it,' he replied airily. 'No, it's not the collar that's special it's what it does. You see it's got something stuffed inside that makes it hop. Look!' He pounced upon the creature which emitted a sort of rubbery squeak before proceeding to lurch drunkenly across the floor. Bouncer studied its progress with bated jaw and twitching tail.

I have to admit that I was impressed by the performance and very nearly stretched out a claw to catch its rump in passing. However, I restrained myself, not wishing to get over-embroiled in the dog's puerile antics.

'Very nice, Bouncer,' I said, 'but I suggest you play with it sparingly otherwise it will lose its hop within the week.'

He had the grace to agree, and pushing it aside changed the subject: 'I'm glad the mistress is back. But we had a good time with the Gaza fellow's mate, didn't we? Plenty of grub in their house all right. And what's more he took me for a walk on that Brighton beach *three* times a day, regular as clockwork.'

'Indeed he did,' I replied. 'It was most restful with you both elsewhere . . . but how do you know it was three?'

Bouncer looked at me scornfully. 'I *can* count up to five you know! It's just the sixes and sevens that are a bit tricky, but I'm getting there. It's like what you say: "slowly, slowly catchee mousey".'

'I say no such thing,' I replied indignantly. 'What I say is *festina lente, carpe musam.*'

The dog snorted. 'It's all the same really – quick or slow you still catch the blighters, except of course when you have one of your off days.'

'I do not have off days,' I replied coldly. 'Just occasionally I am a trifle fatigued, that's all; it's the strain of living with you, Bouncer.'

He gave one of those inane grins, observed that it was a tough old life and resumed his appraisal of the rabbit.

I left the room, intending to lapse into sulk-mode, but was diverted by our mistress who had just come in from the garden trailing bits of twig and burrs. I think she had been hacking at the side hedge again. Humans do that – they have a mania for cutting things down; whereas personally I always feel that the more camouflage a garden has the better. It is one of the few preferences the dog and I share . . . Anyway, on seeing me she stooped down, and before I could take evasive action, had carried me off to the kitchen. Here she dropped me on the rug, and to my slight surprise produced a decent bowl of sardines. I say 'surprise' because it was rather early for supper and the sardines were unusually plump. Naturally one doesn't wish to be cynical, but I suspected such politesse was compensation for having abandoned us to the care of Eric – Ingaza's raucous friend who clearly has an affinity with Bouncer – while she had swanned off to Cod knows where. However, I have to admit that apart from the explosive lungs our temporary guardian had been quite affable, and thus I was only moderately displeased by the change in my routine.

As to the Brighton Type himself . . . well one is never quite sure about Ingaza's movements. He is one of those humans who plays his cards close to his chest (in this respect a little like myself perhaps) and contrives to be at once both elusive *and* ubiquitous with a habit of turning up when least expected – or, in my view, unwanted. Nevertheless, one had appreciated his presence during the recent rumpus with the Topping specimen, when he lent our mistress some mild moral support . . . though *moral* is not perhaps the most fitting term to apply to Ingaza. But he does have his occasional uses. Where he is now I do not know, and I can only hope that when he does reappear he will address me by a seemlier name than his usual *Scrag-arse*. 'Maurice' would be acceptable.

P.O's friend turned up today – the one called Emily and who reminds me of a startled goldfish (a species with which I am well familiar). They had lunch together, and at the end I overheard the visitor say something to the effect that it would be nice to conclude with some of the ice cream she had recently produced. Our mistress gazed blankly and then said curtly that they couldn't because she had already given it to a girl on a motorbike. The Emily person looked even more bemused than usual, and then distinctly pained. However, she said nothing and had to settle for some violently black coffee – which judging from my vantage point on the windowsill, was far from her liking.

From what I observe, the two women are not entirely attuned – or, as my grandfather used to say, as different as cod and coley.

FIVE

The Primrose version

'It will all come out in the wash,' my foot! There are times when I really do wonder about Emily. She may be a very good school secretary and soothes the headmaster's nerves, but she certainly doesn't mine. I mean what was she *doing* up there staring aimlessly at the clouds when she could have been down on the beach making a reconnaissance with me? I thought friends were supposed to give *support* in one's efforts to get at the truth. And just think if I had been knocked over by one of those whopping waves, a fat lot of use Emily Bartlett would have been – communing with the sky miles above!

Still, tiresome though she is, she does have her uses and can be quite companionable when she tries. And one must admit that the woman means well . . . though what was it that Pa used to say? 'Beware the good intenders'? It was something like that, but in Emily's case there's not really much to beware of . . . except perhaps those inane clichés!

Like dear Emily, Nicholas Ingaza can also be companionable but in his case I doubt if he tries and the intent is rarely good. But he is certainly more sharp-witted. And once he gets back from Tangier I must buttonhole him to discuss this strange business of Mrs Travers; he is bound to have a view however slewed . . . But meanwhile I might be able to glean something from the sister. I gather she has come down from London for the funeral and is staying with the Balfours – Melinda and Freddie – over at Firle. If I can avoid tedious Freddie I may be able to wangle an afternoon with Melinda and the grieving guest. Melinda has a library book of mine long overdue – an excellent reason to pay her a visit.

Well, well, that little venture paid off all right: I retrieved the library book, frightful Freddie was elsewhere, and the three of us spent an agreeable and – more to the point – profitable afternoon. That is to say it was profitable to me for I was able to give Melinda's guest my close attention, and thus by dint of dazzling charm and subtle enquiry learn a little more of the circumstances of her sister's death.

I had met Alice Markham only once previously, about a year ago when she was in the throes of putting paid to her husband of ten years, or he was putting paid to her; it wasn't entirely clear. Anyway, a divorce was pending and she had been in a rather febrile state – though whether from pique or relief it was hard to say. I recall a substantial amount of alcohol being consumed, a wedding ring tossed carelessly into the grate (the mammoth engagement sapphire being carefully retained), floods

of tears and gales of wild laughter. As a piece of cabaret –
Divorce à la Figaro – it had had its merits. But it had been
frustrating nevertheless, for I was at Needham Court in the
expectation of making up a bridge four, Melinda also having
been invited. But clearly Alice Markham had been much too
preoccupied to concentrate on the cards, and instead we had
listened to her inveighing against her husband and the baseness
of men in general.

During a brief interval while admiring the dahlias in the
garden, Melinda had whispered to me, 'I can't think why she's
complaining. After all, one gathers she's pretty well stacked and
I doubt if she'll lose out on the settlement – may even make a
profit. Ask her which of them is bringing the case.'

'I will do no such thing,' I had retorted, somewhat shocked
. . . and then of course spent the next ten minutes trying to
discover exactly that. It transpired that the husband was the
guilty party, ostensibly at any rate, having strayed once too
often; and that Alice like the proverbial worm – in this case a
rather rich one – had turned with a vengeance.

Anyway, other than the visitor's state of befuddled fury, my
principal recollection of that afternoon is of Elspeth Travers looking
palely elegant and her remarking it was such bad luck that in the
eyes of men pretty women invariably took precedence, and that
even wealth couldn't compensate for a dearth of good looks. She
had flashed her sister a smile of lavish sympathy which the latter
returned with a glacial (albeit slightly glazed) stare. I went away
with the distinct impression that despite the twin-ship there was
little love lost between the two women. This was confirmed to me
some months later by Elspeth Travers herself, announcing in smug
confidence that while both she and her sister were now without
consorts, at least she was *widowed* whereas poor Alice had 'the
silly stigma' of divorce hanging over her. Although speaking
ruefully of such social bias, it was perfectly clear that she rather
relished the distinction.

Well, since then a year has passed and the pretty widow is now
drowned, and the rich divorcée was seated plumply hale on
Melinda's sofa, sipping tea and consuming a large meringue. It
was just as well I hadn't taken Bouncer with me, for he too has

a penchant for such confections and it would have been unfortunate
had there been a clash of interests.

This time Alice Markham's demeanour was more orderly than
when last seen (the trauma/inconvenience of divorce having
presumably faded) and instead she presented an image of stoical
dignity . . . or she would have done were it not for the flakes of
pink meringue besmirching her lap and lapels.

'It must be simply ghastly for you, Alice,' I said earnestly,
'but I hadn't realized that your sister was such a keen swimmer.
I don't know why, but for some reason I always thought she had
an aversion to bathing . . . but perhaps I have mixed her up with
someone else.'

'Quite possibly,' the other replied casually. 'We were at board-
ing school in Eastbourne and learnt at the Devonshire Baths
there. Elspeth was rather good actually, always diving for
pennies and jumping from the springboard and challenging the
seniors to races. Occasionally we were allowed to the beach;
too cold for me, but Elspeth enjoyed it.'

She turned to Melinda and started to comment on the vicar's
sermon and the clumsiness of the pallbearers, the former being
apparently vacuous and the latter gross. Having been absent for
the event, I did not join in the conversation – and in any case was
too preoccupied trying to decide which of the sisters' aquatic
versions to believe. Their narratives were not exactly marked by
consistency.

Such discrepancy I would explore later. But my immediate
aim was to learn a little more of the circumstance of Elspeth's
unfortunate sinking. Thus during a pause in her sister's description of the funeral, I said, 'So you think she just decided to
go for a swim on a sort of whim, and then found she couldn't
cope? How dreadful to be all alone and to have that happen
to her. Had she told anyone of her intention? And what about
her clothes – where had she left them? On the beach?' (I had
visions of the rocks being strewn with beleaguered nether
garments.)

Alice hesitated before taking a further bite from her meringue,
and then said rather indistinctly, 'They had been left in the car:
her grey raincoat, a skirt and some underclothes. I suppose she
had driven there in her coat and swimming costume intending to

round I was quite surprised to see that the Prim had followed me. She had scrambled all the way down and was standing staring at the waves with her feet apart and hands on her hips. She had got that stern look on her face that generally means trouble, and at first I thought she was going to give me a wigging. But she just kept gazing at the sea and the rocks, and then turned and shouted to the Enema person who was hovering about on the turf above.

'Come down here, Enema,' she bawled, 'and you'll see for yourself.' Well I don't know what Enema was supposed to see but she didn't come. Just shaded her eyes and looked the other way. It was as if she hadn't heard – but *I* know she did hear. We dogs are good at sensing when humans are playing silly beggars.

It was obvious that the Prim didn't like her just standing up there, because she started muttering and hurling pebbles into the water. And then when it was time to go she didn't half make a cat's cradle of getting up the cliff again – huffing and puffing, slipping and cursing. A right old fuss she was making. I think Maurice is right: there is something about human beings that makes them a bit *slow*, and it's what the cat calls CON . . . CON-GEN-IT-AL. At least I think that's the word; it means bred in the bone. (Trust the cat to avoid mentioning bones – he hates 'em!)

Still, the mistress wasn't slow to give an earbashing to Enema when we were back in the car. I couldn't understand it really, but she seemed to be saying that she had expected her mate to give her more *sport*, or at least that's what it sounded like . . . Funny really, as I don't think her friend is the sporting type. I mean, she never throws any balls for me or runs a race when I want her to; and when I once offered her my rubber ring to inspect all she did was squeak and cry 'UGH!'

Anyway, after the Prim had stopped grumbling that she wasn't getting any sport, she calmed down and started to burble about somebody called Travers who was dead and that it was all nonsense. The Prim often says things are nonsense, so I didn't pay much attention and went to sleep. But now I am back in my basket and have had time to think, I've got this feeling that she is on the trail of something and is sort of scenting the air like I do when I get the whiff of a funny smell. The last time she got a whiff of something there wasn't half a shindig. I quite like shindigs but the cat can get tetchy; so I won't say anything to Maurice just yet. But meanwhile Slyboots Bouncer will watch and wait . . . QUIETLY!

SEVEN

The Primrose version

Arriving home from my encounter with Peggy and the garrulous daughter, I was ready for the crossword and coffee. Neither materialized, for as I rounded the corner of the drive I was confronted by the familiar black shape of a Citroën Avant sprawled in front of the dining-room window. At the same window I caught a glimpse of the cat's face squashed angrily against the pane. For once I was pleased to see Nicholas Ingaza, but as usual Maurice was not.

My visitor explained that he had only just returned from his Tangier jaunt (headlong flight might be a more accurate term), and being in the Lewes area thought he would enquire if there were any evolutions regarding the Topping affair.

'If you mean is the coast clear, and can you continue your *unimpeachable* life without let or hindrance from the law, then I think the answer is "so far so good",' I told him. 'I have only been back a short while myself, but it would seem that the initial excitement has died down and that no one, least of all Superintendent MacManus, is any the wiser about Topping's dastardly deeds – or indeed our enforced manoeuvres in the matter.'

He gave a wary smile. 'Well, I suppose that's promising. Still, it doesn't do to relax one's guard: it's amazing how obstinate the authorities can become when faced with a blank wall. They'll snatch at any straw, however innocent, to create an illusion of progress.'

'Exactly,' I agreed, 'one cannot be too careful. After all, just think of the way that wretched little Sergeant Sidney Samson hounded poor Francis in Molehill, always sneaking around and being disagreeable.'

Ingaza raised a hesitant eyebrow. 'Ye-es . . . but then Francis wasn't exactly innocent, was he – or at least not in any conventional sense.' He paused fractionally, and I thought I heard him murmur, 'Or in any sense really,' but I affected not to hear. 'Whereas,' he continued, '*we* have merely infringed one or two regulations of civic protocol by attempting to dispose of a body expired on your premises in unforeseen circumstances.'

'*Most* unforeseen,' I exclaimed. 'I mean, really when one considers—'

'Yes, yes,' he cut in impatiently, 'but we don't want to go over all that again, do we; my nerves won't stand it . . . Now, what I suggest is that to parry any future threat we toast our discretion with a soothing glass of your late parent's whisky – and not that dreary grocer's stuff you keep for the vicar. As Winston Churchill doubtless said: the stronger the measure the better the effect.' He gave a sly grin, and I dutifully fetched a bottle and two glasses.

When I returned he was gazing abstractedly out of the window and seemed unaware of my presence. Hmm, I thought wryly, doubtless still reliving the recherché delights of Tangier. And for a few seconds my own bolthole – Nice and its sun-bleached *plage* – floated before my eyes . . . Strange really, the way that one's most recent locations can exert such an insistent hold whatever the distance.

And then setting down the drinks, I asked brightly, 'Your Aunt Lil, is she still looking for a fancy man?'

The question evidently destroyed the guest's reverie; for turning from the window he replied morosely, 'Huh, she's found one all right.'

'Well, that lets you off the hook a bit, doesn't it? Presumably no more Saturday afternoon jaunts to the Eastbourne bandstand.'

There was a tired sigh. 'Actually, Primrose, he is ninety and a rugger-bugger.'

'Oh well, as long as it's only rugger I can't see the problem,' I said gaily. 'It must give you some respite.'

'Far from it,' was the acid reply. 'I am now expected to drive the pair of them to muddied fields to watch muddied oafs chucking a misshapen ball in the air. Give me the frigging bandstand any day.' He gazed gloomily at Maurice, who promptly hissed.

The idea of Nicholas squeezed between two antediluvians bawling their heads off and waving lurid woollen scarves while a mob of hefty rumps vied for a piece of leather, was not easy to conjure. However, a partial image did emerge and I started to grin. 'I get the picture,' I said. 'All very *trying*, as the referee might say!'

He rolled his eyes to the ceiling. 'Your wit will slay me, Primrose. Execrable puns: it's an Oughterard trait, I suppose. Francis was just as bad.'

I shrugged. 'I was merely attempting to divert you from recounting your Tangier activities.'

He leered. 'Ah, not for your ears, dear girl. Not for yours.'

'In that case,' I said eagerly, 'I will tell you something of *mine*. Now, while we have both been absent something rather intriguing has occurred . . .' And giving him another slug of Pa's best, I embarked on the Travers event and my belief that all was not as it seemed.

The account took some time; and when I had finished Nicholas looked a trifle dazed, and observed in rather tired tones that he was sure I would deal with the matter in my inimitably subtle way, and meanwhile would I mind awfully if he drove on back to Brighton. 'All this exploration of foreign parts makes one a little fatigued,' he explained.

'Depends on the nature of the parts,' I observed mildly . . . and then added more sternly, 'I think you are being most uncooperative, Nicholas. After all, I believe you were acquainted with Mrs Travers, weren't you? She told me she had recently bought a couple of pictures from your *estimable* art gallery . . . though presumably not seascapes.' I nearly added, 'Rather a rash purchase on her part,' but fortunately prudence prevailed.

He nodded. 'Yes, a pair of Tom Calder's; he has become fashionable again.'

'Genuine?' I enquired.

Ingaza shrugged. 'I doubt if it matters: his stuff is so awful that even a fake would be preferable.'

'Fakes or not,' I said briskly, 'you had dealings with the woman and therefore ought to be concerned about her mysterious death.'

'Actually, Primrose, the only thing that concerns me at present is avoiding the eye of your pernicious cat. Old Scrag-arse has been staring at me for the last five minutes. It's an oppressive experience. And as to being mysterious – well, on the face of things it looks simple enough. For some reason, though perhaps a little untypically, the woman decided to take a swim and was drowned. End of story. Take a tip and leave things alone.'

'That's what you said about the Topping affair,' I reminded him tartly, 'and look what a can of worms my instincts dug up there!'

He closed his eyes and gave a slight shudder. 'All the more reason to control your instincts now. Despite the Moroccan sun, one still bears the scars of that last excavation; I don't think I could face another.'

'Huh,' I exclaimed, 'you could face anything provided it was lucrative.'

'Perhaps. But that's just it: there never was any chance of lucre – either filthy or fragrant. And in this case I certainly cannot see the drowned Mrs Travers yielding anything useful whatever the circumstances . . . No, dear friend, I am afraid Nicholas Ingaza must leave the bloodhound business to you and resume his "unimpeachable" life – as you so kindly put it – flogging pictures to the gullible and feeding the aesthetic egos of the pretentious.' He winked. 'A bit like your business really.'

'*Not* like mine,' I retorted. 'At least I paint my own pictures; you have to procure yours.'

'Ah well,' he sighed, 'each to his own artistry . . . Now, Primrose, I really must be off. There's a limit to how long one can stand the stare of that cat.'

He drained his glass and stood up. 'Take my advice: avoid the chief superintendent, forget Travers, and stick to painting sheep and church steeples. Far safer . . . Oh just one more thing: you owe me for the dog food your hound consumed. Eric said he had never seen such a trencherman. I'll invoice you. Bysie-bye.'

Really, sometimes I could throttle Nicholas Ingaza! But equally I felt like throttling my gluttonous companion as he wandered in and settled heavily in front of the fire. 'See what you cost me, Bouncer,' I grumbled; 'you eat twice the amount of any normal dog. It's disgusting!' He burped gently and closed his eyes.

EIGHT

The Primrose version

The Penlows were giving their annual drinks party, invariably a congenial affair. And held at noon and with Agnes's choice of caterers being impeccable, it meant that no one had to face the chore of lunch. In fact, I suspect that, sated with sherry and canapés, most guests skipped the afternoon altogether and retired to their beds until the six o'clock G&T. (Not a practice of mine, having far too much to do: haranguing the town clerk, for example.)

Anyway, it was a jolly little get-together and as always a plentiful source of gossip.

Inevitably one such source was Melinda Balfour, looking really rather svelte in a perky red hat (Freddie Balfour mercifully absent massacring the Seaford golf course). Discoursing on the marital difficulties of a mutual acquaintance, Melinda was inveighing against the multiple defects of the husband. I vaguely knew the woman but had never met the defective spouse, and hadn't realized he was so dire.

Melinda must have seen my look of surprise, for adjusting her hat to an assertive angle, she leant towards me. 'Oh yes,' she breathed, 'he was *unspeakable*, you know.'

I was intrigued. 'Oh really?' I said brightly. 'In what way?'

'I couldn't possibly mention it,' she said darkly, 'but I am sure you can imagine.'

As it happens, I couldn't especially . . . After all, there are so many options, and I really wasn't prepared to waste my time dwelling on colourful hypotheses. Instead I asked when she had last seen him.

She closed her eyes fractionally and then opening them, said, 'I had that misfortune at the Parrys' party about a month ago. He was being beastly to the dog.'

'Oh dear,' I said, 'did it complain?'

She shrugged. 'No more than anyone else: he was being beastly to everyone – rude, sarcastic and boorish. And then, all of a sudden, he left, dragging Octavia alongside. Why that woman puts up with him is beyond me. I mean, either she is utterly gutless and sees herself as some kind of latter-day holy martyr *or* she derives a perverse enjoyment. Frankly, having known her mother, I rather suspect the latter. It's amazing what gives people pleasure.' Her eye swept the room and fell on the commanding figure of Chief Superintendent MacManus dragooned into a corner by Emily. 'Take him for example,' she murmured. 'I have it on good authority that when off-duty he spends most of his time collecting Mongolian postage stamps and sticking them into an album. Does it for hours apparently.'

'Goodness!' I said, genuinely surprised, my own information being slightly more lurid. 'So when does he find time to go to Bognor?'

She looked puzzled. 'Bognor? Why on earth should he want to go to Bognor?'

For a moment I was flustered, realizing that I had made a most stupid gaffe. MacManus's activities in the backstreets of Bognor – as reported by Nicholas Ingaza during our previous imbroglio, the Topping affair – had involved the patronizing of an establishment primly termed a place of ill-repute (though apparently 'knocking shop' is the favoured nomenclature these days) and whose speciality, as I had subsequently discovered, was the enactment of playful charades. Such frivolities included the donning of a pantomime bear suit and being chastised by a lady dressed as an ostrich clad in silver lamé tights. Quite by chance photographs featuring the superintendent thus engaged had once come my way, and which in the interests of safety I have retained. After all, *trouvailles* of that kind should be accorded a proper respect . . . having, what Ingaza might term, insurance potential.

Naturally I could hardly divulge this to my companion, so instead said hastily that I thought he visited Bognor for recreational purposes (true enough, one might say) – something to do with ice skating or was it perhaps amateur dramatics? I sounded suitably vague and quickly turned the conversation to other matters: her recent success in the Eastbourne cake-making competition. The result was tedious and sickly, but at least it covered my indiscretion.

The cake saga finished we were about to split up, but were joined by Melinda's bosom pal Blanche Aubrey. After the rapturous greetings, the latter glanced towards the plump figure of Alice Markham, who, despite the plumpness was looking rather smart in a blue tailored two-piece. However, this clearly did nothing for Blanche's discerning eye. 'My dear,' she murmured to Melinda, 'diamonds in the daytime? *Not* what Lewes is used to.' Briefly her fingers fluttered to her throat to adjust her own unimpeachable pearls.

'Perhaps she has an early dinner engagement in London,' I ventured.

'Can't think with whom,' Melinda replied charitably.

Neither could I. But I was less interested in Alice's social calendar or the outré diamonds than the fact that she had positioned herself at MacManus's elbow and was clearly intent on manoeuvring Emily aside. The latter stood her ground and affected not to notice the interloper. Despite her twitterings Emily can sometimes be surprisingly bolshie, a useful trait in a school secretary, especially one employed by Mr Winchbrooke at Erasmus House. But she had met her match in Alice who, with wider girth and ringing laugh, quickly attracted the chief superintendent's gaze. Doubtless he had told one of his ponderous jokes at which normally no one laughs.

As the others wafted away I was joined by the Reverend Albert Egge, who, unlike my late brother, is endowed with a relentless bonhomie. 'Quite a little gang here,' he chortled. 'I trust this means there will be a good turnout for tomorrow's service. I've sweated hours over the sermon!'

'Oh, bound to be,' I said with a smile, gesturing to an empty tray, 'after all, we shall all be so indebted for those lovely éclairs you have brought.' I must explain that among Egge's secular devotions is a lust for patisserie both its consumption and its making, and from which his flock will sometimes benefit.

'Exactly. Got it in one, Miss Oughterard! What one might call a sort of quid pro quo, a sound working arrangement: pieties in return for bonbons. Pull 'em in somehow, that's my motto. The good Lord moves in mysterious ways: it's all to do with ways and

I nodded, but pressed my query. 'So where is the son now? Did he feature at the funeral?'

Melinda ruminated. 'Well, not noticeably . . . though I do recall Alice having some young man in tow: tall with fair hair, and I suppose he did look a bit like Elspeth now I come to think of it. Still, if it *was* the son he can't have stayed for long; he wasn't at the bun fight afterwards. I think he must have slipped away immediately after the service.' She paused, and then gave a broad wink. 'But I tell you who was there, though only for a brief time – the *boyfriend.*'

I must have looked bemused. 'Didn't you know?' she asked. 'There was definitely a "follower" in Elspeth's life – although whether *free* to follow one wouldn't know.' She leered.

'Who?' I asked. 'Do you mean someone local?'

'Oh yes, local all right . . . Reginald Bewley.' The words held a glint of triumph.

'Who's he—?' I began, unimpressed, and then stopped as light dawned. 'Surely you don't mean *Bewley*, chairman of the town council?'

'That's the man,' she replied breezily. 'They had become rather matey over the last few months, although naturally one doesn't like to . . .'

What Melinda liked or did not like was undivulged, for at that moment her eye fell on Duster, Charles Penlow's mournful cairn terrier, grimly laying siege to her handbag. Recklessly she had put it on the floor while balancing her plate. The creature's hind leg hovered speculatively; but with a yelp of horror Melinda intervened. Both dog and owner assumed expressions of pained surprise and hastily melted in the direction of the French windows.

'Typical,' she seethed, 'the Penlows dote on that dog and it thinks it can do anything it wants!'

I was about to remark that naturally my Bouncer was far more mannerly in that respect; but the smug lie went unheard, for having snatched up her precious Rayne handbag, Melinda was clearly all set to leave. And thus the Bewley topic was left hanging tantalizingly in the air . . .

However, the reference stayed in my mind. And on the way home while giving Emily a lift back to Erasmus House, I

remarked casually that I hadn't realized that Mrs Travers and
Reginald Bewley had been friends. 'He seems a curious choice,'
I murmured.

'Just because you can't stand the town clerk,' Emily observed
rather tartly, 'there's no reason to disparage the council's
chairman. Personally I think he is rather a pleasant gentleman,
very courteous – he always lifts his hat to me. And after all, he
does keep Lewes on an even keel. That's so important, wouldn't
you say?'

'An even keel,' I mused. 'I'm not entirely sure what you mean
by that. If you mean its equilibrium is maintained by having the
litter bins painted a lurid yellow and by endorsing the rates increase,
then I suppose he has his uses – though I have to admit they are
not *my* uses.'

Emily sniffed and tut-tutted. 'Oh really, Primrose, you can be
so critical at times! I mean to say . . .' The words trailed off, as
reaching the school gates she began to collect her things and I
was able to decant her without suffering further reproof.

Later that evening I telephoned Nicholas. 'It's all getting very
peculiar,' I said.

'What is?'

'This Travers business. Apart from the sister I haven't met a
single soul who has said that she definitely liked swimming –
quite the reverse, in fact.'

There was silence from the other end. 'So what do you think?'
I urged.

A weary sigh filtered down the line. 'What I think is immaterial;
you will pursue it just the same.'

'Pursue what?'

'The bloody bee in your bonnet,' he rasped. 'Now leave me in
peace. I've got enough on my plate listening to Eric moaning about
his perishing darts match without having to listen to gossip from
sodding Lewes.'

'This is not gossip,' I retorted, 'it is my serious and shrewd
deduction. That woman's death was no accident, and I very
much doubt if it was suicide . . . Oh, and by the way, the Artists'
Guild of "sodding" Lewes is extremely keen to hear you lecture
on the "Intricacies of Attribution". They seem to imagine you

might have some insight and have asked me to chair the event. And incidentally, as they are currently in considerable funds you can expect a substantial fee – plus no doubt some new gullible clients.'

As I had hoped, Ingaza's tone turned from acerbic impatience to unctuous charm. 'My dear Primrose,' he oiled, 'what could be more entrancing: me dulcet-tongued on the podium, an enlightened audience, and you in the chair receptive and charming as always.' There was a pause, and then a little more sharply, 'How much do you reckon?'

I told him that that the exact sum would rather depend on my negotiating skill but I was sure the result would be to his satisfaction, i.e. walnuts not peanuts, and that it might be an idea if he were to drop in one afternoon to discuss things further.

It is amazing how compliant Ingaza becomes when there is a whiff of money in the air. And thus we briskly fixed a date of mutual convenience for him to come over to Lewes to 'discuss terms'.

NINE

The cat's memoir

'I've got a new friend,' Bouncer announced.

'Oh yes? And what is his name?' I enquired.

'Louis Lionheart.'

I gave a sceptical swish of my tail. 'Hmm. And what sort of name is that? It has a thespian ring.'

'Don't care what sort of ring it's got,' the dog answered truculently. 'It's a jolly fine name. It's what you might call, uhm . . .' He knit his brows clearly struggling for the word. 'PRESSING,' he barked, 'that's what it is, Maurice, PRESSING!'

'If you mean "impressive",' I observed, 'let us hope that his manner matches the name . . . I mean, for all we know he may have a *sheep's* heart.' I flashed him a kindly smile.

Actually, I don't think he found it especially kindly, for the next moment he roared, 'He has NOT got a sheep's heart, he is like a LION. And what's more, Maurice, if you're not careful I'll send him after you!'

Naturally there were a number of ripostes I could have made but it seemed prudent to emit an indulgent purr instead. As my esteemed grandfather used to say, there is no point in goading the natives when disadvantaged. Disadvantaged? I hear you ask. Yes, during a recent skirmish with an intemperate mouse I had the misfortune to sprain my left paw, the white one that I use for special effects. It would have been foolish to chance it further.

Thus, purr over, I suggested that Bouncer tell me more about his new friend. 'Is he big like O'Shaughnessy?' I enquired a trifle warily. (O'Shaughnessy was the Irish setter who had been the dog's bosom pal in our days with the vicar at Molehill; a wild and rumbustious creature whom Bouncer had idolized. If this Lionheart fellow was remotely like him I should need to take cover!)

Bouncer shook his head. 'Legs a bit shorter though he springs higher. But I tell you what, Maurice, he's just as cheery and full of good jokes and wheezes. Do you know, yesterday he even made old Duster laugh!'

'Well, that's an achievement,' I said dryly. (Duster is the rather austere cairn terrier who belongs to Penlow, P.O.'s tweedy friend. He is notable for his reticence and blank expression. Admittedly he does have animate moments, but it rather depends on the day of the week. Evidently L. Lionheart had struck the right day.) 'And am I permitted to meet this ball of fun,' I enquired, 'or is he nervous of cats?'

'Nervous of cats? I should say not! He loves 'em!'

I twitched my ears, not sure whether that was a good or bad omen. But before I could enquire further, Bouncer announced that the following day he intended showing Lionheart the two chinchillas, Boris and Karloff. These creatures occupy a hutch behind the potting shed and are a source of endless fascination for the dog who delights in circling their cage and pulling faces. Naturally they cannot stand him.

'You see, Maurice,' Bouncer added eagerly, 'he is coming to play tomorrow morning. So you could meet him then. That would be nice, wouldn't it?'

Being slightly dubious of this, I murmured something to the

effect that I might be otherwise engaged spreading panic among the sparrows.

'Not with that wonky paw, you won't,' he said with a matey grin. 'You'll be limping and bored out of your mind. But I can tell you, Louis Lionheart will soon fix that!'

'Is that so?' I said, suddenly feeling very tired.

'You BET!' the dog bellowed.

I was about to move away when a thought struck me. 'Oh, and who are his people?' I enquired.

'They are very tall,' he replied, 'and very polite and live in that big house by the river . . . And do you know, Maurice, they spoke to me!'

'Really? And what did they say?'

'They said I was "a little baba". Now that's what I call pretty pally, don't you?'

I considered this for a few moments and then asked if he was sure he had heard correctly. The dog replied that of course he had, and what else could they possibly have said?

I remained silent but thought the more . . .

I will pass a veil over the advent of Louis Lionheart. Suffice it to say that he was as Bouncer had described: mad, bold and with an insatiable affection for cats. You might think this latter trait carried a novel charm. It did not. I was harried unmercifully – not with a keen savagery so typical of canines, but with thunderous endearments and rapturous grins. Indeed, at one point when I was taking sanctuary in the branches of a tree, he kept circling its trunk intoning *More Maurice, more Maurice – more, more, more!*

I suppose some cats might be flattered by the adulation, but I felt not so much flattered as flattened. One can have too much of a good thing and this was one of those rare occasions. Nevertheless, it would have been churlish not to acknowledge such acclaim, and I was just about to raise a gracious paw in his direction when I heard Bouncer snort to him, 'Watch out, you idiot! More of him is just what we don't want. Enough's enough – and I should know!' And the next moment he had butted Lionheart in the rear and hustled him into the shrubbery.

I have to admit to feeling distinctly miffed, torn between relief at the ensuing silence yet stung by Bouncer's graceless remark.

That dog is lucky to have one of my breeding as his companion, and it's about time he knew it! I resolved to speak sternly to him that evening.

But in the meantime I had a more pressing matter to deal with: namely our mistress. She is clearly in one of her detecting moods – something that bodes ill for all. I once heard the Brighton Type refer to her as Deadly Primrose. I hesitate to agree with Ingaza (an objectionable piece of work in my view), but in this case he may have a point. Our mistress's pursuit of those she deems base and nefarious (among others, the town clerk) has been a source of some disturbance . . . to me at any rate; though not to Bouncer who, needless to say, relishes every minute. Still, I suppose living with an amateur detective is mildly easier than sharing a home with a homicidal cleric. However, in my view both siblings, F.O. & P.O, must have inherited the same gene of lunacy. And we poor creatures of Nature's benison are left to cope with the consequences!

TEN

The Primrose version

I was just taking a well-earned rest from my labours in the studio and from writing a thank-you note to Agnes Penlow when I was interrupted by a loud knock at the door. I was startled, not expecting anyone. Besides, who knocks rather than rings these days? Perhaps it was the second post with a delivery of paintbrushes from my London suppliers. Not at all. It was the looming figure of Chief Superintendent MacManus, last seen being tedious at the Penlows' party.

After a polite greeting and clearing of throat, he thrust a carrier bag into my hands, explaining that it was a little gift from his wife. Knowing he would be in the area, she had apparently suggested he deliver it in person. 'Books,' he explained. 'She has been clearing out the attic and thought you might find these helpful.'

'Oh really?' I said, doubtful of their use and fearing the worst. 'How very kind.'

I do not dislike Mrs MacManus – one can hardly dislike a nonentity – and sympathize with her plight. To be married to a pompous bore like MacManus must be a trial . . . though who knows, perhaps the role of grey-clad lackey (Mrs M. always wears grey – albeit of different shades) was what she liked. After all, to be towed through life in the wake of one as assured and inflexible as the chief superintendent might be quite restful: no decisions, no demands, no responsibilities – a sort of languid limbo really.

However, what suited MacManus's wife was hardly my concern, but the books she had foisted upon me were. I glanced at the three titles and shuddered: *The Blithesome Palette: thoughts of an Art devotée*; *Learn to Paint in Six Easy Steps*; *Mr Titian's Little Quiz Book*. I stared dumbly at these offerings trying to muster a smile of gratitude.

It was a difficult process, and while I struggled, MacManus said, 'Yes, she thought these might be your cup of tea. Could be quite inspiring, I daresay. I mean, I suppose you must get a bit bored with church towers and the backsides of sheep – or the front sides, come to that. Ho! Ho!'

Oh ho! Bloody ho! I thought. Sheep and country churches are what keep me in gin and allow me to live in a sizeable house in its own grounds and not in some faceless red box like his own. But naturally I refrained from making such a retort, and instead told him earnestly that the noble intricacies of church architecture were an endless challenge, and that (as obviously noted by Rubens) all posteriors were different, even those of sheep. It crossed my mind to include those of ostriches, but prudence prevailed.

Slightly to my surprise, having completed his mission my visitor seemed reluctant to leave and hovered awkwardly in the hallway. Really, I wondered, hasn't he something useful to do at the police station such as patrolling the Rogues Gallery or serving a summons on someone? Evidently not. For, clearing his throat, he said, 'As a matter of fact, Miss Oughterard, since I'm here I wonder if I might pick your memory about a little matter. It won't take long.'

I froze. Pick my memory? Little matter? How little – my brother's dispatch of Mrs Fotherington? I had always feared that case would be re-opened, and doubtless there was a hotline between the Surrey police and our Sussex squad. To quell panic I told myself that it was doubtless to do with my annual donation to the Police Benevolent Fund. Perhaps my subscription had lapsed. Yes, that would be it, and how typical of MacManus to seize on such a paltry thing. I flashed a dazzling smile, offered some bland beverage and ushered him into the sitting room.

When I returned from the kitchen it was to find him smoking a pipe (no by-your-leave, of course!) and staring fixedly at the dog snoring gently on the hearthrug. I set down the tray and made a bright and lying reference to Bouncer: 'Such a sweet little treasure!' I exclaimed. 'Do you have a doggie companion, Chief Superintendent?'

'No,' he said shortly. 'I am too busy.'

'Oh, of course, of course,' I agreed. 'Catching all those criminals, it must take so much time and energy.'

'It does,' he agreed woodenly. 'And that's what I want to ask you about.'

My stomach muscles clenched and my smile stiffened. 'So how can I help?' I enquired benignly.

'Doubtless you recall the recent Topping case – that Latin master found dead in the car on Beachy Head?'

Oh my hat! So not Fotherington but *Topping*. Relief and fear mingled as I composed my features into an expression of polite enquiry.

'Well,' he continued, 'we are not entirely sure that his death was due to a heart attack after all. It seemed obvious at the time and the coroner evidently thought so, but after a bit of probing we have certain reservations. In fact, it could conceivably have been something involving criminal activity and linked to the incident on Caburn Hill, that knife attack you may remember. It's a possibility that the two deaths were not unconnected.'

In this of course he was right, but not in the way he may have imagined!

'*Criminal* activity? Oh dear, how dreadful,' I said, sounding suitably shocked. As a matter of fact, the shock was far from assumed. I was rattled to think that what I had feared, namely the enquiry into the Topping affair (and something I had decamped to Nice to escape) was still ongoing. But recalling Pa's advice – *when in a blue funk sit tight and smile* – I did just that and offered the visitor some more tea.

He took a gulp, and then said, 'You see, Miss Oughterard, we have a witness who seems to think that on the afternoon prior to the body's discovery he saw the deceased heading in the direction of your house as if he was about to pay a call. Do you remember if he made that call, and if so, how would you describe his manner?'

Huh! I recalled Topping's manner only too well: odious and malign, but I could hardly tell the superintendent that. I wondered what tiresome local had seen his approach and why this had not been mentioned earlier. Presumably because the witness had a defective memory and was unsure anyway. If that was the case then I would jolly well brazen it out – X's word against P.O.'s: Primrose Oughterard's!

I gave a thoughtful frown and shook my head. 'Oh no. Pleasant though he was, I only saw Mr Topping on two or three occasions – we weren't on visiting terms. And even if he did call, then I certainly wasn't aware of it. Besides, dear Bouncer would have barked the house down; he gets excited by strangers and there would have been an awful racket!'

'Hmm,' MacManus said expressionlessly, 'I see. Well, naturally these things have to be checked, you understand, all part of our routine enquiries. Normally I would have sent Sergeant Wilding, but as I was here with the books it seemed sensible to kill two birds with one stone, if you see what I mean. No point in wasting resources.' He gave a sombre smile.

Two birds with one stone, my foot! What did he think I was – another ostrich? I felt like asking him how Bognor was these days, but naturally didn't.

Instead, and on a sudden whim, I heard myself saying, 'So awful about poor Mrs Travers, though her death does strike one as being rather odd. I mean to say, what on earth was she doing in the sea when she was known to dislike it so – or at least so one had gathered? And rather strange, don't you think, that she should have been all on her own?'

If I had expected this to draw him into the subject I was disappointed. He looked utterly blank and then muttered something to the effect that people were full of oddities and presumably she had changed her mind, and that in his experience it was something that ladies often did.

Naturally there were a number of replies I could have made, but restricted myself to remarking sweetly that doubtless his experience ran very deep. If he had detected the veiled sarcasm he certainly did not show it. Indeed, he even gave a nod of agreement, before adding indifferently, 'It's always the way with sudden deaths – the public loves a mystery. And with all due respect I daresay you are no different in that way, Miss Oughterard. Just like my wife, she's suspicious of everything!' He emitted a loud and patronizing laugh. I gritted my teeth and gave a cheerless smile.

After a few stilted pleasantries he stood up to go and I took him into the hall. Here he paused and murmured, 'Oh, by the way, I happened to be up at the Yard the other day and had a chinwag with Detective Inspector Samson, as he now is. He sends you his regards and says he hopes the cat and dog are settling to their new life after the reverend's demise.' He gestured towards the still recumbent form of Bouncer glimpsed through the open door. 'It must have been difficult for them – and for you, of course.'

I can't be sure whether it was my imagination, but he seemed to regard me intently – a look suggestive less of solicitude than of suspicion. 'It was,' I replied stonily. 'And do reciprocate my good wishes to Mr Samson.'

He nodded and returned to his car.

As the noise of the engine faded I gathered the 'art' books and one by one dropped them into the wastepaper basket. And then with mounting fury I strode to my desk, wrenched open the top drawer and withdrew those absurd photographs. I stared at them grimly. 'Well,' I muttered, 'try any funny business and these might just arrive at the office of our local newspaper.' For a moment I was gripped by a savage pleasure, picturing the recipient's face when confronted with the ursine capering of the chief superintendent. Hmm, that would settle the basket's hash!

However, such pleasure was short-lived as my mind plunged back to MacManus's words. Revenge is all very well, but what about the interim cost? If that cost revealed that I had been remotely connected with Topping's demise, it could be embarrassing to say the least. Why, despite my undoubted innocence, they might even pin his fate on *me*. One assassin in the family is quite enough . . . which explains my disquiet at MacManus's mention of the ghastly little Samson. During the investigation into Mrs Fotherington's death, he had held the rank of detective sergeant and was the investigating officer's sidekick. Subordinate he may have been, but with whippet-like tenacity he had pursued the case – and poor Francis – with paranoid zeal. I won't say that the latter outwitted him (my brother's calculations were not of the sharpest), but somehow he had managed to elude his clutches and the case had been shelved. Later, after Francis's death, Samson was promoted to inspector and sent to the Yard, where doubtless that twitching nose is yielding all manner of truffles . . . Naturally one can be oversensitive, but I strongly suspect that his good wishes were far from well-meant and instead a sort of coded message to the effect that he is still excavating the past.

However, no one can accuse the Oughterards of being cowed by circumstance (even Francis had his moments) and I have no intention of letting oafish MacManus or the weevil Samson dictate otherwise. *Neither* will I allow their intrusions to impede my research into another issue: the curious Travers affair.

Despite MacManus's casual dismissal, there is something decidedly bizarre about that drowning, and the more I glean of the matter the more I am convinced that it was *not* as it appeared. I have a nose for skulduggery (no doubt inherited from Ma, who, despite our elaborate smokescreens, invariably knew when her offspring were cheating) and I shall jolly well use it! But naturally caution must be the keynote. The last thing one wants is to have the chief superintendent muddying the waters. I mean to say one is all in favour of the 'strong arm of the law' (naturally standards must be maintained) but in my experience some of its representatives are more trouble than they are worth. The same might equally be said of the Church, whose officers when unchecked can be tiresome in the extreme . . . Bishop Clinker having been a case in point.[5] However, in mitigation of foolish Francis, I have to say that as a cleric my brother was much respected by the Molehill congregation – and especially so after his heroic death rescuing that ninny Mavis Briggs from being hamstrung on the church gargoyle.

Ah well, it has been a long day, and as a prelude to bedtime I think a bracing walk with Bouncer would do us both good. The idle dog has been half asleep for hours. I shall take him across the fields and we can inspect the sheep . . . fore and aft.

ELEVEN

The cat's memoir

As I had feared, it didn't take long before the Brighton Type re-emerged. Ingaza must have returned from his 'holiday' (aka escape) at about the same time as our mistress, for it was shortly after we had been repatriated by that odd person on a motorbike that he came slithering into the hall one afternoon. The sallow features were a little browner than usual, but other than that his manner was much the same, i.e. offensive (*Scrag-arse* still being his preferred mode of address to me). Unlike the dog I am not given to soft-soaping humans, and like to think that I made my distaste abundantly clear. This had no noticeable effect – although in one so louche such indifference hardly surprises. However, despite my displeasure I elected to remain *in situ* as it is always useful to know what these lesser creatures are up to and what absurdities lurk in their fragile minds.

Despite their respective absences, I cannot say that much had changed. There was the usual downing of copious tots of that putrid amber stuff, the sitting room became increasingly smoke-laden, our mistress spoke volubly and Ingaza's nasal responses were typically oblique.

But what was not oblique was his reluctance to get drawn

[5] See *A Load of Old Bones* & other Francis Oughterard novels.

into any plans she may have regarding the death of that Travers woman. Alas, the Prim's imagination is becoming increasingly stirred by that particular event (which she is convinced is sinister), and she was clearly keen to engage her guest on the subject. But Ingaza was having none of it, for after listening to the long spiel of her suspicions, he made a few dismissive remarks and then hastily withdrew to his car pleading fatigue after the Tangier trip.

As often mentioned, I am not enamoured of the Brighton Type – but in this instance I felt a twinge of empathy. He had that look in his eye which I suspect may be seen in mine when deluged by one of Bouncer's more idiotic vagaries: shifty alarm.

After he had gone, I could see that P.O. was none too pleased with the lack of interest, and when the dog sauntered into the room she grumbled loudly. Bouncer of course took not a blind bit of notice and fell into a snuffling stupor on the hearthrug. It was time to seek other diversions and, leaving the pair of them, I went to pursue mild sport among the rhododendrons.

Here I spent a gratifying hour unsettling the hedgehogs and practising my stalking skills. This latter game is not really essential, as having received my O.C. (Order of Cat) some time ago, such skills are well proven. But I enjoy the exercise, and as I frequently have to remind Bouncer it doesn't do to become complacent . . . And besides, I think it time that I seriously began to consider the prestigious C.F.E. (Companion of the Feline Empire), thus attention to niceties of the chase is vital. Few cats in this part of Sussex can boast such an award, and I have every intention of joining their exclusive number. It is only right that the family tradition be upheld. To this end therefore I shall seek out Sir Perivale Puss-Coley, a cat of impeccable pedigree and well versed in the honours protocol. If I can elicit his aid all should be well.

Dwelling on these pleasant possibilities and with palate poised for supper, I made my way back to the house. Here I was confronted by Bouncer who insisted on pushing me into a tight corner.

'I've got some news,' he growled.

'What news?' I asked. 'You've been fast asleep. How would you know anything?'

A crafty look came into his eyes and he said, 'Ah, but you see, Maurice, I only slept for a bit and when I woke up I kept my eyes SHUT. The Prim thought I was sleeping, but I wasn't: I was LISTENING.'

'Really?' I murmured casually. 'And what did you hear? Little of consequence, I imagine.'

He plonked a paw on a passing beetle, and then said truculently, 'Well, that's where you're wrong, Maurice. I heard something rather important. Still, I can see you want your grub so I won't bother to *die-vulge*.' (Bouncer has only recently learnt the word 'divulge' and uses it widely, relevant or otherwise.)

He started to move away but, nettled by his reaction, I summoned him back. 'Tell me immediately,' I demanded.

'No fear,' he grinned, 'you might get indigestion. She's put a whole heap of haddock in your bowl *and* there's a saucer of cream, not just that thin stuff.' He trundled off towards his own bowl, and I was left in a state of tension – hungry for haddock, piqued by his cheek.

Hunger eclipsed pique, and I spent a happy twenty minutes savouring the excellent fare which P.O. had thoughtfully provided. Her offerings are not always so lavish and one frequently has to make do with inferior cod and silver-top milk. As with those earlier sardines, I rather suspect that this current largesse has something to do with our having been uprooted to stay with Ingaza's friend in Brighton while she vamoosed to foreign parts. Guilt, presumably.

Anyway, having partaken of this feast I felt sufficiently mellow to smile at the dog – a rash gesture for it resulted in his bounding over, butting me in the chest and with merry chortles snatching at my tail. Mercifully the chivvying didn't last long for it was plain he was eager to talk and, shoving his snout in my ear, he snuffled, 'I expect you would like to hear my news now, wouldn't you, Maurice?'

Somewhat winded by the onslaught, I merely nodded my assent.

'Well,' he began, sitting on his haunches with paws splayed, 'when I woke up I heard this deep voice droning on and realized she had got another visitor. So like I said, I lay doggo for a while but then I opened just *one* crafty eye . . . and, Maurice, who do you think I saw?'

'No idea,' I replied, feeling a bit sleepy.

'Guess!' he roared.

I shrugged.

'It was that person she can't stand.'

'Which of the many?' I enquired.

After the requisite pause for dramatic effect, Bouncer told me. 'MANUS,' he boomed, 'the police geezer, the one she's got the photos of wearing a bear suit, that one playing silly beggars with the ostrich bint!'

'So what did he want – his photographs back?'

'Don't be daft,' the dog said scornfully, 'he doesn't know she's got 'em . . . but I tell you what, Maurice, he soon may.'

'Really? And why should that be?'

'Ah well, you see,' he replied smugly, 'it's my sixth sense.'

'Which doesn't exist. As I've told you before, it is one of those absurd figments of your imag—'

I got no further, for with a lunge and a snarl the dog had pinioned me to the floor. 'Pax?' he panted. ''Cause if not, you're as dead as a dormouse and I shan't tell you a sausage!'

Naturally no self-respecting cat wishes to be likened to a dormouse, whether living or dead; but what really riled me was being kept in the dark – especially by Bouncer. Like my brethren, I am insatiably curious. Thus clamped under his hulking foot, I mewed dulcetly, 'Proceed. I am all ears!'

For a few moments the dog seemed to ponder; and then, lifting his paw from my chest, he bent his head and said, 'Well, Manus was burbling something about our old master F.O. and Mrs Fotherington (couldn't catch what exactly, he speaks funny – but then of course most of 'em do). Anyway, P.O. was looking pretty po-faced, like she does when she's miffed or putting on a front, and I *knew* she was rattled. They rambled on for quite a bit; and then after he had drunk some of that awful brown brew they put in cups, he got up and sloped off.'

'Hmm,' I observed, 'I can understand her being rattled about the reference to our late master and his tiresome victim, but what has that to do with MacManus soon learning of the photograph?'

A crafty grin appeared on Bouncer's face. 'It's to do with what I saw after he left and what I *sensed.*'

'Oh yes,' I replied affably, 'and what was that?'

'The moment he had gone, her face went all red and angry
like it does when I've nabbed a cake from the table. And then
she rushed to her desk and pulled out those pictures, stared at
them and muttered, "Huh! Any tricks and I'll wave these under
his nose. Repellent basket!".' The dog chuckled, and added, 'Now
those are two words that I really do understand. It's what she
often says about my bed in the kitchen . . . But what I learned
from our old master the vicar, and since living here, is that humans
also say *basket* when they mean *bastard* or *rotten blighter*. Isn't
that right?'

I agreed that it was and complimented him on his deduction.
The tail wagged and he continued, 'So it's my belief that the police
geezer has been doing some snooping about F.O.'s hand in the old
girl's death – sort of putting his hooter in where it's not wanted.
And what's more, I think if he goes on like that the Prim will
jolly well give him a BIG KICK and spill the beans! So how about
that, Maurice?' Bouncer gave an excited snort, scrabbled inele-
gantly in his nether regions, and then with fixed gaze awaited my
response.

'Hmm . . . on the whole,' I mused, 'you could be right. After
all, why has she kept the photographs all this time unless for some
purpose? There's enough clutter in that desk as it is, without its
being added to by images of MacManus dressed in a bear's outfit
and romping with a pantomime ostrich encased in pink sequins.'
I gave a sharp hiss and flicked my tail. 'It just goes to show that
my noble grandfather was so right in his dictum that *omnes homines
insanitos sunt*.'

I flashed Bouncer an indulgent smile – but have to admit to
being not only startled but a trifle put out when he replied solemnly,
'Oh yes, Maurice, off their blithering rockers, they are.'

Well, really, I thought, since when did the dog understand Latin?
And then of course I remembered. He had picked it up from the
church crypt in Molehill, the Surrey parish where we had lived
with the vicar. Bouncer had developed a liking for that dark place
and would retire down its tortuous steps to gnaw his foul bones and
to meditate – i.e. to brood on rabbits. He used to say that being
in the dark soothed his nerves. (Nerves? The dog hasn't a nerve in
his body!) Anyway, he would spend long periods there, consorting
with the ghosts and gazing at the inscriptions on ancient plaques

and tombs. It was during these interludes that he had absorbed a number of Latin phrases which occasionally he would repeat. But since our coming to Lewes and living with F.O.'s sister, such classical relics had seemed to evaporate and one had heard no more.

Thus, it just goes to show how things learnt at an impressionable age never quite desert us but remain embedded in the psyche . . . even in the outlandish psyche of dogs.

TWELVE

Emily Bartlett to her sister

My dear Hilda,

Thank you for your long letter telling me how you are coping with Mother. As you rightly say, it is my turn next – although I fear my own ministrations are not nearly as effective (nor so welcome) as yours. However, the weeks fly by and it will soon be time for my own little 'pilgrimage of grace', and to that end I am already knitting her a new pair of fluffy bed socks. She didn't say much about the last pair I brought (in fact nothing at all), but I have since obtained a charming pattern from this month's copy of Women & Flowers *– an intricate design of rabbits interweaved with marigolds which, assuming she can find her spectacles, she is bound to like. Yes, I know that when I sent the pretty handkerchief sachet for her birthday she asked why it hadn't been wrapped round a bottle of Scotch . . . but naturally that was just one of her little jokes. Our mother's humour has always been a trifle obscure, and some of her cryptic comments not easy to grasp. But I am sure she will appreciate the socks and I must press on with them 'tootie-sweetie', as the Erasmus boys insist on saying!*

And talking of cryptic comments, Primrose too has been making more curious remarks – specifically about that Mrs Travers, the poor lady who drowned. You may recall that in

*my previous letter I recounted the rather taxing afternoon I
had spent on the cliff at Birling Gap while Primrose and the
awful dog patrolled the beach below. Primrose was absurdly
convinced that there was some mystery attached to the
death and had been searching for clues among the rocks, if
you please!*

*Well, since then I have been desperately busy at the school
dealing with the vagaries of Mr Winchbrooke (as wayward
as Mother really) and doing battle with the stationers
who as usual have misread our order for the new term. Thus,
other than briefly during the Penlows' party I had not seen
Primrose for quite a while. But yesterday when I slipped
into town for a little shopping (Mr Winchbrooke being in
London at a headmasters' conference, i.e. beanfeast) she
happened to appear. I had just settled in the peace of Grange
Gardens with a sandwich and my library book, when I saw
her striding towards me. Mercifully she was without the dog.
But her face looked grim and I feared she had been jousting
with the town clerk.*

*My assumption was correct, for sitting down beside me,
and without preamble, she launched into a customary
diatribe. 'Do you know what that man had the gall to
suggest?' she exploded. 'He actually had the nerve to . . .'*

*I cannot recall the exact nature of his offence, but in any
case managed to forestall further elaboration by telling her
that I rather gathered Mr Winchbrooke was considering
purchasing two of her sheep paintings to hang on the walls
of his study. His predecessor had favoured a graphic
print of stampeding wild elephants – a scene popular with
the boys but which does little to calm those parents
summoned to discuss their offspring's defects. The image
seems to stir the simmering belligerence and makes them
difficult to handle. Mr Winchbrooke is convinced that the
presence of milder scenes – sheep gently grazing – would
help soothe their truculence and shorten the interviews.
He could be right . . . Anyway, as hoped, the topic of the
purchase also soothed the wrath of my companion, whose
lowering expression was instantly replaced by a quizzical
smirk.*

Thus, with the air softened, we chatted most amiably, and I told her all about my new knitting pattern and Mr Winchbrooke's plans for the staff party. Actually, the plans are the same as always except that this year he proposes cutting the alcohol allocation to one glass per head – something which Primrose, not being one of the staff, seemed to find very funny.

So we continued chatting about this and that and I offered her a sandwich (declined). And then I foolishly made an observation about Mrs Travers – that she had always struck me as having impeccable dress sense: elegant and understated, and how she always eschewed the frilly and silly. Styles becoming only too popular in my view! As a matter of fact, I think Primrose's attention may have been wandering a little, as she looked at me vaguely and said, 'Oh sorry, Emily, what was that?' So I carefully repeated what I had been saying; and by way of example added that I had once bumped into Mrs T. in the newsagents leafing through a copy of Vogue, *and that she had shown me a beachwear page featuring a busty girl wearing an exotic bathing hat made to look like a bouquet of poppies. 'Such absurdity,' Mrs T. had laughed, 'I wouldn't be seen dead in a thing like that – far too fussy. What will they think of next?'*

Well, Hilda, I thought, my little anecdote was quite amusing – but not so Primrose. She stared at me with fixed expression, before muttering, 'Oh . . . my . . . God.' And then she stood up abruptly, knocking my sandwiches to the ground, and without further word made off across the garden. I have to admit to being none too pleased. I had taken a lot of trouble over those sandwiches – my favourites, you recall, egg and potted meat – and to have them dashed to the gravel in that cavalier way was too bad. I did think of picking the bits off them, but remembering Mother's tales of lethal insects decided against it.

And so you see, Hilda, the mere mention of poor Elspeth Travers seems to provoke an unsettling (and clumsy!) response in Primrose, and I must take care to avoid all reference to the subject in future.

Oh, and talking of care, I do hope you will be a little more sparing of Mother's nightly port and lemon. Such generosity may induce silence, but I do feel that three glasses are more than enough for her. Besides, think of the cost!
Your devoted sister,
Emily

THIRTEEN

The Primrose version

I had a stimulating conversation with Emily the other day – well, hardly stimulating, but certainly *revealing*. I hadn't seen her since the Penlows' party, and thus when I spotted her sitting on a bench in Grange Gardens, I felt it my duty to approach and engage in social chit-chat. Besides, having just left the town clerk's office in some dudgeon (that man is utterly impossible!) I needed an outlet for my annoyance. There being no one else immediately available Emily could provide that.

However, barely had I started my narrative when she rather took the wind out of my sails by telling me that Mr Winchbrooke is keen to purchase a couple of my paintings for his study . . . something to do with quelling the parents, I gather. But the reason is hardly relevant, what *counts* is the sale itself. It is almost three years since Erasmus House has bought any of my work – and that was at a discount – so it is high time they bought some more, and at full whack! After all, going there to judge the boys' painting competitions and having to listen to the art mistress's oozing banalities is damn hard work – especially the latter. And it is all very well Winchbrooke introducing me as 'our esteemed artist friend and counsellor', but to quote Nicholas Ingaza, a little *quid pro quo* wouldn't come amiss.

So certainly news of the impending deal is good, but much more intriguing was Emily's reference to Elspeth Travers' dislike of frothy bathing caps: a revelation which surely supports my belief that her end was unnatural. Naturally Emily had no idea of the significance of her words, but they certainly made an impact on me . . . an unusual event in our relationship. Anyway, we had been chatting away for a few minutes (well, Emily was; something to do with her mother and woven rabbits or some such – I had rather lost the thread by then), when I suddenly heard her saying that Elspeth had hated showy clothes and had once been very sniffy about some girl modelling one of those exaggerated bathing caps. In fact – and this was the real jolt – Emily quoted her as declaring she wouldn't be seen dead in such a thing. Well, if that's not an irony I don't know what is! In fact, I was so stunned that I rose at once, eager to get home to collect my thoughts. (Collecting thoughts on a bench with Emily when one's ears are being assailed by rabbits and knitting patterns is not an easy task.)

Unfortunately I rather think that in my haste I may have dislodged Emily's sandwiches – those awful potted meat ones she guzzles. They had been beside her on the seat and I did sense something fall as I stood up, but thought it best not to look back for fear of ructions. Doubtless she will apprise me of the matter when we next meet.

Engrossed in Emily's news and keen to get home, I then collided with Charles Penlow going in the direction of the White Hart. I think he was eager to talk, but being so preoccupied, I hurried on up to the car park. I was about to unlock my car when I heard a voice say, 'Hmm, a bit over the line there, aren't you? I mean to say, my aunt could barely get hers in. Any closer and it might have scraped her mirror.'

'But it didn't,' I snapped, glaring at the gangling young man who had accosted me. His hair was very fair, white almost, and blended well with the pasty skin. I took an instant dislike. And then out of the corner of my eye I saw a woman in the driving seat of the adjacent vehicle. Yes, he was probably right really: a bit too close for comfort. But then so was its occupant, Mrs Alice Markham.

She wound down her window and cried, 'Ah, Miss Oughterard, what a pleasure again! Take no notice of Aston, he is *so* pernickety . . . although I must say, your car *is* a trifle skew-whiff.' She wagged a mocking finger. I seethed, gave a wintry smile, and then watched as with some effort she squeezed her plump frame out on to the tarmac. She gave a breathless laugh, and turning to her companion, said, 'Come along, boysie, off to the shops we go!' And then looking at me she added, 'I expect you know I shall be staying in Elspeth's house for a couple of months – have to get it straight for the sale and there are so many things one needs, a thinner eiderdown, for example. Poor Elspeth so hated the cold!'

'Boysie' nodded. 'Yes,' he murmured, 'we must leave Miss Oughterard to concentrate on some rather careful reversing.'

Bastard, I thought vaguely as I watched them move off in the direction of the High Street. I was struck by their difference: the short, dumpy Alice and her tall, etiolated nephew; the one moving with a teetering trot, the other languidly strolling. My goodness, he certainly had long legs. What a contrast! Had I been less irritated I might have been amused. As it was, I jumped in the car, reversed abruptly and in some pique sped off home.

Here I was greeted by a bounding Bouncer and a nonchalant Maurice. The latter seemed in an unusually mellow mood for he extended a paw to toy with my shoelace. Such pleasantries are rare from the cat and I made the appropriate responses. And then relaxing in what as children we had dubbed 'Pa's Thinking Chair' (sleeping more like), I contemplated the fate of the late Mrs Travers and the oddities surrounding her accident. These were that from all accounts, except her sister's, she had been averse to sea bathing – or at the least not notably enthusiastic; that she had been disdainful of the fashion for ornate swimming caps; and that, as just declared by Alice, she had hated the cold. How strange therefore to think that such a one – head smothered in pink rubber roses – had decided to plunge herself amid the perishing waters of Birling Gap, a site notorious for its fearsome currents and pounding waves. And this entirely on her own. For from all reports of the tragedy she had been unaccompanied – no hearty companions to share her boldness, not even a devoted dog to bark and frolic. What on earth had the woman been up to . . . Or what exactly had someone *else* been up to? Gripped by a sudden excitement I leapt from the chair and rushed to the telephone.

*   *   *

'Nicholas,' I gasped, 'I know I am right! There *is* something wrong and I wish to discuss it with you immediately.'

'Well, you can't,' said Eric's throaty voice, 'because he ain't here. His Nibs is aht on a mission. It's a bit delicate like, and he may be some time.'

I snorted. 'Mission? You mean he is soft soaping some gullible punter.'

'*Nevah!*' was the bellowed response.

'Hmm. Well, when he comes in could you possibly tell him that Primrose Oughterard called and needs to speak to him urgently?'

'Right-o, Primrose! I always knows your voice and I'll tell him the good news.'

'What good news?' I asked sharply.

'That you wants to speak to him, o'course. He's bound to like that!'

I raised a sceptical eyebrow.

'Anyway,' he continued, 'while we're on the blower I expect you'd like to know what Phyllis said about you after she had dropped off your furry pals the ovver day.'

Did I? 'Er, well . . .' I muttered warily.

'I'll tell you: she said you was the tops. "A real nice lady," those were her very words – and what's more, she don't say that about many. Very picky, is our Phyllis. You've made a hit there, Primrose!' A loud guffaw hurtled down the phone line, and I winced. Nevertheless, I couldn't help feeling mildly flattered . . . until he added, 'And she likes that long drive you've got – it suited the motorbike just fine! Most impressed, she was.' Images of the bomb-struck gravel came to mind, and I closed my eyes.

I murmured something to the effect that I was glad she had enjoyed her morning. And then with renewed thanks to him for entertaining my 'furry pals' and a reminder to alert Ingaza, it was with some relief that I replaced the receiver.

Much later that evening, when Nicholas eventually deigned to return my call, I started to tell him of my encounter with Alice Markham and what she had said about Elspeth always hating the cold.

'You see,' I said, 'there *is* something fishy and I want you to—'

'Yes, yes,' he replied, 'but I think we already have a date to discuss my lecture to the Artists' Guild. Can't it wait?'

'Not if you want to hear of MacManus's enquiry into the Topping affair. He called the other day and it's perfectly obvious that he is still pursuing that case, and he actually hinted that in his view there was something not quite kosher about Topping being found dead in the car on Beachy Head. *We* know that we are blameless, of course, but not being of the subtlest mind, will MacManus? There are certain complexities regarding that business which I doubt he would grasp. I think it might be useful if we had a little pre-emptive pow-wow just in case he starts to sniff again. It's as well to be prepared, and the sooner the better. Don't you agree?'

There was a silence followed by a long sigh, or it could have been a groan. Either way Ingaza was clearly not at his sparkling best. 'No peace for the frigging wicked,' was the muttered response. And then he added testily, 'Not that I am wicked – straight as a die, that's me, and I don't deserve this persecution.'

'Nonsense,' I said briskly, 'you're as curved as a sickle and always have been. And just as sharp – which is why I want you to help me get to the bottom of this Travers business. Besides,' I added alluringly, 'I happened to bump into Polly Fox-Findlay yesterday and she told me that she and Lance were most keen to hear your lecture at the Artists' Guild. Little Lance is *big* on the committee, treasurer actually, and with consummate subtlety I have managed to wangle you a really fat fee.'

I waited for the gasp of joy. None came, of course. 'Hmm,' he grunted, 'in guineas, I trust.'

'Oh naturally. And incidentally I have opened another bottle of Pa's Talisker. It's very good.'

Ingaza said he was sure it was good and enquired if I might also be making my renowned lobster bisque. That had not been my intention but it immediately became so. And thus, having established that he would come two days hence for a late lunch, we concluded our conversation.

Back in the sitting room I turned to Maurice crouched in front of the fire and gazing fixedly at one of his rubber mice. 'Honestly,' I said, 'what it is to have supportive friends!'

The cat shifted its attention from the mouse and for a few seconds regarded me with a speculative stare; and then with the merest mew and a twitch of its tail returned to contemplating the mouse. I had the distinct impression of being cold shouldered.

FOURTEEN

Charles Penlow's account

Agnes was awfully pleased with the party – and rightly so as she's a splendid hostess and works her socks off to get it just right. A merry time was had by all, although I fear Duster nearly disgraced himself, naughty little fellow. He clearly had urinary designs on Melinda Balfour's smart new handbag, which didn't exactly enamour him to the good lady and she left shortly afterwards. Still, she's a decent sort and will doubtless recover. But apart from that little blip it all went swimmingly.

And talking of swimming, Primrose Oughterard still seems obsessed by Mrs Travers and her unfortunate drowning at Birling Gap and I heard her asking pointed questions of some of the other guests – e.g. the Haskins who rarely listen to anything, but also the Reverend Egge who does listen but on the whole rarely produces a cogent reply. I doubt if her enquiries got her very far. Whether she consulted the chief superintendent on the subject I don't know but suspect not. She is not enamoured. And actually, I rather share her aversion – he isn't the most stimulating cove. But Agnes was keen to invite him as she thinks it sound policy to keep in with the constabulary. According to her, in 'these dastardly days' one never knows when they might be needed. My wife has a dramatic imagination and I doubt whether Lewes's genteel routine has much experience of the dastardly . . . unless of course you count that business of the corpse in the dewpond and the foreigner knifed on Caburn Hill. But we were in Tobago at the time and the whole affair rather passed us by.

From all accounts an odd business and one likes to think a total exception to the general calm!

No, on the whole this neck of Sussex is mercifully couth and free from alarm, something which suits me very well. After all, one saw quite enough action in the war; and I can't say that post-war London was much better. No bombs of course but the noise and frenzy was bad enough (still is really). Yes, it was a good move of ours to retire down here. And renovating the derelict Podmore Place is a damn sight more exciting than a desk job in Whitehall. The east wing is now fully up and running and I've already dynamited the outbuildings to make way for the Orangery. For some reason Agnes seemed to take exception to the dynamite and went away for the weekend. Still she is all right about it now and is eagerly scanning fruit catalogues trying to select the right type of inaugural pip. Who knows, this time next year we may have a flourishing orange tree – provided of course that the builders play ball. In my experience builders, like God, move in mysterious ways and it takes time and guile to fathom their intent.

In fact, I was saying that very thing to Mrs Alice Markham during our party. I gather she proposes staying at Needham Court for a short period before putting it on the market, and wanted to know if I could recommend anyone to make a few renovations. I gave her the name of a small local firm – being reluctant to suggest my own contractors for fear of giving them an excuse for further delays!

It may sound ungallant but I can't say I was especially drawn to the lady. As a comparative stranger to the area she had not featured on our original guest list (confined largely to the Lewes 'old guard'), but in the course of attending the sister's funeral and in a moment of rash altruism, Agnes had invited her. In a cool sort of way Elspeth Travers had been attractive and, I think, intelligent – qualities which I did not immediately discern in the sibling, and still do not. Her manner was dissonant, being an unsettling blend of the coy and assertive, and the voice not exactly what you would call mellow . . . Mind you, my judgement may be clouded by the fact that she wanted to know where I lived. Slightly bemused, I told her that it was here, in Podmore Place. 'Oh,' she laughed, 'so *you're* the host, are you? I thought you might have been the gardener!' Having delivered that merry quip she went off to swallow some more of the 'gardener's' champagne.

When later that evening I mentioned this to Agnes, she said that I was clearly becoming oversensitive in my old age, and that if I must go about with a roll of garden twine trailing from my pocket what else could I expect? She had a point, I suppose. I do recall tying roses on the terrace that morning and must have shoved the thing in my pocket when the first guests arrived. Oh well, such things happen . . . But all the same, I still think Mrs Markham's manner was a bit off and I am not endeared.

This morning I bumped into Primrose – literally, I mean. We collided in the High Street. I was just coming out of the fishing tackle shop and wondering whether I might take a late-morning snifter in the White Hart, when all of a sudden, wham! – and there was Primrose.

'Steady on,' I exclaimed, 'people will think we are drunk!'

'Speak for yourself,' she retorted breathlessly, but then apologized, saying she hadn't noticed me as she had been thinking.

'Pretty deep thoughts,' I said jovially.

'Hmm,' she replied cryptically, 'you could say that. But how useful, it remains to be seen.'

'Oh really? That sounds intriguing. Are you going to divulge?'

She shook her head and said I wouldn't understand.

'Try me.' I laughed.

She gave an impatient sigh. 'I really must be off, Charles. I'm in a hurry.'

'Oh come on, just a clue.'

'A clue? Yes, it's a clue all right: it's the bloody bathing cap!' And with those words she turned on her heel and pushed on up the hill, head down and mac flapping.

Initially of course, she was right; I didn't understand, and it was only when I was settled with my drink in the pub that the penny dropped. Silly me, wouldn't you know! Bound to be the ruddy Travers affair. What else?

FIFTEEN

The Primrose version

Normally I am rather a good sleeper – sign of a clear conscience, Mother was keen on saying – but for some reason that night gave me difficulties. I toyed with the usual distractions: read for a while, compiled a mental shopping list, tried to calculate when Bouncer had last had his toenails cut, and even debated whether I too might indulge. (According to Melinda an excellent pedicurist has just opened shop in Alfriston of all places). But none of these really displaced the sheer boredom of insomnia . . . Until something did. And how!

As a further distraction I had been vaguely recalling aspects of the Penlows' party, when quite by chance the name of one who had not been present came to mind: Reginald Bewley, Chairman of the Town Council – and who, according to Melinda's sly assurance, had been a so-called 'follower' of Elspeth Travers. Idiot! Why on earth hadn't I thought of him before? Surely I might glean some more information from that quarter. After all, if he really had been cosy with Elspeth (covertly or otherwise) he could surely be an important piece in the puzzle. Indeed, a crucial key perhaps!

Such was my elation at finding a 'lead' to follow that I leapt out of bed, grabbed a wrap and went down to the kitchen to make tea and *think*. In my experience being upright on a hard chair at a hard table is more productive of thought than when lolling in bed. Bouncer, who had been snoring loudly, woke up and gazed at me reproachfully; and then exploiting the chance whined insistently to be let out. 'Be quiet,' I snapped, 'you'll just have to wait.' He wouldn't of course, but cussedly danced and scrabbled at the back door until I obliged. In the ensuing silence I sipped my tea and dwelt on Bewley.

As I had observed to Emily, he wasn't a type I would readily have linked with Elspeth. Nothing wrong with him exactly but nothing especially remarkable either. The term *grey bureaucrat* is perhaps unduly disparaging, but from what little I have seen of him he hardly has the dash of an Errol Flynn, and even less the suavité of George Sanders – or for that matter Leslie Howard's legendary charm! Blandly polite and a competent administrator I would say, and not much more. Still, as my brother once told me reprovingly, tastes differ and it is futile to foist one's own preferences on others. (Dear Francis – despite his somewhat oblique qualities I still wonder why on earth Mrs Fotherington became quite so obsessed with him. An unfortunate choice given the result.)

So, I surmised, they must have had something in common – though whether romance played quite the part Melinda had suggested, one cannot be sure. Fond as I am of the girl, she does have a fanciful turn of mind – prurient? – and so one can't always rely on her news and views. But I decided to telephone her as soon as possible and probe a little further. After all, presumably something must have tweaked that eager imagination. I could also check with Emily to see if she knew of any sign of a wife, a detail Melinda had been vague about. But best of all I would engineer a meeting with the man himself: engage him in conversation about some council matter, speak fondly of Elspeth and generally get his measure – or to quote Pa, 'case the cove'!

With those plans in mind I finished my tea and was about to leave the kitchen when I suddenly remembered the dog. I opened the door expecting to see the creature agitating to come in. Not a sign, of course. I peered into the dark and bawled his name. Nothing. An owl hooted and in the far distance I heard the shunting of an early train . . . Silence. So I tried again.

'Bouncer,' I yelled, 'come in immediately, damn you, or no bones!' That did it. Like an explosion from a canon which nearly knocked me flat, the dog hurtled past and fell panting into his basket. From the airing cupboard in the passage I detected a note of peevish protest. Maurice had been disturbed and we should all suffer for it in the morning.

Thus, the morning came, and as predicted the cat was in one of its contrary moods. But ignoring such feline petulance, I marched to the telephone and dialled Emily at Erasmus House. 'Emily,' I demanded, 'when did you last see Reginald Bewley?'

She seemed surprised, and mumbled that she couldn't remember.

'Of course you do,' I insisted, 'try to think.' There was a silence, presumably part of the thinking process.

And then she said, 'I am really not sure, Primrose – a week ago perhaps. I think it was at the Rotary, but—'

'In which case you will know whether he has a wife, and if so does she live with him?'

For some reason Emily sounded more bemused than usual. 'Er, well I really couldn't say . . . I mean why do you want to—'

'So you *don't* know if he is married?'

'He may be, I suppose, but it's hardly my business to . . . Ah, I'm so sorry, Primrose, Mr Winchbrooke has just come in to say that he needs me to take the minutes at a meeting with some parents: something to do with their son and a twelve-bore. If you don't mind I must just—'

I banged the phone down. Really, it is amazing how obtuse one's friends can be!

I then tried the Balfours over at Firle. Just my luck that it was the tiresome Freddie who answered.

'Wonderful to hear you, Primrose my dear,' he galumphed. 'So sorry to have missed you at the Penlows but I was busy wielding my mashie up on the Links, if you see what I mean.' There was a hoot of laughter and I blanched at the image of Freddie's mashie in full swing.

'I hope it was a success,' I said, 'and, er, is Melinda there by any chance?'

'Not today she isn't. The naughty girl is up in London spending all my well-earned money. But she'll be back this evening – at least I *assume* so – and I'll tell her you called.'

I thanked him and firmly replaced the receiver.

Huh! So far, so rotten useless. However, there was of course a third and vital string to my bow: contact with Bewley himself. That surely would yield the best intelligence. So to this end I made some strong coffee, removed the cat from the sofa, and brooded. How exactly could I buttonhole the man? What pretext could I use? Perhaps a complaint about the town clerk's obstructiveness or the uselessness of the Watch Committee . . . No. Such topics might rankle or at least be counterproductive. Something more neutral, more anodyne was required. The problem of cats in the castle grounds? A plea to reduce the unholy glare of the civic litter bins? The potholes in the approach to the priory? Hmm . . . not really. Too dull, too negative. I thought instead of Ingaza's methods: flattery laced with guile, applause calculated to disarm.

And thus, inspiration came. I would bang on about the dazzling spectacle of the annual Guy Fawkes bonfire and the accompanying fireworks, and how this year under his watch the event had surpassed itself: a display so masterful that even poor Fawkes himself might have approved! (Actually I hate the business, as do Bouncer and Maurice, and we take cover under the eiderdown till dawn.) But yes, that was it: a gushing encomium to soften him up; and then, his defences down, I could ply him with questions about his 'friend', the late, lamented Elspeth Travers.

Triumphantly I grasped my handbag, applied a slash of crimson lipstick, waved to the animals and set off briskly for the town hall.

Mindful of my recent encounter with Alice Markham and her officious nephew, I parked my car with scrupulous exactitude and started to make my way to the town hall. The route passed a newly opened tea shop, and I paused by the window to inspect its menu. My eye had just travelled as far as 'Our Fresh Pastries and Speciality Ices', when I suddenly saw a vaguely familiar figure seated at one of the tables. Yes, it was Reginald Bewley himself. What a stroke of luck. To engage him now would save not only time but a possible encounter with sour-faced Purvis at the front desk. (Normally the town clerk lurks malignly in some corner recess, but occasionally, unsought, he will emerge eager to block whatever it is one requires.)

Thus, with ingratiating smile and all ready to gush about the annual display on Caburn Hill, I opened the door, walked briskly across the room and stood in front of his table. 'Why, if it isn't Councillor Bewley,' I exclaimed. 'Such a coincidence. We must be on the same mission – to case the new joint!'

He jumped up, set his book aside and invited me to join him. (What else could he do?) The usual pleasantries were exchanged, the tea shop assessed and the weather disparaged. And then

I launched into my Guy Fawkes eulogy. The result was just as I had hoped. He seemed both surprised and gratified; and then, presumably encouraged by my look of rapt enquiry, embarked on a meticulous account of the event's logistics and the council's plans to introduce subtle modifications the following year.

Frankly it was all rather fatiguing. And after murmuring something to the effect that perfection needs no adjustment, I ordered a large ice cream. I also persuaded him to do the same . . . After all, there was a limit to how long one could talk about municipal bonfires, and now that he was suitably softened it was time I broached the topic of Elspeth.

'Such a sad business,' I sighed, 'and such a waste. I fear it is just as they say – the good die young, and in her case the attractive too. Admittedly I didn't know her well but she always struck me as a person of great style and charm, which somehow makes it seem doubly awful that she should have ended like that: beleaguered and alone, washed up on some bleak and desolate shore . . . Wouldn't you agree, Mr Bewley?' I gazed pensively at the vanilla concoction before me, wondering if I had over-egged the tragic scene. There was silence, and for a few moments I feared that I had.

But then with a faint cough and clearing of throat, he leant forward and said, 'You are so right, Miss Oughterard – oh, and please call me Reginald – I couldn't have put it better myself. Just why sympathy for tragic victims should be heightened by their attractiveness I'm not sure – but I fear that is often the case and I share your feelings of Mrs Travers' untimely end. A most agreeable person and a stalwart of the community, she didn't deserve to die like that.' He gazed at me with earnest eyes, and while mentally querying the term 'stalwart' as applied to Elspeth, I nodded my agreement.

'But you know,' I said casually, 'I hadn't realized she was such a keen swimmer – she certainly wasn't a member of the Brighton Breakwaters. Though perhaps that boisterous clan wasn't quite her thing. I imagine Elspeth preferred more languid aquatics.'

If I expected that to elicit anything useful I was disappointed. 'One might think so, but I really have no idea,' he replied vaguely. 'I don't recall her ever mentioning the topic. We talked about art and travel mainly . . .' There was a pause. And then he said, 'Yes, I have to say it has all been quite a shock. Most unsettling. And it may sound trivial, but I fear my whist will suffer.'

'Your whist?' I asked, somewhat taken aback.

'Oh indeed, she was an excellent player – and certainly taught me a thing or two. I shall miss those little sessions, most invigorating.' His voice held a melancholy note and for an uneasy moment I thought I saw a tear in his eye, but perhaps it was a trick of the light.

'Well, of course one does get used to a partner's style,' I said sympathetically. 'But what about your wife, doesn't she play?'

He looked startled. 'My wife? Oh no – or at least I don't think so, unless she's taken it up recently. I fear we are "estranged" as the newspapers quaintly put it, not divorced exactly but she is down in Hampshire and we live separate lives. On the whole it's more comfortable that way. She leads a quiet life tending her beloved garden, and I beaver away up here organizing bonfire displays and keeping the rates and the council in check.' He gave a dry smile.

'A sound arrangement,' I replied. 'It's a pity more couples don't do that – enforced co-habiting must be an awful strain!'

'You could be right,' he murmured, and glanced at his watch. 'If you will excuse me, duty calls – or at least Mr Purvis does. We're scheduled to meet in ten minutes and it would be dangerous to keep him waiting.' He laughed, and with a few additional pleasantries got up and approached the exit.

Left alone I ordered some fresh coffee, finished my now melting ice cream, and cogitated. Not that there was much to cogitate about. Pleasant, mannerly, confiding up to a point but only so far . . . Was Reginald Bewley the arch diplomat or simply a bland bureaucrat? It could be either, but I suspected the latter. I gathered my things, paid my bill and stood up to leave. It was only then that I noticed he had left his book behind.

Slipping it into my bag to return to him later, I saw its title. It was Compton Mackenzie's *Thin Ice.*

SIXTEEN

The dog's view

She's gearing herself up again. Oh yes, I can always tell, just as I could with F.O. It's my sixth sense, it sort of sniffs out what's going on inside 'em, or what the cat calls their S.O.M. – their STATE OF MIND-LESS-NESS. Of course, Maurice doesn't believe in my sixth sense, says it's all hooey. But I know what I know, and I can tell you that the Prim is getting all excited and nosy again and she's on the track of something – or more like some*one*! And when that happens she's a bit like me with a bone or a bunny, TEE-NAYSHUS . . . Hmm, I like that word and it's easier to say than some of the other words Maurice uses. Anyway, so that's it: our mistress is definitely on the warpath again and I bet you that there's going to be a big HULL-A-BALLOON. Trust Bouncer, he knows!

Take the other night, for example. I was having a really good kip in my basket, knackered with playing Top Dog with my new friend Louis Lionheart (cor, he's a one!), when there's a mighty crash and in comes P.O. all got up in her night clothes and curlers, and muttering something about having to *think*. That made me a bit fed up 'cause I'd been having a really GOOD dream, all about chewing the tail off the cat's toy mouse. So I gave a growl and said a few rude words, but she went on crashing about and rattling the kettle and stuff.

Huh! No sleep for the wicked, as Maurice is always telling me. So I thought I might as well stretch the old ham'n' eggs – or as the cat would say 'savour the night air' – and force her to let me out. As a matter of fact, I quite enjoyed that, though I was still a bit miffed at being woken up. So when later on she opened the back door and yelled at me to come in I hid behind the potting shed and made her blooming well wait. That kept her cursing for a bit! But then I heard her bawling something about no more bones. Don't suppose she meant it; still, you can never be sure with humans and it doesn't do to chance your whatsit, so I raced in pretty smartish.

The next morning she was still in an odd state (so was Maurice, all yawny and sulky) and sat on the sofa frowning and swilling coffee. Then up she leaps, and scoots from the house like a ferret from a trap. Oh ho! I thought, something's up. I mentioned this to Maurice but all he did was twitch his tail and look po-faced. I suppose he thinks his night's sleep was disturbed. *His* sleep? What about mine! Anyway, the cat was in one of his IN-COMMUNI-CADO moods and I left him to it.

And then I started to feel a bit bored, so I visited Boris and Karloff in their hutch and shouted the odds. But nothing happened (out for the count in the back, I suppose). Then a really good wheeze hit me: I would trot along to the tall house and stir up Louis Lionheart. He's always ready for a romp. So with the Prim out and the cat sulking, it was easy to squeeze through the hedge and out into the lane without any beggar seeing me.

It doesn't take long to reach the spaniel's place . . . and do you know what? Just as I got there I saw his people leaving together by the front gate and *without* him. So I lurked behind a lamp post for a while just to see them out of sight, and then sloped up and took a crafty peek through the hedge. And what do you think I saw? Old Lionheart stretched his length on the lawn gnawing a rubber toy! Things couldn't be simpler. 'Lion,' I barked, 'come here quickly!'

'What-ho!' he yelped, and came bounding over to see me. 'If it's not old Bouncer,' he cried. 'How did you get out?'

'Easily,' I said, 'with a bit of low cunning. No fleas on Bouncer!'

'I should think not,' he said, 'I wouldn't mind having some of that.'

'It'll come,' I told him. 'And meanwhile what about a little jaunt somewhere?'

He nodded eagerly and, twirling around, tried to do a somersault. It wasn't very successful. 'But which way have my people gone?' he asked, panting slightly.

I told him that I thought they had wandered off down to the river.

'Oh yes, they like doing that, always at it – so we'd better go the other way.'

I agreed and, grabbing his collar in my teeth, tugged him through the hedge.

We wandered towards the edge of the town, sniffing this and growling at that. And then as we passed a pair of wide gates, Lionheart said, 'I say, Bouncer, have you ever been in there?'

I shook my head.

'Shall we go in? You never know, we might find a cat.'

So we slipped in and looked around. There didn't seem to be any cats about, and I thought it all looked a bit boring: a square white house, big lawn and some empty flowerbeds. I mean there were no nice molehills, no long grass or bunny hutches, and not even a shed – not like at MY house! I was just about to say that we could probably find somewhere more fun nearer the town when I saw a garden seat by one of the windows and someone sitting on it. Louis saw it too. 'Who's that?' he asked.

'Dunno,' I answered, 'but it looks like a lady. Never seen her before.'

Louis screwed up his eyes and then wagged his tail. 'But *I* have,' he chortled, 'and I don't like her. She's not nice.'

I asked him how he knew her and why she wasn't nice.

'Well,' he explained, 'I was in the grocer's the other day with my mistress. She had put me on my lead and I was being very good. Or at least I was only doing a *little* bit of prancing – just by those nice biscuit stacks in the corner. Anyway, that roly-poly person was there, and she pointed at me and frowned and said I was in her way or something stupid like that. I thought that was a bit rotten as I was being really nice and chummy to everyone!'

'So what did your mistress say?'

'She didn't say anything. Doesn't need to. When she's annoyed she just gives one of her looks. I think it's called' – Lion sniffed at a patch of grass – 'uhm . . . *withering*. Yes, that's what it's called, and when she withers you don't half know it! Anyway, she had a good old wither at this person who went all pink and tossed her head. I don't think they liked each other, you can generally tell with humans.'

'Oh yes,' I said, 'nearly always. So what did she smell like?'

Lion wrinkled his muzzle. 'Nothing much, just boring. I mean, she didn't smell of DOG or even of CAT. All the best people smell of one or both. If you ask me, Bouncer, that lady is not of the best.'

'Cor,' I said, 'you've got a sixth sense just like mine!'

He grinned and wagged his tail. 'It's getting better: it's the company I keep.'

We had a laugh and a quick roll on the grass, and I was just about to lift my leg against a handy watering can when this thin weedy-looking chap comes out of the house and sits next to the lady and starts yacking.

We watched for a bit, and then Louis Lionheart started to fidget and growl. 'Ssh,' I said, 'we'll play a game. Let's pretend we are bloodhounds and see how close we can get to them without being seen. Whoever is seen first is a ninny. And then we'll scarper!'

'You're on,' Lion whispered.

So that's what we did – edged on our bellies alongside the hedge like collies do, until we reached a couple of big stone pots with flowers stuck in them. We crouched behind these and were so close to the humans that we could hear what they were saying . . . No, that's not quite right, *I* could hear; Lion was too busy snuffling and chuckling. I told him to CONTAIN himself, like Maurice says to me, and cocked my ears.

You know, when I was a young pup I hadn't a clue what humans were on about (they grunt and burble), but now that I am big I am getting the hang of it. Not as good as the cat, of course, but not bad all the same – and MUCH better than Duster, the Penlows' cairn terrier, who only knows six words: *walkies*, *haggis*, *badboy*, *NO*, *ochaye* and *grub*. Well, Bouncer knows lots more than that! So I listened very carefully and heard the weedy one say something about having to take care as they were treading on thin mice. Pretty rum really . . . I mean, what's the point of treading on 'em? Much more fun to chase the blighters like Maurice does. And in any case, why *thin*? Ah well, you never know with humans – daft as a fox's brush, and no mistake!

Anyway, the lady gave a fat laugh and said he was a dear boy and shouldn't worry so much. Hmm. He didn't look very dear to me – kick your rump as soon as look at you! But then he said something which made her look rather fierce and she wagged her finger at him. It was to do with pills. (Now I know about pills because the Prim shoves them into me when the old gut is playing up or she thinks I've got worms.) So I pricked up my ears even more and concentrated really *hard*. And this is what I heard: 'Oh, Auntie, I do hope you are taking your pills, you know you like them. And whatever happens we must stay calm, mustn't we?'

Can't say this made much sense to me, but I didn't have a chance to think, because just then the Lion gave a deafening sneeze. And that did it: our cover was blown and we had to skedaddle fast. So we tore across the lawn and through the gates like cats out of hell. I looked back once and saw the roly-poly lady shaking her fist. Not that that bothered me – I mean humans do that all the time, don't they.

Well, after that BROO-HA-HA as Maurice would call it, we decided to go back to our own homes and lie doggo for a bit. It doesn't do to hang about. Besides, I wanted my nosh. Oh, and by the way, who was the ninny? Well, it wasn't Bouncer, that's for sure!

SEVENTEEN

The Primrose version

That afternoon I had a dental appointment, and as I returned to the waiting room to collect my coat, I bumped into Melinda Balfour. She was leafing restlessly through some outdated copies of *Vogue* and looking distinctly out of sorts.

'What's wrong with you?' I asked cheerfully. 'You look as twitchy as a jack rabbit.'

'So would you be if you had my delicate disposition; we don't all have a rock-hard carapace. I can't bear that awful drill!' she replied irritably.

I cannot say that Melinda had ever struck me as having a delicate disposition, but I assured her briskly that the ordeal would soon be over and not to worry.

She didn't look particularly reassured, and then said, 'And what's more I've got Alice Markham coming to tea tomorrow. Not the most exciting prospect, but she pushed me into a corner and I couldn't get out.' The frown suddenly turned into an ingratiating smile and she said, 'I don't suppose you would care to come, would you? It might be quite helpful.'

I hesitated. 'Well, er . . . but what about Freddie? Won't he do?'

'Freddie? Good lord, no. He'd ruin any tea party. No, this will be girls only. Come on, be a pal.' She winced theatrically and moaned, 'Oh Christ, that bloody drill!'

The rock-hard carapace softened slightly, as presumably it was intended to, and I told her that provided there were doughnuts and Huntley & Palmers' wafers I would be there.

She gave a relieved nod. 'Yes, yes of course, I'll get some of those . . . But don't bring the hound, Alice doesn't like dogs.'

Thus the following afternoon, having told Bouncer that his presence would not be required, I dutifully drove over to the Balfours' place at Firle. I was a little late and there was already a blue Talbot parked in the forecourt, which I took to be Alice Markham's, but also another car I didn't recognize. It turned out to belong to Peggy Mountjoy who, like me, had obviously been dragooned into swelling the ranks and to give diversion to Alice and support for Melinda.

Swelling the ranks further was Peggy's 'Freudian' daughter. In the library where tea was already being served I saw her closely examining one of the bookcases. Perhaps, under the tutelage of the 'brilliant' Dr Bakeshaft, she was hunting for significant insights into the Balfours' buried identities. Since that particular bookcase shelved old copies of *Punch*, *Wisden's Almanack*, volumes of Surtees (*Mr Sponge's Sporting Tour*, etc.), and a collection of Sapper novels and Enid Blyton, I feared she would draw a blank.

Peggy and I exchanged cheery greetings, while Alice Markham gestured graciously from behind a large doughnut. I was reminded of my first encounter with her over a year ago and in the same surroundings. Then, being in the throes of a messy divorce, she had been in what might be called a 'heightened state' and we had been treated to a febrile display of fury and self-pity. The more recent encounter at Melinda's had been void of such drama though I cannot say my view of the woman had been especially enhanced.

Nevertheless, she now seemed civil enough and, though garrulous and forthright, moderately stable.

We sipped our tea and talked of this and that – the delights of the Lewes flower show, the improved train service to London and Eastbourne, the state of the government and poor Mr MacMillan's cough, Princess Margaret's dress at Ascot – and the latest peculiar sermon from the Reverend Egge.

'It was very interesting,' Melinda said, 'all about fairies and tree-felling. Riveting really, but I couldn't quite see where God came into it. Still I suppose He was in there somewhere, although I'm not entirely sure whether . . .'

'Lost in the foliage presumably,' I said.

'Or hanging on to a branch purloined by the fairies,' laughed Peggy.

Her daughter frowned. 'You are being *so* facetious, Mummy. The Reverend Egge is a very complex person and his sermons deeply symbolic, and—'

'How do you know he is complex?' I asked her. 'He seems perfectly straightforward to me: pleasant and a bit daft.'

The girl shook her head and gave me an indulgent smile. 'Ah but the *trained* eye can discern things the layman can't. I have been making a study of the gentleman and I just know that in those veiled depths there lurks a network of needs and impulses of which the subject is totally unaware.' She paused to stretch out a hand for a sandwich, before adding, 'And besides, nobody is straightforward, Miss Oughterard. Dr Bakeshaft says that under expert analysis the psyche yields up simply fascinating material. We all have our hidden neuroses and dark crevices' – she turned to Alice – 'wouldn't you agree, Mrs Markham?'

'What?' the latter spluttered, having just bitten into another doughnut.

'Dark crevices, Mrs Markham – don't you think we all have them?'

'Oh doubtless, dear,' Alice replied, the morsel of doughnut safely swallowed, 'but unless the doctor is known to me personally I prefer to keep mine covered!' She emitted a crash of laughter. The girl turned pink and the rest of us raised startled eyebrows.

There was a brief silence. And then hastily changing the subject, Melinda said, 'You know, Alice, I still can't get over how stoical you were at Elspeth's funeral. It must have been *such* an ordeal. I think you've coped splendidly!' She wore the kindly expression that she assumes when Freddie has said something particularly crass.

Alice gave a modest shrug. 'Oh well, one does one's best, you know – but you're right, it's not been easy since dear Elspeth died. So many memories . . .' She sighed wistfully.

'And so, what are you going to do about Needham Court?' asked the practical Peggy. 'Sell it or rent it?'

'Oh, a clean break is the best, hard though that will be. Once I have made it ship-shape it will be on the market. Renting out a property means one still has to keep in touch, however tenuously. And you know, I really don't think I could bear to see other people living where Elspeth had once been.'

I understood the sentiment, but somehow coming from Alice Markham it didn't quite ring true though I couldn't explain why. Perhaps an instinct spawned in one of those dark crevices?

We turned to other matters, during which my eye fell upon a vase of small roses displayed on a corner table. I hadn't noticed them before and was taken by their perky charm. Inexplicably they struck a chord, for gazing at them I was suddenly confronted by an image of Elspeth's rose-decked bathing cap bobbing wildly amid swirling waters.

It was an unfortunate chord, as without thought I heard myself saying, 'But it still strikes me as odd that given Elspeth's dislike of the cold, she should have taken the plunge in that particular week. I was abroad at the time so wouldn't know, but I gather we had been having the most unseasonable weather – quite Arctic by summer standards.'

'Oh yes, frightful!' chimed Peggy.

I realized as soon as I had spoken that my words might not be well received, but was unprepared for the intensity of the reaction. Alice Markham glared at me and then picking up her teaspoon drummed the table loudly (rather like a headmistress impatiently rebuking a pupil). 'You seem to have a fixation about my sister's swimming habits, Miss Oughterard. I recall you showing the same kind of interest not so long ago. I consider it tiresome and intrusive.' She released the spoon with a clatter and angrily twitched her napkin.

Before I could make a hasty apology (not that I felt apologetic) Peggy's daughter had intervened. 'Ah but you see people *do* act irrationally sometimes. It's all to do with their neural—'

Alice switched her glare from me to the girl. 'You know nothing about it,' she snapped, 'and if you take my advice you will find yourself a nice young man. At your age you ought to be playing tennis and going to parties, not bothering your head with all this mental nonsense!'

I suspect Peggy might have shared that view, but she made loyal protest nevertheless. 'Oh, I say, steady on!' she gasped, and cast a nervous glance at her daughter who for once looked mildly flummoxed. Alice glowered across the tea table, and for an instant I saw our hostess close her eyes. (In prayer?) And then something miraculous happened. (An answer?) There was a loud crash in the hall, followed by a curse – and Freddie appeared.

'Who on earth has left that blithering—' he began, and then stopped short. Faced by the group of ladies, his tone changed from testy protest to unctuous gallantry. 'Oh I say, aren't I the lucky chap! I come home worn out with honest toil' – he is a stockbroker – 'only to find a bevy of beautiful birds!' He bellowed a laugh and winked roguishly. And then seeing Alice, added, 'Including the lovely Mrs Markham – and with such a splendid hat! I'm sure Melinda is jealous; I'll have to get her one just like that!' He advanced and made much show of clasping our hands. Had Freddie been on stage he would have been accused of over-acting. As it is, such fulsome nonsense is second nature and it comes pouring out whenever in the company of the opposite sex (except for that of his sister, mother and wife).

I can't say that I have ever thought of Freddie Balfour in the role of a *deus ex machina*, and I doubt if Melinda has, but that day he was timely and superb. Turning back to Alice, he said, 'Do you remember once asking me about the best pot plants to impress prospective buyers for your sister's house? Well, just come and look at mine on the terrace. They're on pretty good form and might give you some ideas.'

Somewhat disarmed by the attention, Alice allowed herself to be ushered outside. Freddie's invitation was no diversionary ploy. Like Charles Penlow, he is a keen gardener (the one thing the two men have in common) and will take any opportunity to show off his planting skills – regardless of audience.

After they had gone there was a brief silence, during which I heard Melinda's breath being slowly expelled like a punctured tyre.

'That was a bit hairy,' Peggy observed. 'If you don't mind my saying, Melinda, she's not exactly the perfect guest. Quite a touchy madam!' She giggled.

'Touchy? Unhinged you mean!' the hostess yelped. 'And did you see the way she was rattling that teaspoon, if you please? It's from one of my best sets. It's probably bent by now.' Melinda rose and, picking up the spoon, scrutinized it closely. She said nothing and one assumed it was unscathed.

'But wasn't Freddie wonderful!' I exclaimed quickly, fearing I might be seen as the cause of the outburst. I was.

'Oh, he has his moments,' she agreed. 'But honestly, Primrose, for God's sake steer clear of that swimming business or it might set her off again. If you hadn't said what you did she'd have probably been all right.'

I nodded meekly. As a rebuke it could have been worse.

'It did seem to touch a nerve,' Peggy agreed cheerfully. 'Still, I suppose that's death for you, it shakes you up and casts you down.' She glanced at her daughter and with the merest twinkle said, 'She certainly had it in for you, my girl!'

The latter had evidently recovered from her slight, for with a doleful shake of the head she replied, 'I fear poor Mrs Markham had simply no idea of what she was saying, no concept at all.'

Personally I felt that Alice Markham had a very clear concept of what she had been saying. However, I remained silent; and at that moment the cause of the disruption returned from the garden in obvious high spirits and gaily clutching Freddie's arm. 'Your hubby's such a charmer,' she chortled to Melinda, 'what a lucky girl you are!' Her hostess gave a pinched smile while the rest of us laughed politely. And on that merry note the tea party broke up and Alice was waved a fond goodbye.

Staring after the departing car Freddie was heard to mutter that he was in need of a stiff drink. To which his wife replied that her need was somewhat stronger than that – i.e. to be taken to the

Grand Hotel at Eastbourne that very evening, plied with cocktails and be given a slap-up supper.

As I got into my own car Peggy edged up and murmured, 'By the way, did you see her hands? They were shaking.'

'What, Melinda's?'

'No! What an absurd idea. Alice's, of course.'

'But they weren't,' I frowned, 'she was bashing that spoon on the table.'

'But the left hand was in her lap and shaking like a leaf.'

'D.T.s?'

She shrugged. 'Who knows? That or dope.' And then with a leer she added, 'I wasn't terribly sure about that hat, were you?'

'Frightful,' I said.

EIGHTEEN

The Primrose version

As arranged, Ingaza turned up for our late lunch – very late as it turned out, well after two o'clock. 'What took you so long?' I protested. 'The lobster is not at its best, and neither am I.'

He had the grace to apologize and explain that he had been delayed by a recalcitrant client. 'Someone you know, actually.' He smirked.

'Oh, really? And who might that be?'

'A Mrs Alice Markham, sister of the Travers woman you are so obsessed with.'

I was taken aback. Why on earth should Alice Markham be patronizing Nicholas's money-trap? Had she inherited spare funds from her sister's will and thus eager to fritter them on paintings of questionable worth and ambiguous provenance?

Naturally I didn't say that exactly, but instead asked blandly, 'Oh, and did she want to buy something? Perhaps her London flat has a wall space?'

'No,' was the curt reply, 'I wouldn't know about her London

flat and do not care. What the lady wanted – if thus one can call
her – was not to purchase, but to *sell*.' He glared at the cat, who
glared back.

I must have looked puzzled, for he then continued, 'Yes, the
old bat actually had the nerve to say she didn't like those two
Calder pictures her sister had bought and would I kindly take
them back! When I enquired what price she had in mind, she
gave a sour look and said, "The original naturally!" I wasn't too
keen on that and told her Calder's popularity had taken an unfortunate nosedive since that sale and thus any reimbursement would,
alas, be minimal.'

'You don't say,' I laughed, 'and what was her reaction?'

He winced. 'Made a scene, if you please, quite embarrassing
really – an awful racket, and then flounced out bawling the odds
and declaring she would do better at Sotheby's . . . Huh, and
much good that'll do her, I don't think!' He gave an indifferent
shrug but I could see he was piqued. 'Mad as a hatter,' he
muttered.

To soothe ruffled feathers I hastily introduced the lobster bisque
and a bottle of chardonnay, which gave mutual pleasure and a
mellowness we rarely shared.

Over the cheese (the grocer's best mousetrap) we discussed
the terms of his talk to the Artists' Guild and touched lightly on
MacManus's recent visit. About the latter he was fairly insouciant:
'I shouldn't worry. Take my advice and hang on to those photos;
they could be dynamite. A chap in his position can't afford to be
caught romping about with some tart dressed as a stork.'

'An ostrich actually,' I murmured.

'Either way it would be curtains for his career. Play that card
and he'll be putty in your hands.' He spoke with confidence and
I was reminded that having once upon a time been gaoled for
dubious antics in a Turkish bath, Nicholas Ingaza would surely
know what he was talking about.

He consulted his watch. 'Ah! Time for liquors if you have any.'
He grinned encouragingly, and I dutifully supplied some port
while he produced cigarettes. We settled back in our chairs in a
swirl of scented Sobranie, and he winked. 'Quite like old times
really – all we need now is dear old Francis . . . God, what a
bumbler! What a lovable effing bumbler!'

I nodded, and tacitly we raised our glasses. For a moment there was silence as we lapsed into private unspoken nostalgias. I suppose it was the heady blend of wine and port, but for a brief moment I was back in my student days carefree and unencumbered. 'Youth is so far away,' I sighed wistfully, thinking of my dalliances at the Courtauld.

Rather to my surprise Ingaza seemed in agreement, for he nodded and gave a rueful smile. There followed another silence. And then he said brightly, 'Fortunately my tango is still superb, of course, but I fear my singing days are over. Out of practice . . . a pity really. I don't think you ever heard my rendition of "La Mer", did you?'

I was about to say something polite to the effect that I had missed that particular joy, but an awful memory seized me. Oh yes, I had certainly heard it: once in the Auvergne when the three of us – he, Francis and I – were embroiled with an unhinged pseudo-religious sect on the heights of Le Puy[6]. Yes, that was the time. In a moment of careless bonhomie (prior to the onset of darker matters) Nicholas had launched into an excruciating imitation of Charles Trenet singing that haunting chanson. Affected, reedy, nasal and overlaid with a distinct cockney twang, Nicholas's version had been hard to bear. But bear it we did, on the assumption that such a performance would be a rarity . . . And so it had been until this moment – when, with a sharp clearing of throat and a bracing of thin shoulders, the crooner manqué stood up, spread his arms and began to give voice.

Dutifully I listened with rapt features, but just as he reached the end of the sixth line, '"*La mer au ciel d'été*",' spinning it out for all it was worth, the doorbell rang. 'Fuck!' the crooner snapped, and stopped.

Saved by the bell, I went to open the door.

'Hello, Miss Oughterard,' piped the diminutive Richard Ickington, 'I've brought you some flowers. Matron said you might be in.' Why Matron imagined that I have no idea. The boy thrust a mangled bunch of chrysanthemums towards me. Colourful they may have been, but as I politely held them to my nose I was assailed by that characteristic odour of old vestries and rancid cheese.

[6] See *Bones in High Places*

I beamed down at the child. 'How lovely,' I murmured, 'and to what do I owe this nice surprise? Has Grandpa won on the horses again?' Grandpa was His Honour Mr Justice Ickington, formidable High Court judge and whose soubriquet, Sickie-Dickie, his grandson shared.

Dickie giggled. 'No, not for quite a bit actually, and the air is really blue! Even the court ushers are beginning to complain.'

'Ah well,' I replied vaguely, 'I daresay something will romp home . . . So, er, why have you brought me these pretty flowers? I hope you haven't spent all your pocket money on them.'

He shook his head, saying that a mere ninepence had been spent as they were some of the florist's rejects.

I complimented him on his grasp of economy, but asked again why he should have produced such a bouquet. 'What an unexpected pleasure,' I twittered. 'A passing whim, perhaps?'

He looked puzzled. 'What?'

'A *whim*, Dickie. Was it something you suddenly thought of on the spur of the moment?'

He shook his head. 'Mr Winchbrooke said that if I called in with the invitation he would let me off my lines. So here I am!' He beamed, and then looking past me, added, 'And is your nice dog still here?'

I confirmed that Bouncer was still in residence and that he could see him shortly – but in the meantime what invitation was he talking about?

Thrusting a hand into his blazer pocket, he drew out a crumpled piece of cardboard and passed it over. 'It's time for the school concert again,' he explained, 'and Mr Winchbrooke said that personal delivery would save on the postage.' Typical!

'I see,' I said dryly, 'so I take it the flowers were not his idea.'

'Oh no, Miss Oughterard,' the child exclaimed earnestly, '*that* was my idea. It's what Grandpa calls "useful gallantry", and Grandpa knows a thing or two!' He seemed to cogitate for a moment before adding, 'Probably a bit more than Mr Winchbrooke, I expect.'

A just assessment no doubt, but before I could say anything, Dickie's eye had again turned to the end of the passage where Bouncer was now hovering. 'Good old Bouncer!' the boy squeaked rapturously. 'I say, Miss Oughterard, have you got any of those nice custard tarts that I could feed him with? I think he likes them!' He turned to Bouncer. 'Don't you, old boy?'

After a faint hesitation the dog wagged its tail obligingly, and I shoved the pair of them into the kitchen to gorge themselves sick.

Returning to the drawing room I found Nicholas slumped on the sofa in a cloud of smoke, a languid hand rhythmically stroking the air. Fearing he was preparing for a further assault on 'La Mer' I looked for a diversionary tactic and hastily supplied him with another glass of port.

This worked, for taking a sip, he said, 'Your visitor sounded not unlike a castrated elf. Who was it – one of those poor little tykes the Jehovah's Witnesses always seem to have in tow?'

I explained that it was not a Jehovah's Witness but merely Judge Ickington's grandson delivering an invitation to the Erasmus Revels, an annual event of searing sobriety to which half the county was summoned in the hope of augmenting the school's reputation and revenue . . . mainly the latter.

Nicholas looked vaguely interested. 'Oh, was that the kid who found the naughty photographs in Topping's study?'

'Yes, but fortunately he doesn't have a clue what they were about, and thanks to me thinks it was some rehearsal for a pantomime.'

Ingaza gave a mirthless laugh. 'Poor little sod, he'll learn soon enough.' We exchanged knowing nods as elders do when speaking of the young.

We chatted some more and even put on a jazz record. But its sinuous strains were suddenly echoed from the doorway where Maurice stood looking thunderous. He gave another yowl, and tossing his head stared indignantly towards the kitchen. From that region I heard faint sounds – a dog's bark and a squeal of laughter. O lord, I had forgotten Sickie-Dickie! Excusing myself to Nicholas, I went to investigate.

'Well,' I said, surveying an upturned chair and the crumb-strewn kitchen, 'you've obviously both had a good time.'

'Oh yes, Miss Oughterard,' Dickie exclaimed, 'it's been wizard. I've been practising leapfrogging with the chair – we do it at school. And dear old Bouncer let me have half his cakes. Wasn't that nice?'

I glanced at the dog who looked distinctly bilious. 'Yes, he has his moments of generosity,' I murmured. 'Now, Dickie, I think it's time you bustled off, otherwise Matron will be worried, and I have a visitor who I must attend to.'

He nodded. But then, slipping his hand in his trouser pocket, said, 'Oh, I quite forgot, would you be kind enough to translate this for me, Miss Oughterard? Some of it's in English but there's a lot in French. We've only just started that and I can't do it for toffee – can't tell a *de* from a *le*. Can you?'

'Well,' I said modestly, 'French is one of my few accomplishments, so perhaps I can help.' I put out my hand, into which he thrust a piece of crumpled paper.

'It's the new French master,' he explained, 'he says we have to collect little ponces and copy them out and put them into English. I don't know what a ponce is but I expect this will do. I got it out of Mrs Markham's coat pocket.'

'You did what?' I said sharply. 'That doesn't sound very polite.'

He shrugged. 'Oh, I don't suppose it matters. She came to visit Mr Winchbrooke and he said I should help her off with her coat. It was a jolly big coat and jolly heavy and I nearly fell over. This slipped out of the pocket and I was going to stuff it back, but just then Smidge Minor came by and gave me a whopping wink and I started to giggle. And then when I did pick it up Mr Winchbrooke had already taken the lady into his study. So Smidge and I ran off to play. Anyway, here it is, and I don't suppose she has missed it.'

I ran my eye over the note. It was hardly a *pensée* but a brief little missive, terse yet oddly effusive – and fortunately did not strain my linguistic skills.

> *Ma plus chère,*
>
> Well, it's over. Mission complete – and thanks to you it all went brilliantly! *Quelle triomphe!! Il faut fêter ça. Mais pas encore – un peu trop dangereux* (so hold on to your *châpeau*!). Will contact when the dust settles *et quand tout va bien.*
>
> *Entretemps, <u>vagues</u> des baisers*

If the note had once been in pristine condition it certainly wasn't now, being crumpled and grubby and with a splodge of ink covering

what presumably had been a signature. It bore the hallmarks of
Sickie-Dickie's paws.

'You've made an awful mess of it,' I said sternly.

He gave a rueful grin; and then as I guided him in translating
the French bits, asked, 'But why are the kisses vague?'

I explained that they were not vague but waves. 'It's a figure
of speech. It means lots and lots of them. That's rather nice,
don't you think?' I said brightly. The child looked dubious and
said he thought it was soppy – and in any case why was it
dangerous to celebrate? He liked celebrating, especially when
it was his birthday which, he informed me with studied care, was
very, very soon.

Luckily before the vital date could be confided Nicholas came
in to announce his departure – which was just as well for I was
feeling tired and the dog looked seedy (or possibly vice versa).

'I'm off,' he announced. 'Got to see a man about a Rembrandt.'

'Huh! That'll be the day,' I snorted, and was about to hustle
him out, when there was a squeak from Dickie.

'Oh I say, are you that Mr Ingaza?'

'What Mr Ingaza?' Nicholas replied cautiously.

'The one that Mummy says is as sharp as a ferret and the best
slippery art dealer on the south coast.' The boy beamed up at
Nicholas and added, 'I think that is very im . . . im . . . *pressive*!
It is an honour to meet you, sir.' (Clearly Matron had been teaching
the boys their social graces.) A small hand was extended, which,
after a moment's glazed hesitation, the ferret shook.

Exploiting such burgeoning camaraderie, I suggested that as it
was getting dark Nicholas should give his young admirer a lift
back to Erasmus House. I sensed it was not a proposal that the
former favoured, but pressed on regardless. 'Oh yes,' I said gaily
to Dickie, 'and Mr Ingaza's French is very good. He can tell you
all the words for sea, sky, gulls, clouds and even angels. That will
impress your French master! In fact if you are lucky he might
even sing you a famous French song which contains all those
words. Wouldn't that be nice?'

Dickie nodded, while Ingaza closed his eyes.

After they had gone I set the kitchen to rights, swept up the
pastry crumbs, removed some globs of custard from the dog's
basket (evidently too much even for Bouncer's gross palate), and

with a sigh of relief lit a cigarette and settled down with the evening paper.

Such repose lasted for about five minutes as for some reason the contents of Dickie's note kept playing in my mind. It had been a curious little thing and not quite what one would expect to find in the pocket of Alice Markham's fur coat. Still, it is amazing what people stash away in moments of distraction or impatience. I recall Francis as a boy raiding Pa's overcoat for some loose change; he was out of luck, but instead fished out a silk stocking and a partially chewed gobstopper – both presumably stowed in some haste, though whether at the same time we could never decide.

The note's scrawled brevity and casual mix of French and English suggested it had been dashed off in a mood of rapt elation – albeit tinged with wary relief. Obviously something of mutual benefit had been gained but whose disclosure, initially at any rate, might be unwise. The piece had a collusive, intimate ring and the emphatic use of '*baisers*' clearly indicative of a close relationship. But was Alice the recipient, or had she herself penned the thing and failed to send it?

Such musing was curtailed by Maurice, who, having eventually gained access to the kitchen yet evidently finding Bouncer unresponsive, had sidled in to needle me. This I endured for a brief while; and then tiring of the game thrust him aside and went up to the studio to put finishing – and with luck lucrative – touches to my current canvas.

It was only later, in the middle of the night and unable to sleep, that my mind once more turned to the wording of Dickie's note. Again the style struck me as somewhat gushing and the bits of French affected – and wasn't the term *waves* of kisses a trifle excessive, especially when underlined? I sighed and gave a mental shrug . . . oh well, presumably some people were like that: emotionally florid. I turned over and had just closed my eyes determined to sleep, when I was suddenly assailed by an image of the spume-topped waves lashing the shore at Birling Gap and of Elspeth's pink bathing cap dipping and diving like some beleaguered duck. Despite the warmth of the bed I shivered. *My God – rather her than me, poor woman!*

Fortunately sleep did come but it was hardly soothing. The grey waters continued to pound, the cap bobbed helplessly . . . and splashing about like a roguish walrus was, of all people, the Reverend Albert Egge, shouting, '*Ma chère, ma chère, n'ayez pas peur.* Be not afraid – let us frolic in the briny, just *toi* and *moi!*'

It was with some relief that I awoke to Bouncer's cold nose and the morning sun.

NINETEEN

The Primrose version

C learly supper's ancient cheese followed by nocturnal thoughts of Dickie's grubby note in its fractured French had played havoc with both mind and digestion. But why the vicar, for goodness' sake? Perhaps his 'marine' sermon had gone deeper than I had realized! I resolved that that night's supper would definitely include a good sleeping pill!

Thus to banish the bizarre and embrace the reassuringly bland I decided to visit the public library. Clasping a bag of overdue books and a full purse I set out briskly . . . but at St Anne's Church was stopped by the sight of a familiar figure bearing down with beaming smile.

'Good morning!' cried the Reverend Egge, removing his hat with a flourish. 'What a lovely day at last, we've certainly had our share of rain. But now we bask in the Lord's benison!'

'Er, oh indeed we do,' I replied brightly but vaguely embarrassed, recalling his chilly flounderings of the night before.

We chatted inconsequentially for a couple of minutes. And then he told me he had just been talking with Mrs Markham, who apparently had been in a state of great exuberance: 'Almost literally bubbling over.' He laughed.

'Oh yes?' I said, not especially interested. 'You surprise me – I should have thought she'd be far too busy with the house sale to find anything very exciting at the moment. It must be quite a task, shifting all that stuff and dealing with solicitors and house agents, etc.'

Egge agreed but said that the reason for her high spirits was her nephew, who was on the verge of landing a lucrative job locally selling exotic lingerie to cabaret artistes.

I blinked. 'Selling lingerie to . . .?'

Egge simpered. 'Yes, it does sound a little risqué, doesn't it, but apparently it pays well – and we musn't be too harsh on the young, must we? This is 1958, not '38, and the world moves apace. We old fogies must learn to adapt to new trends! You may recall the Bible's words that . . .'

I have to admit that I was less concerned with biblical injunctions than with being included among the Reverent Egge's 'old fogies'. He could speak for himself! But I was also intrigued by Travers' unexpected trade, not something I would associate with the etiolated character who had been so patronizing to me in the car park. 'So this lingerie,' I asked him, 'where does he get it?'

Egge shrugged. 'Oh, some warehouse in France, I gather. I believe Mrs Markham knows the director well and has pulled the odd string to get an exclusive deal so it's virtually in the bag. But keep it under your hat – she tells me the formal offer from the local firm is yet to be made and there are still rivals in the wings so it's all been rather hush-hush. In fact, I don't suppose I should be mentioning this at all.' In a gesture of sly conspiracy, he tapped the side of his nose and then bustled off muttering something about ordering new hymn books.

Well, I reflected, that certainly explained the contents of Dickie's crumpled message. Presumably the note had been penned by the nephew rejoicing in his good news. Yes, its reference to danger and the need for discretion (*keep it under your* châpeau) would certainly seem to fit with what Egge had been saying about the negotiations being top secret. He had also said something about Alice having an influential contact. Thus if 'Auntie' had indeed pulled a lever to secure the deal, no wonder the nephew's thanks had been so fulsome.

I continued to the library, paid my colossal fine and then treated myself to coffee and scones in Lewes's best tea shop. I don't normally indulge in 'elevenses' but perhaps like Albert Egge was inspired by the sun and the 'Lord's benison' and felt a sneaking halo of virtue for having paid my library dues. But whatever the reason, the scones and their liberal helpings of cream and jam were demolished with gusto and followed with a reflective cigarette.

I say reflective because, perhaps triggered by the previous night's dream, my mind once more turned to the fate of Elspeth Travers. Deep in my bones I remained convinced that there was something distinctly odd about that drowning. There seemed too many anomalies – her rooted aversion to the sea, to the cold, to frothy bathing caps. Why then should she have donned such headgear (had she bought it specially?) and ventured alone among those rough and icy waters? Summoned by mermaids? Hardly. Alice Markham might be sufficiently perverse to have taken the plunge (and in such florid millinery) but surely not the fastidious, self-preserving sister. It simply did not add up. I still smelt a very large rat and was determined to hunt it out. If the police had not cottoned on to these strange anomalies then Primrose Oughterard had! It would not be the first time that my instinct had sounded alarm bells – and in the case of the perfidious Topping it had been spot on. So yes, undeterred by my recent mistake, I would jolly well continue to follow my nose! With such thoughts revolving in my mind, my ears were also busy. For from the past I heard two dissonant voices: my father's and my brother's. *Atta girl, that's the spirit!* roared Pa. *Oh I say, Primrose, must you really?* moaned Francis. But then suddenly, cutting in on both of them came a third voice – but this time from the present.

'When we last met you were just about to prang my aunt's car,' Aston Travers said languidly. Without waiting he drew up a chair and sat down. 'Hope you don't mind if I join you. This place is so popular there's not a spare table to be had and I'm dying for a cuppa. Shopping with Auntie all morning can be hard work! But I've sneaked a pit-stop while she's chivvying the estate agents.'

'By all means,' I replied distantly. 'Actually, I am just waiting for my bill. And incidentally I was not about to prang anyone's car; it is not my habit.'

'Oh, of *course* not!' he said laughingly in a voice clearly meant to disarm. Yet underneath I detected a note of snide mockery and my original distaste deepened. But as Ma used to say, one should always be polite to the ignorant; it makes them uncomfortable. And thus I asked how the house sale was proceeding and how much longer he expected to be staying in this part of Sussex.

'Well, I was intending to go back to Brighton once we had settled the sale of Needham Court but I may revise my plans. You see, I have certain business concerns and I've just landed a rather nice little coup locally and may have to stay on for a while to oversee things. Up to now negotiations have been under wraps as I've been waiting for the green light concerning supplies from France, but that's all fixed now so all wraps are off. I haven't told Auntie yet so you must be the first to congratulate me.'

'Oh certainly,' I replied politely, guessing this would be the deal to supply racy nether garments to cabaret artistes as coyly mentioned by the Reverend Egge, and wondered where the performers would gain access to such essentials. Brighton doubt-less; it caters for all sorts.

But I was wrong. 'Oh no,' he replied when I later enquired, 'not Brighton. Bognor.'

I blinked. It is amazing the power of coincidence.

He must have seen my surprise, for he laughed and said, 'Ah, you are thinking of King George the Fifth and his dying words: "Bugger Bognor". Sheer piffle, I imagine, but it's an amusing tale.'

As it happens my thoughts were far away from the good king, but rather with MacManus and his bespangled companion galumphing around in that Bognor bordello. I wondered vaguely if Aston Travers' supplies of lingerie would include theatrical tights for ersatz ostriches brandishing whips, but hardly liked to ask. Instead I enquired casually whether I would know the premises.

'I shouldn't think so,' he replied cheerfully, 'unless you were looking for a pair of plumed knickers or a sequined vest. Are you?'

'Not really,' I murmured.

'Thought not. Still, should you change your mind you'll find there's a theatrical costumier not far from Mercer's Music Hall. It's been there for years but recently has been getting a bit moth-eaten and the new owner wants an injection of fresh merchan-dise and someone to manage the business while he's away. That's where I come in. I'll soon have the thing smartened up. And who knows, I might even consider a partnership; I daresay it'll be offered.' He gave a nonchalant smirk, before adding, 'Money for old rope really – unless it interferes with my other interests.'

Whether I was supposed to ask what those interests were, I don't know, but if so he was disappointed. Instead I said briskly, 'Well, that all sounds very nice for you. I'm sure your mother would have been delighted.'

'Mother delighted? I doubt that *very* much. Few of my enterprises ever received her prissy accolade, and I don't imagine she would have approved of this particular venture.' The sardonic smile was replaced by a petulant shrug and my distaste sharpened.

'That's a shame,' I lied, 'but I expect your aunt will be pleased.' I started to consult my bill, ready to leave.

'Oh yes, Auntie will approve, she always does – no problems with that one!' The laugh held little warmth.

Rather frostily, I said I was glad that was so, and bade him good day. As I made my way to the door, I heard him hail the waitress (Martha, aged sixty): 'Just a pot of tea will do – oh, and don't take your time over it. Chop, chop – there's a good girl.'

Opening the door, I heard not just the tinkle of its overhead bell, but my father's voice: *Arrogant young pup!*

After making a couple of domestic purchases I wandered back to the car park, my earlier sunny mood now considerably dulled. I had been discomfited by my encounter with the charmless Travers. How frightful to have a son or nephew like that! I felt a sudden sympathy for the dead Elspeth – and even a mild twinge for the living Alice. The latter had appeared to dote on the oaf, but contrary to the spirit of Dickie's note, I suspected that the dotage was unreciprocated – except perhaps when expedient.

I drove home in some irritation, and when there told Maurice and Bouncer that they were very lucky to have such a thoughtful and well-mannered mistress. This was not greeted with notable applause, in fact none at all. They stared at me in silence and then went their separate ways, Bouncer to his bone and Maurice to his seat on the gatepost.

TWENTY

The Primrose version

I think it was Cyril Connolly who, as a sly variation on the William Congreve original, once observed that there is no fury like an ex-wife searching for a new lover.

I came across the quip years ago and at the time found it amusing, if a trifle exaggerated. However, since then events have conspired to make me revise those feelings, for I have now discovered the comment to be entirely true. I am also less inclined to find it funny. The reason for this change? Mrs Alice Markham.

Out of the blue she appeared on my doorstep one afternoon, explained that she had been driving past and wondered if I might have a few minutes to spare. Given the little fracas at Melinda's her sudden presence rather surprised me, but as I had been reluctantly poised to scrub out the chinchillas' hutch I was only too happy to oblige. Delay in the form of a visitor was a welcome respite. In retrospect, I realize that an hour cleansing the Augean stables of Boris and Karloff would have been peanuts compared with what I instead had to endure.

I ushered her into the sitting room, settled her on the sofa and offered tea. This she declined, and I had the impression her mind was set on more pressing matters. In this I was right. Initially she was smiling gaily and even made complimentary remarks about my vases of arum lilies and the rather imposing sketch of Pa looking fearsome above the fireplace. And then small talk over, she cut to the chase.

'I saw you, Miss Oughterard,' she declared accusingly. 'I saw you with him – and very cosy you both looked!'

I blinked. 'Er, saw me with whom – you mean Mr Ingaza?'

She gestured impatiently. 'No, not that little barrow boy, someone of far greater worth. I mean Councillor Reginald Bewley, of course. I saw you both in that new café off the High Street.

You were sitting at a table in the corner, heads together and exchanging coy looks. Wrapped up in each other, you were. Oh yes, I know the signs by now!' She gave a bitter laugh, while I stared uncomprehendingly.

I have to say that my memory of the meeting with Reginald Bewley hardly tallied with hers. Heads together? Absurd! Exchanging coy looks? What nonsense . . . in fact, I don't recall having passed one of those for *quite* a number of years! What on earth was the woman talking about? I was about to enquire but didn't get the chance.

'Oh yes,' she snapped, 'I've met your sort before – always ready to poach another's fish, just like my *dear* sister. But don't imagine you can try that with me, Miss Oughterard. It won't work; I will not be upstaged – Reginald is mine!' She glared and tapped her foot.

Goodness, so that was it – she saw me as a rival and the decorous Bewley was her intended catch! Did he know? I wondered. I stifled a giggle and suggested coldly that she may have mistaken me for someone else. However, she assured me that she had not been mistaken and had seen it all before.

When I asked what she seen exactly, she stormed, 'The whole bally sexual betrayal, of course! My husband was always at it, which is why I divorced him. Still, the philandering toad suffered for it all right – I got him to pay me a pretty penny, I can tell you. Very satisfying. But later, later . . .' She leant forward flushed and furious. 'What do you think I discovered?'

I shook my head dumbly.

'I found out that one of his mistresses had been none other than my *own* sister! Oh yes, he and Elspeth had been having a merry old time, had been for months – and me not knowing a thing. So what do you think of that?'

'Oh dear,' I said lamely.

'Of course she had always hated me, since we were children really. Nice on the surface but deadly underneath. And can you guess what she said when I showed her the hat I had bought to celebrate the divorce?' I shook my head. 'She actually had the nerve to declare that it looked like a pudding and that she had always thought my face fundamentally flawed.'

'No!' I cried, as if aghast.

'Oh yes, that's what my dear sister had the brass neck to say. Smug little bitch!' Alice's 'flawed' features contorted in a spasm of rage. It wasn't a pretty sight and I was inclined to agree with the sister.

But then, just as suddenly, the features relaxed and the eyes turned strangely blank. Unnervingly so. In a toneless voice, she said, 'And so that was that. When I learnt of her affair with my husband it was the last straw and I knew what had to be done. There are ways and means. After all one cannot allow predators like that to thrive, can one, Miss Oughterard? It musn't be allowed. She had to *go*.'

She paused, studying me intently, and I felt that something was required. 'Er, go where?' I enquired politely. Deep down I sensed the answer, but her words when they came still struck an icy chill.

'To her death, of course. Where else do you imagine?'

It is curious how in moments of shock one's attention can be caught by things entirely inconsequential. Thus I recall noticing how low the water was getting in one of the Waterford vases, that the silver salver on the bookcase could do with a polish and that Maurice, sliding in through the open window, was looking unusually amiable. Perhaps he had just done for a sparrow.

Such trivia impinged for a matter of seconds, before a sudden movement opposite returned my gaze to Alice . . . and to the pistol she was firmly pointing in my direction. The previous shock at her words was as nothing compared to the shock I now felt, and this time there were no distractions. 'My God, what *are* you doing?' I exclaimed in horror.

She gave a mirthless laugh. 'What does it look like? Feeding the cat? No, I am merely demonstrating that should you persist in your intrusive attentions to *my* friend Councillor Bewley you just might go the same way as my dear sister. I can assure you I am not to be trifled with.'

Trifled with? Like hell. She would get more than trifle from me given half a chance! The problem was that at that moment there seemed no chance of doing anything, partial or otherwise. I was much taller than Alice and so theoretically could have easily overcome her. But height does not deflect a bullet. And in her present state I felt she could pull that trigger at the drop of a hat; it would only take one false move. The woman was clearly raving

and the best thing surely was to calm her down, apply copious
soft soap – and then, exploiting an off-guard moment, lunge boldly
forward, knock her to the ground and grab the weapon. A graphic
image of 'Primrose Triumphant' flashed through my mind. Yes,
that was how I would proceed.

And thus in a voice of unctuous interest, I asked how on earth
she had managed the dispatch. 'It must have been fearfully difficult,' I said earnestly, 'and all on your own too!'

The lowering look softened and she said airily, 'Ah, but you
see, I had a loyal helpmate.'

'Oh really? Well that must have been handy.'

She narrowed her eyes. 'Don't try to be smart with me, Miss
Oughterard – it won't do.'

I murmured what passed for an apology and asked casually if
the 'helpmate' was anyone I knew.

For a second she seemed to pause, and then said impatiently,
'My good woman, you don't think I would tell you that, do you?
Besides, you wouldn't know the name anyway – one of my
London friends.' (Her voice assumed what she clearly felt to be
a rather grand tone.) 'We've been friends for years. This person
couldn't stand Elspeth either and not without cause – she let
them down appallingly. Such treachery deserves punishment.
Anyway, what was *handy* – as you would doubtless put it – is
that they keep a boat in Newhaven. So we did it with that. The
whole thing just needed very careful planning – though I must
say it was quite tiring.'

'Oh, I am sure,' I murmured in evident sympathy; and then,
clearing my throat, enquired casually where her helpmate might
be. My interest was real enough. After all, the maniac might have
been skulking in the garden!

'They have gone away,' she replied shortly, 'on their boat.'

Gone away? Fled the country, more like! I nodded vaguely, and
then rather foolishly added, 'Ah . . . a little holiday perhaps. I am
not surprised after all that strenuous activity.'

My voice must have held just a dash of sarcasm for again Alice
frowned and narrowed her eyes, a gesture that did little for her
features. 'Don't be facetious, Miss Oughterard. Any more of that
lip and I'll fill you with this!' She brandished the pistol.

I performed a hasty back-peddle, and in tones of oily empathy said, 'But surely the whole thing must have been simply *awful* for you! I mean I can see it was what you planned, but at the actual time it would have been a nightmare!'

Still gripping the butt, she lowered the pistol's muzzle and replied musingly, 'Oh I wouldn't say nightmare – rather exciting really. Exhilarating in fact. But latterly it seems to have got on my damn nerves. They say the aftermath is the worst, and I have to admit that sometimes I don't know whether I'm coming or going!' She emitted a hyena-like laugh. 'Do you ever feel like that?'

'Frequently,' I replied with some feeling.

'Luckily I have my pills,' she continued, 'and they buoy me up no end. Invaluable they are. Little lifesavers!'

Hmm. A pity her sister hadn't had a few of those, I thought grimly. She might still be mistress of Needham Court. I think I may have allowed my mask of sympathy to slip – replaced perhaps by what Ma used to call the Primrose Pout.

But whatever the look Alice clearly didn't like it, for, leaning forward, she waved the gun under my nose and hissed, 'And you're a nasty piece of work too, Miss Oughterard! I know your type – all snooty and full of airs and graces but interfering and deadly! And if you think you are going to trump me over Reginald Bewley, you can think again. I had your measure the moment I set eyes on you. Oh yes indeed, a nasty piece of work altogether. I've told my friend and they agree.'

Whether that final comment was supposed to be the coup de grâce I wasn't sure and didn't care. Frankly, what enraged me was to be called 'a nasty piece of work', if you please! No Oughterard has ever been thus described, and to have that insult hurled at me by a rampant harpy who by her own admission had just drowned her sister in the English Channel was a bit much. I was incensed! My immediate instinct was to stand up and administer a good clip round the ear.

Fortunately prudence prevailed: the thought of Elspeth's fate and the proximity of the pistol having a somewhat sobering effect. Thus although inwardly seething I contained myself, and instead of delivering the deserved clip enquired soothingly if she would like to confide the logistics of the dispatch. 'After all,' I said, 'it must have been awfully tricky . . . and given her dislike of the sea how on earth did you entice her on to the boat? Quite a feat, I imagine.' To my relief this seemed to defuse her wrath, and whether it was a matter of pride or the instinctive need to 'unburden' herself (as Peggy's daughter would doubtless say), she gave a surprisingly succinct account.

Apparently the sisters' birthday had been imminent, and to celebrate the event Alice and her accomplice had made a surprise visit to Elspeth announcing that a champagne supper and a visit to the casino at Le Touquet had been arranged for that very night. A smart hotel had been booked and instead of flying they would go by sea. Elspeth enjoyed the bright lights – provided they were sufficiently stylish – and in the past had made some lucky gains at roulette. Thus other than being assured of a calm crossing, it hadn't taken much to persuade her to take the trip. 'All she needed was her overnight bag, hair curlers and an evening dress, and she was ready,' Alice chortled. 'We set off at once in a *very* merry mood!'

I have to admit that despite feeling vaguely sickened I was totally gripped. Was she really telling the truth? Perhaps after all, this whole tale was just some lurid wishful thinking, one of those signs of early dementia people talk about.

'You look surprised,' she said.

I cleared my throat. 'Er, isn't Le Touquet rather far from Newhaven, I mean—'

'Oh, that didn't matter. Elspeth's geography was hopeless! We could have told her Timbuctoo and she'd have believed us.'

'But what about her other clothes – the ones that were found on the beach? How did you—'

'Simple enough,' she replied casually. 'Once we returned to Newhaven we drove hell-for-leather back to Lewes where we picked them up and then went over to Birling Gap and strewed them on the rocks. At that time in the morning it was pitch dark and not a soul about.' She paused, and then said ruefully, 'Quite a marathon really, but it was worth it; but my goodness I was fagged out!'

'I can imagine,' I said dryly.

She seemed not to hear, for without pause she had launched into additional details: 'And then you see there was the disposal itself – not half as difficult as I had expected.' She beamed. 'In fact, the whole thing went off like clockwork!'

I said nothing, vaguely wondering whether I should suggest she took another 'lifesaving' pill. With luck that might be a distraction and provide the chance I had been waiting for. However, in her febrile state such a suggestion might be injudicious, for having already accused me of being interfering she might see it as yet further proof of my villainy and unleash God knows what. Thus I kept silent but raised my eyebrows in quizzical surprise.

'Oh yes, it was quite simple really,' she explained. 'My companion gave her a rabbit punch behind the ear, followed by a quick bash on the temple. And then while she was nicely stunned we thrust her head into a bucket of water and held her there. It didn't take long.'

I shut my eyes.

'Oh, don't worry,' she said breezily, 'there was no thrashing around or anything beastly like that – well, only mildly, otherwise I couldn't have stood it . . . No, she was amazingly pliable really. That first blow on the neck must have made her pretty groggy and the other was simply a sort of belt and braces job. Anyway, once it was obvious she was dead we put her into the bathing togs and then . . . uhm . . . well, slipped her over the side.' Alice spread and closed her hands as if to say, 'And that was that.'

'I see,' I said faintly. 'You make it sound so easy.'

She nodded. 'Yes, on the whole it was. Although of course there was the problem with the cap, that frothy thing I bought from Plummers in Eastbourne; now that *did* complicate things a bit.'

I was intrigued. How murder should be incommoded by a floral swimming cap I was at a loss to know.

She must have seen my surprise, for with a little gasp of annoyance, she said, 'Yes, it was that wretched girl behind the counter. I expressly told her the size I wanted but she obviously hadn't listened, because when we tried to put Elspeth's head in it the thing was far too small and made the whole process rather tricky – she had very thick hair, you know. So we had to do quite a bit of shoving. Still, we managed it in the end.' Alice smiled, evidently reliving the tricky moment.

I gazed silently at the plump, complacent face, wondering

what means of disposal she had in store for me. A simple
squeeze of the trigger? Or something more challenging? Perhaps
I should take the bull by the horns and make that sudden foray
after all. It might just work . . . But studying the plump finger
caressing the thin trigger, I fear I lost my nerve; and so still
playing safe (or safer) remarked how rarely things went
according to plan but that this had obviously been one of them.
The comment produced an unexpected response. For in a
moment of careless good humour she laid the gun aside and,
leaning forward, swept up the unsuspecting Maurice crouched
quietly on the rug. 'He is such a sweet little boy,' she crooned. 'I *so*
love cats!'

That was her mistake. There is nothing sweet or especially little
about Maurice, and I think he objected to being patronized. He
reacted with a fractious hiss followed by a brisk right hook to
her cheek while his left paw struggled to pull the feather from her
hat. The hat came off. Bouncer came in.

Seeing the hat, the dog promptly pounced upon it, emitted a
whoop of joy, and with tail wagging full-tilt bore it triumphantly
back to his lair in the kitchen. At last this was my chance, a chance
which I deftly exploited. I leapt to my feet, and in a trice had
lunged forward to grasp the discarded revolver, levelling it at her
in menacing mode.

However, standing there like James Cagney I was somewhat
nonplussed to see that she seemed more perturbed by loss of hat
than by loss of gun, and was clearly intent on pursuing Bouncer
into the kitchen. I cleared my throat to stay her exit and waved
the weapon assertively. 'Can't you see the game is up, Alicia,' I
cried, 'this is the end of the line!'

She stopped abruptly and, looking me up and down, snapped,
'The name is Alice, not Alicia, you may recall. And if you think
you are going to harass me with a toy gun I fear you will be
disappointed.' With those words she turned, and with surprising
agility for one so plump, swung her leg over the windowsill and
hared off across the front lawn to her car. The next moment, with
a crash of gears and churning of gravel, she was speeding up the
drive like a demented Fangio.

I stared after her in numbed wonder, and then looked down
at the now obviously toy gun in my hand. My eyes turned to the

desecrated gravel; and a sense of weary déjà vu enveloped me as I recalled Eric's niece on her motorbike and the gardener's extortionate bill. Should I be bold and have the whole surface spread with tarmac? If the future held such similar comings and goings it might be wise (though admittedly less aesthetic, but definitely cheaper in the long run). As I pondered the matter, from the top of the drive there came a searing screech of tyres. I winced, gritted my teeth and hastily retreated inside for a fortifying brandy.

Of course, maddening though it was, the issue of the drive was hardly the only thing that occupied me. There were other issues: issues which danced before me in the now chewed remnant of Alice Markham's ridiculous hat. Tired of his trophy, Bouncer had thoughtfully laid it upon the hearth rug in front of my chair.

I took a sip of my drink and contemplated the macerated headgear. Was the woman barmy? Short odds – up the bleeding spout, as the eloquent Eric would doubtless say. Was I barmy? Oh, assuredly long odds. Would I tell the police? Absolutely zero odds. My 'story' with no corroborative details except for a child's pistol of the sort Sickie-Dickie might brandish would be laughed out of court and I should look a fool to say the least. True, Alice had made an elaborate confession (well, less a confession than a brazen admission), but without a shred of evidence it would be my word against hers. Naturally I am not averse to fighting my corner (one has to in this life) or, as Pa would have said, 'giving 'em what for'; but frankly unless the 'what for' is likely to be constructive and one is assured of triumph what is the point? Far better to be cautious and canny like the sterling Montgomery: bide my time, make an assessment, wait for an opening in the enemy's flanks and then capitalize like hell with no holds barred.

'Wouldn't you agree, Bouncer?' I asked.

A fruitless question. It was of course greeted by an inane leer and a resounding burp.

I had just closed my eyes to soothe the pounding in my addled brain when the doorbell rang: not lightly, but with brisk insistency.

I caught my breath. Surely it couldn't be the wretched woman returned to demand her revolver?

Warily (and wearily) I rose and went to the door and opened it a fraction.

The figure confronting me was not the mad woman, but rather, to my surprise, Charles Penlow.

He raised his hat and before I had time to greet him, said, 'I say, Primrose, do you know about that car at the top of your drive?'

'What car?'

'The one that has smashed into one of your gates. It's slewed across the path with the driver's door open. A couple of struts are buckled and the top of one of the posts has fallen over. I wondered if you were aware.'

'Is the top broken?' I asked.

'Oh yes,' he said cheerfully, 'it's in little pieces.'

'What make of car?' I heard myself asking in chilly tones.

'A Sunbeam Talbot – blue.'

Yes, it was hers all right. Not content with putting the fear of God in me with a fake pistol, she now had to destroy my gates and gatepost. With manners like that no wonder Elspeth had pinched her husband!

'But there doesn't seem to be any sign of the driver,' Charles went on, 'so I suppose having done the damage he took off – or she did. Anyway, it couldn't have been a visitor, otherwise I assume they would have mentioned it.'

Huh, I thought grimly, you don't know my visitors. But I nodded in agreement and then asked casually in what direction the car was facing.

'Well, that's the odd thing, it looks as if it may have been coming from down here' – he gestured at the drive and flower beds – 'though I daresay it was some silly ass charging at an absurd speed who took a wrong turn and tried a lightning three-point turn. Drunk, probably.' He then suggested that I went with him to take a look, after which we should call the police.

Still dazed by Alice's bizarre behaviour and shocking revelations (assuming indeed they were true), I accompanied him up the drive saying nothing. My instinct of course was to blurt it all out in relief and anger. Charles has a steady mind and is a good listener, but for some reason I held back. The crashing of the car and Alice's obvious flight might well have strengthened my tale of her confession and the threats to me, but one couldn't be sure. She could still brazen it out and there might be repercussions not exactly to my benefit. (Having had a homicide for a brother one knows the value of reticence.) So for the time being I kept quiet, trying to arrange my churning thoughts.

The silence was broken by Charles taking my elbow and saying, 'There you see, the damn thing is virtually blocking your entrance, and just look at that gatepost!' He paused, and then added, 'I don't suppose the cat will like it.'

'Blow the cat, what about me?' I exclaimed irritably. 'Maurice will just have to sit on the other one.' I glared at the wreckage, mentally cursing Alice Markham and cursing the insurers who were bound to be difficult.

Charles made a reconnaissance of the abandoned car, scrutinizing the broken wing-mirror, dripping radiator and dented bonnet. He looked inside to see if there were any signs of ownership. He needn't have bothered: once the number plate was identified Alice's name would come up in a trice. I frowned. But where the hell *was* the woman and what on earth had she been playing at!

We were just about to retrace our steps – and at Charles's insistence to telephone the police – when there was the drone of an engine and glare of headlamps. We stepped aside, but the vehicle drew up and two uniformed figures emerged wielding flashlights.

'Ah,' the taller figure said, 'it's Miss Oughterard, isn't it – and if I am not mistaken Mr Penlow. Perhaps you heard the shot, did you? Or maybe there was more than one.'

I stared at Chief Superintendent MacManus. 'What shot? What do you mean?'

'I mean, Miss Oughterard, the shot that has just killed Mrs Alice Markham.'

TWENTY-ONE

The Primrose version

The words hit me like the proverbial thunderbolt and I gasped in disbelief. 'But she was—' I began, then stopped abruptly. I had been about to say that she had been with me less than forty minutes ago, but bit my lip, and instead heard myself mumble inanely that she had been so charming.

'That's as maybe,' MacManus said brusquely, 'but she's dead, so somebody didn't think so.'

I continued to stare at him, absorbing the extraordinary news. Who? Why? How? Where? The questions tumbled in my mind.

In answer to the last, MacManus gestured down the road. 'She's there, just round that bend where the trees are, by the ditch at the boundary of your field. Sergeant Wilding found her on his way home, said he fell off his bicycle with shock. She has been hit in the back with a single bullet – which isn't to say that others weren't fired. My men are dealing with it. You are quite sure that you didn't hear anything?'

Charles muttered something like, 'Absolutely not,' while I shook my head dumbly. MacManus regarded us intently before fixing his eye on the backdrop: the blue Talbot and my rammed gatepost. 'So what's all this then?' he demanded sternly. 'Is that vehicle yours, Miss Oughterard?'

'Certainly not,' I replied indignantly. He knew perfectly well that I drive a Morris Oxford. 'I would hardly prang my own gates, let alone inflict that kind of damage!'

'Hmm. People do funny things when they are in a hurry, and even ladies have been known to overindulge.' (Insufferable man! I thought of the bear suit and those spangled tights.)

'Well, this one doesn't,' I lied icily.

Charles cleared his throat. 'You know what,' he said, 'I believe I recognize the car. Now I come to think of it, Mrs Markham drove a blue Talbot – and if I'm not mistaken it's the same number plate, JK 100.'

I sighed inwardly. Oh well, at least that saved the police lackeys a few moments of research. I turned to MacManus and in my most earnest voice said, 'How appalling, Chief Superintendent, she must have crashed into my gates, fled in distress perhaps to get help and then been shot down. It doesn't bear thinking about!'

'You may not bear it, but we have to,' was the gruff reply. Typical of MacManus: no finesse. He stepped aside and muttered a few words to his fellow officer. There were vigorous nods. And then he returned and said, 'Well, Miss Oughterard, in view of the circumstances, and as a formal procedure, I am afraid I must ask you to accompany me to the station.'

'Accompany you to the station!' I exploded. 'What on earth for?'

'Good lord,' I heard Charles mutter.

MacManus turned to him and said, 'You won't be needed just now, Mr Penlow, but I should be obliged if you would present yourself tomorrow morning just to make a brief witness statement. It's merely a formality, nothing to worry about.'

Naturally I demanded to know why Charles was being given preferential treatment.

'The crime occurred on your property, not his,' was the gruff response. 'As such it must be checked immediately.'

'She may have ruined my gates,' I protested, 'but she wasn't killed there.'

'Ah, but the *body* was found on your boundary and it is quite likely that the shot came from behind the laurels at the top of your drive. Your property, you see.'

I thought I detected a hint of satisfaction in his words and suspected he was enjoying himself. My hackles rose but I retained my customary cool. 'Oh dear,' I gasped, 'how dreadful. But naturally I will give any help I can, Chief Superintendent . . . Oh yes, I can quite see one needs to be quick off the mark!' I wasn't aware of MacManus ever being especially quick off the mark, but a little compliant flattery rarely goes amiss.

Charles had gallantly offered to accompany me – something I appreciated but which I declined. My mind was still swimming in a maelstrom of confusion, yet I needed to do some fast thinking; though well-intentioned, Charles's presence might have been a distraction.

Thus as I sat in the back of the police car I reviewed the situation – and didn't like it. Although agog to know who had done in the wretched Alice, my principal concern was to keep quiet about her visit. This had also been my initial instinct when Charles had called, but it was now strengthened by what MacManus had said about it being *my* property on which the foolish woman had been found, and indeed from where the shot had been fired. And being the last person to have seen the victim was hardly to my advantage; invariably in such cases it is the last witness *pre-mortem* who gets the keenest grilling! And who knows what that might lead to: it is amazing how suspicious these officials can be. No, there was no point in supplying grist for MacManus's turgid mill. If the insufferable Sidney Samson began to seriously suspect that Francis had been responsible for Mrs Fotherington's death and persuaded MacManus of that, who is to say they wouldn't pin this current dispatch on the sister? Just think, they might think that such behaviour ran in the family! *Sauve qui peut* as my father used to say, i.e. be charming and lie like a trooper – not that I can recall charm being one of Pa's more obvious attributes. However, the precept was sound enough.

After my ordeal I was in no mood to spend more time than absolutely necessary among the denizens of Lewes's police station. Naturally I was politely cooperative but kept my answers as brief and bland as possible. Mercifully MacManus had disappeared into some nether region, leaving a subordinate to conduct the interview. His replacement seemed perfectly civilized – rather pleasant, in fact. And thus, spared the long pauses and bovine looks of the chief superintendent, I found the experience moderately painless.

Well, painless for me but presumably frustrating for my interrogator. All he was able to elicit was that I had known Mrs Markham only slightly, having met her at the most three times in the last year; that I had not seen her on the day of her death; that I had heard no gunshot, nor seen anyone lurking around my property or in the lane outside; and that I was only aware of the collision at the top of the drive when informed by Mr Penlow. As it happens, apart from that second answer the others were perfectly true.

However, negative though my responses were, I did not wish to appear indifferent or chary. And thus to dispel any suspicion that I might know more than I admitted, I displayed an avid curiosity about the event and the culprit. 'I mean to say, who on *earth* would want to mow down an innocuous lady like Mrs Markham?' I protested in wonder. 'It's too grisly for words!'

Closing his notebook, the other nodded. 'Yes, it's a funny old world all right – still, it keeps us in business, I suppose.' He gave a lopsided grin and offered me some tea.

A little later, being driven home by Sergeant Wilding with whom I have always got on well, I asked the name of my interviewer.

'Ah, that would have been Speakeasy,' he replied, 'he's new.'

'Speakeasy?' I echoed. 'What an extraordinary name! Is he in the habit of frequenting illicit drinking holes?'

Wilding chuckled. 'Well, that's what we call him, but his proper name is Inspector Spikesy. Quite a nice bloke really. Leastways,' he added wryly, 'better than some I wouldn't care to mention.' I could guess who he meant.

As we approached my shattered gates, Wilding emitted a silent whistle. 'Hmm, that lot's going to cost you a pretty penny I shouldn't wonder. They don't come cheap, posts like that; and those fancy metal bits are difficult to get nowadays. No, not what you'd call an easy job . . .'

It always amazes me how encouraging people can be.

Feeling somewhat mangled, I entered the house thankful to be alone at last; alone, that is, except for Maurice and Bouncer, who greeted my arrival with rowdy acclaim. Or at least the dog was rowdy; the cat merely conveyed its welcome by insistently mewing and tweaking my shoelaces. I am not often accorded such overtures and have to admit to being quite flattered, and as a concession allowed them up to the bedroom where they promptly fell asleep. I did not. Tired though I was, the recent dramas continued to assault my mind, and I sat up in bed munching chocolate and restlessly reviewing the extraordinary events of the last few hours.

Having to fend off the raving Alice had been bad enough, but to be then faced with her sudden annihilation on the edge of my property was really a bit much! The appalling damage done to my gates plus being taken in for questioning by smug MacManus had hardly added to the joy of things. In fact, it was this questioning that was beginning to worry me. Inspector Spikesy had been mild and affable and I like to think I had acquitted myself well, but if MacManus got it into his head that I was concealing something then the situation might turn awkward. Certainly I did have my 'indemnity' photographs, but even so things could be tricky. For a few weak moments I wondered if after all I should have told them of Alice's visit: should have assumed the mantle of the upright citizen eager to do her bit for the maintenance of law and seemly order. In some agitation I tore the wrapping from another bar of chocolate and debated whether to ring the police station the next day announcing that I wished to amend my statement.

But luckily such wayward instincts quickly vanished. I am all in favour of being the upright citizen . . . *provided* that such uprightness is expedient. But it was not expedient, and thus the prone position seemed far the best. The unsolved case of my brother's blunder still casts its shadow; as does MacManus's continuing investigation of the 'dewpond murder' which has so fascinated Lewes. Innocence does not necessarily confer safety, and it would be unwise to furnish Fortune with more hostages than she already has – or indeed to give MacManus that vital inch. To admit that the victim had been with me just prior to being killed would allow him yards of dangerous intrusion. It was a risk I preferred not to take.

And as to the actual significance of Alice's visit – the bragging confession to her sister's murder – well, I argued, as Elspeth's drowning had prompted no interest from the authorities and my querying of it to MacManus treated with such terse complacency, why should I now stick my neck out and gratuitously report the matter? Besides, they were bound to be sceptical – might even think I was batty and had fabricated the whole tale. If I could suspect that of Mrs Markham, might they not of me? After all, one does have one's reputation to consider; being thought a fantasist would hardly enhance my local standing – nor my picture sales!

But would silence make me guilty of thwarting the due process of law? Not particularly. Being now dead, Alice could hardly be brought to book to receive her just deserts. And as to the unnamed accomplice – well, who was I to make allegations against the unknown and possibly non-existent? My information would be merely hearsay and that from a source now firmly defunct. Oh yes, I told myself, reticence was definitely the safer course – albeit a reticence laced with rampant curiosity! I mean to say, who *was* it that had hidden in my laurels and extinguished that wild woman? Was there a maniac in the area, as unhinged as his victim and liable to loose off bullets whenever the chance arose? Should I change my locks? Board up the windows?

Chocolate finished and brain finally anaesthetized by these whirling thoughts, I settled down on the pillows and switched off the light. The room lay silent except for the rhythmic breathing of the dog.

The last twenty-four hours had been eventful to say the least, and when morning came fatigue and reluctance to face inquisitive locals prompted me to stay in bed. A sound instinct but not one I could indulge. That afternoon I had an urgent appointment with Hislop the bank manager, whose crass handling of my affairs had resulted in a misapplication of shares. 'A temporary hitch,' he had unctuously assured me, 'I am sure it can be remedied.' *Sure it could be remedied?* You bet it would! Hence my resolution to harry him until the remedy had been applied. It's amazing how these functionaries will try to fob you off!

Thus a few hours later and ready for the fray I set out in incognito garb (brown coat and hat – the latter pulled well down – plus newly prescribed spectacles) to beard Hislop in his cushy den. Actually I don't think my sartorial efforts were all that effective, because as I approached the bank I heard Emily's familiar voice. 'Oh, Primrose,' she bleated, 'how good to see you! I hear there's been an awful accident near your house and you've been with the police and—'

'Yes, yes,' I said impatiently, 'I'll tell you later. Now if you don't mind, I'm in rather a hurry!' I shook off the restraining hand and hurried on to my destination.

Here too I was immediately recognized by the clerk and promptly ushered into Hislop's office. Initial pleasantries over (luckily with no mention of the Markham affair), we settled down to discuss matters, i.e. the bank's stupid mistake, and I made my views clear. As it happens the discussion didn't take long because Hislop smugly revealed that the whole thing had been resolved and all was well: the correct shares were in place and I need no longer worry. I rewarded him with a generous smile and said I was delighted to hear that as I *had* been wondering whether to transfer my account elsewhere. Slightly to my surprise he looked quite cheerful and said that there was an excellent branch in Brighton.

Mission satisfactorily accomplished, I was almost tempted to indulge in a cup of coffee but, fearful of meeting friends and being subjected to officious enquiry, I scuttled back to the car park.

Parked a few yards away from my Morris Oxford was a very stylish red sports car, brand new by the looks of it. I was rather impressed and was about to look closer when I saw someone striding towards it, presumably the owner. I was just about to enquire the make when I realized who it was – Aston Travers. We had met before in that same place but not in these circum-stances and I felt rather awkward. Should I express sympathy about his aunt or pretend I hadn't seen him? The latter might be simpler, perhaps.

However, the choice was never made for the next moment he had come straight up to me and said abruptly, 'Ah, I expect you've been put through it too – it's like dealing with the Gestapo down there!'

'Down where?' I replied, somewhat nonplussed.

'The police station, of course. Since she was shot from the top of your drive they are bound to have hauled you in for a grilling. God, that Spike fellow is insatiable – nothing but damn fool ques-tions about my aunt's domestic habits, moods, manner, social contacts and what she had for breakfast – or as good as. When had I last seen her? Did she confide anything in me? Could I think of anyone who would want to dispose of her? A number, I had joked – though he didn't seem to like that. Ghastly!' Travers scowled and ran his hand through his hair.

'Oh, ghastly,' I agreed. I was startled by the tirade but intrigued to see that he seemed more put out by his ordeal with Spikesy than by the fate of his aunt. Still, in moments of emotional crisis people are not always predictable in their reactions, and despite my distaste for him I felt a stirring of sympathy.

This was partly dispelled by his next words. 'So what was she doing at the top of your drive anyway – been to tea or something?'

Hmm. It had certainly been something.

'I bet they've asked you about that – probably think you know the killer!'

'I don't know what they think,' I said coolly, 'but I agree, it's all very disturbing – especially for you. You were quite close, I believe.'

There was a silence as he stared into the distance, the taut features slackening. 'Yes, I suppose you could say that,' he murmured. 'She was a funny creature. Generous when it suited her, but also maddening. Utterly maddening, manipulative old bat. Still, you get used to people . . .' Briefly the abrasive tone had assumed a wistful note, and I detected a kind of homage being made, however slewed.

He returned his gaze to me and shrugged. 'Ah well, that's the way of it all, I suppose: in the midst of life et cetera, et cetera . . . Meantime, things to do, people to see. I must be off. Nice meeting you, Miss Oughterard. But take my advice – beware Mr Spikesy! Oh, and if I were you I'd avoid brown in future; not your colour at all. Blue would be nice.' With a grin and brisk salute, he sauntered to his car.

Seated in my own car and consulting the driving mirror I agreed that he was right: brown was distinctly unflattering. I removed my hat; an improvement at least.

TWENTY-TWO

The cat's memoir

After the little contretemps with the visitor in the taste-less hat I felt rather satisfied. I mean, if our mistress insists on parleying with such people she must reap the consequences. To be swept up into a stranger's arms without so much as a by-your-leave is not my idea of amusement and I made my feelings abundantly clear. Why, I doubt whether the insufferable Mavis Briggs at Molehill would have dared to do that!

I expressed these views to Bouncer, who grinned vacantly and said he couldn't remember Mavis Briggs but he was sure I was right. Of course I was right! And I reminded him that Mavis Briggs had been one of our late master's most tedious irritants, and indeed the one who at his own cost he had heroically saved from near death on the church gargoyle.

Light eventually dawned on the dog, for with a slow grin he said that yes he did remember and wasn't she a funny one.

'I don't think F.O. ever found her funny,' I remarked dryly, 'but at least she was more couth than this current specimen, a most objectionable type, I consider.'

Bouncer cocked an ear and sniffed. 'If you ask me,' he growled, 'she's off her rump.'

'Chump,' I corrected him.

'What?'

'Chump – that what's people are off, not their rumps.'

He snorted. 'Chump or rump; it makes no difference. One is top, the other's bottom. Either way she is off it.' To clinch the point the dog tore a piece of meat from his bone and swallowed it noisily. I closed my eyes, and then retired to the garden to think more quietly.

Here, amid the serenity of the shrubbery (or at least in *my* corner – Bouncer's part is disgusting) I was able to cogitate undisturbed. Thus, free from human inanity and canine gurgling I could review the situation and reach certain conclusions. These were to the effect that P.O. was once again deeply embroiled in something unseemly and that to protect our own pelts vigilance was vital. There had been enough near misses with the vicar in Molehill, and one had thought that after our transfer to Sussex peace would prevail . . . well, not on the current showing it doesn't!

When the visitor arrived I had not liked the look of her one bit, but in the interests of scholarly curiosity had made it my business to sit in on their conversation. From what I deduced it was obvious that our mistress was in a somewhat tense mood (she had that steely look in her eye, you can always tell). Tense she may have been, but the visitor was patently manic and disagreeable, and I predicted that it would not be long before an eruption occurred. In this of course I was right – though little had I known that I myself would be the instigator!

Once I had knocked the intruder's hat to the floor things moved apace and Bouncer was quite useful in contributing to the general furore. He smartly fielded the hat and tore with it into the kitchen where he dropped it into his basket and sat on it. The woman promptly hurled herself through the drawing-room window – I think for humans this is known as *defenestration* or so my cat lexicon assures me – and rushed off to her car. As is usual in times of tension, P.O. then made an assault on the brandy bottle.

After those fisticuffs with the intruder and my later cogitations in the shrubbery I felt fatigued, and so returned to the house to recuperate beneath the kitchen table. I slept a little, but awoke to be faced with Bouncer chortling and snuffling and digging me in the ribs.

'Must you do that!' I protested.

'Just thought you might like to know, Maurice,' he said, 'that left gatepost you're fond off – it's gone.'

'What do you mean, gone?' I demanded sleepily.

'What I said, it's gone to pieces. The mad woman's done it. You won't be able to snooze on it anymore.' He looked sympathetic but I noticed his tail was slowly wagging.

'What on earth do you mean?' I hissed. 'This is outrageous!'

He nodded cheerfully. 'Yes, that's just what I thought – OUTRAJUS!'

'So where is P.O.?' I demanded.

'Down in the town with the rozzers. I think something BIG has happened.' He suddenly looked anxious. 'But I hope it's not too big otherwise I shan't get my weekly bone.'

'Blow your bone,' I said testily, 'what about my haddock?'

There was silence as we brooded on our potential losses. And then feeling rather agitated, I jumped up on to the windowsill, and pressing my nose against the pane stared out into the dark. Nothing. I asked Bouncer how long she had been gone. He replied that he wasn't sure as he wasn't good on time but that his tummy was starting to rumble. I flicked my tail impatiently, but at that moment suddenly saw the lights of a car coming down the drive. Paws crossed this would be her. Bouncer had also sensed the lights and, racing into the hall, set up an excruciating racket. Deafened but relieved, I jumped off the windowsill and joined him to await our mistress.

We heard a man's voice saying goodnight, followed by the sound of a key being rattled in the lock. And then, with a loud curse as she tripped over the dog's rubber ring, the Prim came in. I thought she looked rather the worst for wear – but then humans often look like that after they have been out in the evening. Anyway, I gave her a gracious reception while she tickled me under the chin and Bouncer danced about like a delirious bear.

I am glad to report that despite her evident fatigue she had the manners to feed us; and then, unusually, indicated we could accompany her to bed. Normally I do not approve of animals sharing the same sleeping quarters as humans (the latter make such a din) but occasionally it does one good to have a break from routine. And thus with a courteous mew I complied. Bouncer of course wanted to bring his bone, but she frowned and called him a greedy hound – an apt description in my view. But he didn't seem to mind, and giving me a wink muttered that it had been worth a try. Really, these canines!

TWENTY-THREE

Charles Penlow's account

As I remarked to Agnes over breakfast, on the whole I think our decision to come to Lewes and renovate the family white elephant was a good idea. Physically the place is so much more attractive than London – an ideal position in a fold of the South Downs, a beautiful landscape, intriguing history, plenty of fishing, good hunting over at Wilmington, decent pubs such as Jevington's Hungry Monk, and friendly locals. What more could a fellow want?

Agnes said nothing for a moment, intent on spooning jam on to her toast (an exacting process – not too much, not too little, a pernickety ritual which I do not share). But then looking up she said with a twinkle, 'Oh yes, and then of course there is the crime factor: a murder last year on the Downs and now it looks like something *very* murky on Primrose Oughterard's land. You have to admit that does lend additional stimulus to living here! Are you *sure* you didn't notice anything when you were taking your walk the other evening?'

'What – you mean like an assassin lurking in her laurels? I hate to sound dull but as I told our gallant constables, I saw nothing except the unfortunate lady's shattered motor car.'

She sighed. 'What a shame, I thought that would spice things up a bit and deflect your mind from the defective plumbing in the east wing's lavatory. Still, you never know, perhaps something will come to you later. It's amazing how retentive memory can be.'

Agnes is an incurable optimist and has a strong sense of drama, and I was almost tempted to invent something to feed that avid imagination. But I banished the thought, knowing that any hint would be gleefully seized upon and spread far and wide. Prudently I turned my mind to the sombre problems of the east wing's cistern.

* * *

Later that morning, Duster and I made our customary visit to the White Hart. It is strange how conservative some dogs are. Duster is a quiet little chap, but once when I introduced him to an alternative pub he went berserk and expressed his displeasure in the most voluble way. It had been an embarrassing scene and since then I have been careful to remain loyal to our usual haunt.

Normally at that time on a weekday the lounge is relatively empty. Thus on entering I was surprised to find quite a little gaggle of locals clustered around the bar counter. Among these were the Balfours, the Reverend Egge, Peggy Mountjoy (fortunately minus the dreary daughter), Winchbrooke from Erasmus House and even Reginald Bewley, our esteemed council chairman. Of the drinkers he was the only one holding a glass of water. It might have been gin, I suppose, but I rather doubt it.

As soon as they saw me I was greeted warmly and beckoned over. Someone offered to buy me a drink and I soon realized the reason for the gathering: the 'awful Markham murder'. Yes, with a mixture of awe and relish they were picking it to pieces for all they were worth. Agnes should have been there; she would have enjoyed herself.

'Ah,' cried Freddie Balfour, 'in the absence of Primrose you'll have to do! Now dear chap, tell us about the accident – I mean you were there at the time, weren't you? First person on the scene, I gather.' He turned to Peggy: 'A key witness, you know – probably glimpsed the slayer's coat-tail, I expect!'

'Oh, do shut up, Freddie,' Melinda said, 'the poor man hasn't even had a chance to touch his beer.'

I smiled and said I was sorry to disappoint him but that whatever had happened at the top of Primrose's drive, alas, I had seen nothing. 'The smash had already happened when I got there,' I told them, 'and there was no sign of anyone – neither the victim nor anyone else, least of all a marksman lurking in the laurels.'

'But then of course you weren't looking for him, were you?' Bewley said. 'Apart from the signs of a crash you weren't aware of anything else having occurred.' He paused, looking at me quizzically, and then added, 'But I suppose you may have heard something – I don't mean the gunshot, but the sound of stealthy movement, something to suggest that the assailant was still there: the cracking of twigs, rustle of leaves, that sort of thing.'

'Ugh, you make it sound so spooky,' Peggy exclaimed. 'The watcher in the shadows, perhaps biding his time to take a potshot at Charles himself!'

I told her that her imagination was as bad as my wife's, and in reply to Bewley's comment explained that having seen what the car had done to Primrose's gates I was far more concerned with letting her know about it than with hanging around listening for strange noises from the undergrowth. Suddenly Freddie bellowed with laughter, a noise that made Duster give a disapproving yelp. 'Who knows,' he spluttered, 'it may have been Primrose herself. I had the impression she wasn't too keen on the lady, and we know that patience isn't her strong suit!'

'Oh, very funny,' his wife said. 'Besides, she would hardly have been hidden in the laurels, otherwise she couldn't have opened the door to Charles.'

'Ah,' Freddie replied darkly, 'but with those long legs Primrose Oughterard could whizz down that drive in a trice. I tell you I've seen ostriches cover the ground at one hell of a lick. I bet she could do it!'

There were chuckles followed by Winchbrooke informing us mournfully that Mrs Markham's death had been a great blow to the school.

'Really?' I asked in some surprise. 'In what way?'

He explained that for some time Erasmus House had been in need of an annexe and that to his delight Mrs Markham had approached him about the possibility of their making an offer for Needham Court. 'Naturally I told her I would need to consult the governors but that in the meantime would she hold her horses and grant us first refusal. Fortunately the governors gave their assent, and as she seemed so eager to get the thing off her hands I thought the deal was virtually in the bag . . .' He gave a heavy sigh. 'But not so, I fear. Fate has intervened. It's all very vexing.'

'I daresay rather vexing for the intending vendor,' the Reverend Egge was heard to murmur.

'Oh yes, naturally,' Winchbrooke said hastily. But judging from his glum expression I suspected that his concern still lay with the elusive annexe rather than the murdered Alice.

'It's funny about twins,' someone remarked. 'They do say that their lives and destinies follow the same route. This double death would seem to bear that out. Bad luck on the family, I should think – one drowned, the other shot.'

'I don't think there was much of a family,' I said, 'not that one knew of anyway.'

'Oh, but there was Elspeth's son, Aston Travers,' Melinda broke in. 'He came to her funeral. I had an idea he was staying on for a bit to help Alice deal with Needham Court.'

'So where is he now?' Egge asked. 'I expect he will want to discuss his aunt's funeral arrangements with me – not that he did much for his mother's. Still, grief can work like that: induces apathy and numbs the will. Perhaps his aunt's passing will be less of a trial, dreadful though it was. Yes, I am sure the poor man will weather this death better than the last.' He smiled benignly and gave a confident nod.

Reginald Bewley cleared his throat, took a sip of his water and said quietly, 'You could be right, but frankly, according to the late Mrs Travers, aunt and nephew were not always at one. In fact, just recently there may have been a considerable rift. I don't know what it's about but I think it runs pretty deep. I think Mrs Markham has antagonized him in some way and—'

Melinda snorted. 'She could antagonize anyone. Her behaviour at my house the other day was extraordinary, utterly unhinged! I had to lie down afterwards.'

'No, you didn't,' Freddie said, 'you insisted I took you to the Grand at Eastbourne for a lavish blow-out. You ate like a horse and my bank balance is still in the red.'

There was general laughter, not shared by Duster, who gave a disgruntled growl, and I knew it was time to go home.

As we reached the crossroads a few yards from the lane for Podmore we were startled by the loud hoot of a car and a screeching of brakes. I yanked Duster's lead and turned ready to scowl at the driver. No point: it was a black battered Citroën

Avant of the type beloved of Nicholas Ingaza. The driver's door opened and slammed, and sure enough Ingaza's thin figure advanced towards me.

Years ago in the war Nicholas and I had met at Bletchley Park, and while we were never close, there had been a mutual respect which has never quite died; and on the rare occasions when we do collide the encounter is always affable. Although Bletchley is the main bond (though it is never mentioned – DORA's taboo still in operation) Primrose Oughterard also provides a link. I gather that Nicholas had known her clerical brother well – too well, she sometimes says grimly. I wouldn't know about that but gather that Ingaza's past was not exactly spotless (nor now I suspect). However, I speak as I find, and so with nerves quietened after their initial jolt, I was glad to see him.

We shook hands and I enquired after his Brighton art gallery. 'How's trade? Sold any good pictures lately?'

'Not *good* pictures, dear boy,' he leered, 'but I've sold a fair lot – and at a fair price too. *Very* fair you might say. It's amazing what people will snap up! I don't suppose you are after a Landseer reproduction, are you?'

'No fear,' I said, 'it might frighten Duster.'

He laughed and we spoke of other things, the last of those being Primrose. 'I expect you've heard what happened at her gates,' I said. 'A frightful business, and it's bad luck because—'

Nicholas looked blank and asked what was wrong with her perishing gates.

'You mean you don't know?'

'No, why should I? I reside in the metropolis of Brighton, you might remember, not in its rural suburbia. Besides, it's pictures that interest me, not gates.'

I replied mildly that he might make an exception in this case, and proceeded to relate the recent events.

When I finished he was silent for a few moments, and then closing his eyes, muttered, 'Oh . . . my . . . God.' He repeated the words and then groaned loudly.

So strong was his dismay that I was quite perturbed. 'Er – did you know the victim?' I asked.

'Fortunately apart from one violent encounter, no. But I know Primrose.' He gave a wan smile, and then offering a wilting hand said he must be off to brace himself. 'There is bound to be a telephone call,' he added gloomily.

When I got home Agnes had prepared lunch and asked why I was so late. I explained that the pub had been unusually crowded with people discussing the Markham drama and that I had been drawn into the discussion. 'That delayed me a bit and then I bumped into—'

'Did they ask if you had done it?' she enquired brightly.

'Certainly not.'

'I would have.'

'Doubtless,' I said dryly and, changing the subject, told her about my encounter with Ingaza. She said she bet he had tried to flog me the fake Landseer in his gallery window.

I nodded. 'As a matter of fact, I bought it. Delivery is first thing tomorrow morning. It can replace the painting of your grisly ancestor.' That took the wind out of her sails.

Lunch proceeded smoothly. And then feeling sufficiently strong, I ventured into the east wing to supervise matters lavatorial.

TWENTY-FOUR

Emily Bartlett to her sister

> *My dear Hilda,*
>
> *In response to your latest bulletin on Mother and her sudden return to rude health, I must report that here in Sussex we are far from healthy – or at least one of us is not. I refer to poor Mrs Alice Markham (sister of Elspeth Travers whose drowning I told you about). Well, would you believe it, I fear she is now dead too. Yes, and not only dead but murdered!*
>
> *Naturally we are all shocked to the core . . . except for Primrose who has assured me that the woman was obviously deranged and had doubtless brought it upon herself! Really, for an artist specializing in placid idylls of rustic churches*

and docile sheep, Primrose can be awfully harsh at times. (I gather her brother was mildness itself.) Indeed, when she said that about the victim, I was prompted to show my disapproval by making a cautionary joke. 'But Primrose,' I said, wagging my finger, 'a little bird tells me that poor Mrs Markham was found on the edge of your property. Some might draw conclusions!' I gave a sprightly smile and hoped she would feel abashed. But I fear it cut no ice, for all she said was, 'If you talked to the birds less, Emily, and thought more, you might have more pertinent things to say and wouldn't need to make feeble jokes.' She then stalked off saying she was in a hurry and had to take the dog to the vet about its bowels. (Oh, and that reminds me . . . is Mother's recovery to do with the removal of that blockage you were telling me about? Perhaps you took my hint and mentioned it to the doctor?)

But back to the Markham murder. Of course, the boys are in their element and rather ghoulishly are betting on which of Lewes's residents is the prime suspect (all nonsense of course – it was obviously some malcontent from Brighton). The most shrill and vociferous of these 'bookmakers' is that wretched Sickie-Dickie, the grandson of Judge Ickington – not a good influence, I fear – who is offering odds of ten-to-one on poor Mr Winchbrooke. Well, I can tell you that the headmaster is the last one to want to assassinate Alice Markham. Only recently she had come to discuss plans about selling Needham Court to the school as a much-needed annexe. I gather the price was remarkably fair and Mr Winchbrooke was over the moon – so much so that in anticipation of the purchase he had already arranged a celebratory cocktail party. But I have to say that since the tragedy he has been exceedingly cast down, a mood not helped by the caterers demanding a cancellation fee. It is all very sad as negotiations had been going so well!

Another of Dickie's 'runners' is the gym mistress Bertha Twigg (or Big Bertha as Dickie rudely calls her . . . though I have to admit she is rather large), and for some reason he is offering odds at sixty-to-one (pennies). When I enquired about their long length, he explained that given her weight and girth it was unlikely she could have made a sufficiently quick getaway. I was inclined to agree but naturally didn't say so, and instead told him he was a very naughty boy. Like Primrose he shrugged, but unlike Primrose he gave me a toothy grin.

But I can tell you someone who isn't grinning and that is Chief Superintendent MacManus: very curt and down in the mouth he seems. Doubtless he is much burdened by this dreadful Markham affair. I happened to see him and Mrs M. in church last Sunday. They were sitting on the opposite side of the aisle from me. He glanced in my direction so naturally I gave a friendly nod and raised my hand, but the gesture was ignored. I daresay he hadn't seen me as he frowned and looked away evidently preoc-cupied . . . so preoccupied in fact that I couldn't help noticing he put only two shillings in the plate. Five is customary and even Mr Winchbrooke manages three. I also noticed that when the locum vicar embarked on a rather abstruse sermon concerning the sins of the flesh (their exact nature not specified fortunately), I distinctly saw him drumming his fingers on the pew and consulting his watch. Quite why the vicar should have chosen that topic on so sunny a day, I do not know. I cannot imagine the Reverend Egge venturing into those waters! But when he tapped the lectern and declared it was incumbent upon those in authority to set a good example in such matters, the superintendent was overcome by a violent fit of coughing and had to go out. Of course at this time of year the pollen count can be very high and I suspect he had a touch of hay fever. Some people suffer appallingly in that way. Indeed, I used to myself and said as much to him after the service, but he gave me a stony look – the sort that mother often gives – and so I spoke to his wife instead, admiring her hat which was dreadful.

The next day I told Primrose that in my view Mr MacManus was under much strain regarding the Markham case and that he was obviously taking it very seriously. She gave me one of those maddening stares, and then said she thought the Markham case was the least of the superintendent's strains and that the next time I felt like making gay social chit-chat in the church porch I should ask him about Bognor. What she meant by that I have no idea! Why Bognor, for goodness' sake? Like Mother, Primrose sometimes says the most extraordinary things and one is hard-pressed to make head or tail. Ah well, such is life and other people! Alas I fear I must end now as Mr Winchbrooke insists that I compose a blandishing letter to the caterers requesting they withdraw their cancellation fee. They won't, of course, but he lives in hope. I do not.

Be assured, Hilda, I will write again as soon as I have more news of our little town's unsavoury drama – who knows, perhaps to report the fiend has been arrested! Meanwhile do tell Mother to keep on taking the syrup of figs – and if she demands an accompanying gin you must be very firm.

From your devoted sister,
Emily

TWENTY-FIVE

The Primrose version

I t didn't take long for the news of Alice's fate to be bruited abroad. Speculation was rife, as well it might be, and needless to say I was forced into the position of having to lie charmingly to all those eager to hear things from 'the horse's mouth'. I object to being likened to a horse but took solace from the fact that any publicity was good for business and that I could bank on selling more than my usual quota of pictures and prints. Fortunately once it was apparent that the horse knew nothing and was as shocked and bemused as anyone else, attention lapsed, although sales stayed fairly brisk. With Inspector Spikesy in charge the police too were being brisk, having combed my laurel thicket endlessly (or so it seemed), cordoned off the area where the victim was found and padlocked the main gates of Needham Court. A wise precaution in my view: the public can

be disgracefully nosy, and not least those little scallywags from
Erasmus House.

I had feared the local newspaper might be tedious. But its frenzy
has been defused by the drama of two small boys who, having
vanished for several days, have been found bivouacking in a tree-
house near Glynde. Apart from threatening fire and brimstone, the
parents are jubilant; the boys, I gather, less so, complaining bitterly
that one couldn't 'go nowhere these days without some blooming
snitch blowing the gaff'. 'Spies everywhere,' the younger one
grumbled. I felt some sympathy and indeed rather commend their
initiative. And at least the tale diverts the press from pestering me
and gawping at my ravaged gateposts!

My decision to remain silent, while a pragmatic necessity, is frustrating for it means there is no one in whom I can confide Alice's
awful revelation. No one, that is, except for Nicholas Ingaza, who
is being tiresomely elusive. I gather that Charles Penlow bumped
into him recently and told him what had happened; thus you
would have thought that natural curiosity might have prompted
a phone call . . . Huh! An absurd assumption. Ingaza rarely does
the obvious thing if he can help it, and in any case is doubtless
too busy practising his tango routine. (The Brighton Latino Cup
is imminent, and having won the trophy last time he will be hell
bent on another triumph. Primrose Oughterard's astounding news
will be peanuts compared to that challenge!) I did telephone this
morning but couldn't get through; it almost sounded as if the
thing was off the hook, though it was probably just the GPO
engineers being difficult again. Anyway, I shall persist this
evening, and meantime must go into Lewes to take the dog to the
vet and collect the spondulicks for my pictures.

A trio of chance encounters made this quite a busy morning. Thus,
before leaving Bouncer to be manhandled by the vet – surprisingly
something the dog quite enjoys – I was stopped by Emily, who
burbled inanely that since the corpse had been found in the vicinity
of my house I was likely to be a prime suspect. I think she thought
she was being funny. I did not and sent her packing.

Then, afterwards and less tiresomely, I bumped into Councillor
Bewley about to enter the town hall. Naturally we touched on

Alice Markham's shocking death and voiced the usual platitudes about the awfulness of Fate and her not deserving to die like that (oh no?) et cetera. For one who had been the focus of the deceased's jealous ardours Bewley showed no more disturbance than the social norm, i.e. shocked but relatively detached. It confirmed what I had rather assumed, that he had been happily ignorant of Alice's plans to 'net' him!

I was about to move on but he seemed eager to discuss the book he had left behind in the café and which I had completely forgotten to return. 'So remiss of me,' I apologized, 'you must come over for a drink next week and pick it up.'

He said he would like that very much as then we could have a good discussion about Compton Mackenzie. 'My favourite author,' he said earnestly. 'So shrewd, so eloquent – a fine writer. But you know, I think this latest one, *Thin Ice*, is perhaps his most accomplished: such a delicate portrayal of a . . . well, of a sensitive subject. And bold too. Wouldn't you agree? Ah, but perhaps you haven't read it.' He looked at me quizzically.

I replied that indeed I had, having ordered it from the library when it first appeared, and that I thought Mackenzie's handling of the theme most enlightened. He nodded vigorously. Then, raising his hat and murmuring something about a vital meeting to do with municipal drains, hastened inside.

I pressed on to the art shop to collect my recent takings and to suggest to the new assistant that she really ought to display my pictures in a more suitable space. I mean to say who on earth wants their work hung next to a portrait of some 'cute' infant with bulbous cheeks and guzzling an ice cream? Talk about lowering the tone! But as I reached the door, poised to deliver some kindly advice on the subject of aesthetics, I was tapped smartly on the shoulder and a voice said, 'My dear, I've been *dying* to see you. What excitement about the Markham palaver! Have you time for a teeny drink?'

I smiled at Melinda Balfour whose buoyant company, laced with impeccable gossip, I rather enjoy. What with one thing and another the last few days had been somewhat tense, and I realized that I could do with a chat and a laugh. So shelving my immediate mission, I accompanied her to the White Hart for a quick snifter before collecting Bouncer.

Naturally we chewed the cud over Alice . . . or at least Melinda chewed while I listened, smiled, nodded and made observations where it was safe to do so.

'*I* think it was the ex-husband,' she opined cheerfully. 'Do you remember her telling us what a beast he was – greedy, loud and insatiable?'

'Well, that applies to a number of people, men and women,' I said, 'but it doesn't necessarily make them murderers. You may recall we were also told he was a dedicated philanderer – thus I should have thought far too busy to waste valuable time coming down here looking for Alice. He is bound to have more pressing engagements.'

Melinda nodded, but observed that if Alice had been bleeding him white over the alimony payments he might just have been tempted to postpone those current engagements to remedy matters. 'It happens all the time,' she declared airily, 'ex-spouses killing to save money. I tell you, my bet is on the erstwhile hubby!' She spoke with her usual cheery conviction. I pondered the idea, conceding she had a point. Yes, such things were not unknown . . .

But before I could think further, Melinda had jumped to another topic: 'I say, have you heard about the funeral?'

I shook my head.

'Well, I can tell you there's not going to be one, or at least not here in Sussex. The body is being taken back to London by cousins. Apparently the thing will be done at Paddington or Willesden – can't remember which. Anyway, the Reverend Egge is most put out; he likes them.'

'What, the cousins?'

'No, you ass, funerals!'

'Ah . . . so where is the nephew?' I asked. 'I've only seen him once since it happened. Isn't he involved?'

She shrugged. 'Doesn't look like it. No sign, unless he is organizing things from behind the scenes.'

Behind the scenes? Huh, the scenes of Bognor's music hall, no doubt, with its backstage bordello; he was probably absorbed in some vital deal to secure new supplies of underwear for his 'business interests' in that theatre shop he had mentioned. A consignment of spangled corsets would top a funeral any day, even Auntie's!

I was about to say as much to Melinda but stopped – partly because I felt suddenly ashamed of such waspishness but also because I was interrupted by her next words.

'Actually, now I think of it, I'm wrong: I did see him recently. He was outside the Anne of Cleeves House jawing with the Mountjoy girl – or at least she was jawing; he looked bored to tears.'

'She was probably treating him to a lecture on angst and the psychology of familial bereavement,' I said dryly.

'Oh, doubtless.' She grinned.

That evening I was able to contact Ingaza and with supreme tact enquired if his line had been out of order. He muttered vaguely that he thought perhaps it had. I was unconvinced but didn't press the point having more crucial matters to pursue.

'It is essential that I see you,' I told him. 'I have *much* to report!'

'Yes,' he said flatly, 'I know. Your gates are smashed and the Markham woman has been shot.'

'Oh, but there is more to it than that,' I assured him. 'I am now in possession of certain facts denied to others – facts which entirely vindicate my suspicions!'

'My dear Primrose, you have so many suspicions. Which particular set are these?'

'You know perfectly well,' I replied impatiently. 'The Elspeth Travers case, of course.'

For a moment there was silence. It would have been gratifying to think he was stunned by the news, but I knew better.

However, my words had obviously sparked an interest for he then asked if I thought the two matters were related, to which I replied that since the two victims most definitely were then surely there was a fair chance.

'But it doesn't necessarily follow.'

'Exactly, Nicholas, it does not follow – which is why I want to explore the whole business with *you*.'

'Hmm, thought you might . . .' There was the faintest sigh.

'So when can I see you?' I demanded.

'Well, I am a bit tied up with tango steps just now – why don't we wait till I come over to deliver my superb talk on attribution? We could—'

'Certainly not,' I exclaimed, 'that is much too far ahead. I need to . . .' I paused seeking the right term, and for some reason heard the voice of the Mountjoy girl: 'To *unburden* myself,' I echoed.

'Crikey,' he said dolefully.

Thus it was arranged that since he had to spend a morning with the awful Aunt Lil at Eastbourne's bandstand later that week, we could rendezvous in the afternoon at the town's Gildredge Park and watch the tennis. A most soothing venue in which to consider the grim and gruesome and I ticked the date in my diary.

TWENTY-SIX

The Primrose version

You would have thought there was enough drama going on without its being added to by the Erasmus school play. This is an annual event to which naturally parents and trustees are invited, but so also are Lewes's 'great and good' – i.e. those whom Mr Winchbrooke deems useful in boosting the school's finances and prestige. Because I have donated three of my larger pictures, adjudicate their painting competitions and once contributed a glowing article to *Sussex Life* praising the school's virtues (was I drunk?) I too am among the elect. This time, however, preoccupied as I was with other concerns, I nearly gave it a miss.

But I changed my mind, thinking that an evening of frothy entertainment from juvenile thespians might be an agreeable distraction. Emily too was most insistent I should attend and, being the school secretary, she is useful in saving me a good seat and ensuring I am listed for the better wine and not the egregious plonk kept for the staff.

I was just about to leave when I was diverted by baleful grunts from Bouncer's basket. As said, he usually enjoys his visits to the vet, but the previous day's session had been more probing than usual and exploiting the chance for sympathy he was now lolling about looking pathetic. The cat had stalked off somewhere and I think he was feeling fed up. I hesitated and then said, 'Oh, all right. I suppose you want to come in the car, do you?' That did it. He was out of the basket like a shot and trotted purposefully to the front door.

Arriving at the school I gave him a quick run, and then pushed him into the back seat with one of his special toys before joining my fellow theatregoers. Among these, and rather to my surprise, was Mrs MacManus. She seemed to be minus her husband, and I wondered whether this was a bore or a bonus. I suspected the latter for she was looking quite animated and wearing a sharper tone of grey than usual and had added touches of beige. She was also sipping a glass of wine with the Reverend Egge who, giving an expansive wave, beckoned me over. He produced a programme and said, 'I've never heard of this play, have you, Miss Oughterard? I mean, they generally do something like *Treasure Island* or *The Wind in the Willows*, something rather jolly. But this one has a bit of an odd title.' He pointed to the programme cover and the words *Alphonse and the Awakening Vision*.

I shook my head. 'Never heard of it.'

'Oh, I don't think anyone has,' Mrs MacManus murmured. 'I am told the new English master has written it especially for Erasmus House. I gather it's full of rich symbolism and that this is its first performance. Rather exciting really!' I thought she looked a trifle uncertain. As was I, for when scanning the small section of acknowledgements, I noted the following:

> *My thanks to Dr Louise Bakeshaft for supplying such invaluable advice on the complex nuances of character and the subtle interplay of mind and spirit.*

I blinked and turned to Egge. 'Have you seen this?' I asked.

'Yes,' he replied glumly, and went in search of more wine.

I was about to do the same when Mrs MacManus plucked my sleeve. 'I so hope you found those little books I sent you useful,' she simpered hopefully. 'I expect you artists are always on the lookout for inspiration.'

Not from those crass sources, I thought grimly. But, giving a noncommittal smile, I enquired politely after her husband.

'Oh, he's *very* busy,' she said. 'He would have been here tonight but he had a more pressing engagement in—'

'Bognor?' I said slyly before I could stop myself.

'Bognor?' she replied vaguely. 'No, in London. At Scotland Yard with Detective Inspector Samson. They are having dinner together, they often do. I gather Mr Samson is keen to re-examine an unsolved case he was once associated with, somewhere in Surrey, I think, and Alastair is giving him some advice. He's good at that.'

Served me right! Ask a cheeky question and get a rotten answer.

In fact, Mrs MacManus's answer worried me for the whole of the play's opening scene. Samson and MacManus were getting too close for comfort. Surrey was a large county and there could be a number of unsolved cases they might be discussing, but given the prevalence of Sod's Law it could well be my foolish brother's.[7] I brooded bleakly.

However, by scene two I had managed to put the thing out of my mind and could concentrate on the theatricals. These I found virtually incomprehensible, as I suspect did the cast. In fact, when in the interval I bumped into one of them, Sickie-Dickie still in his costume, he seemed to think the same, for when I asked him which of his fellow thespians was playing the eponymous Alphonse and to explain his own role, he said he hadn't a clue.

'But you must have some idea, Dickie.'

His brow furrowed and then he said slowly, 'I think I am a metaphor.'

'A metaphor for what?'

'What?'

'As a metaphor what exactly do you represent?' I said patiently.

He shrugged. 'Not sure what you mean, Miss Oughterard. I'm just a metaphor. I say, do you think you could possibly lend me sixpence to buy an ice? It's awfully hot in this robe!'

---

[7] See *A Load of Old Bones* & others in the series. The Fotherington murder case had been shelved for lack of evidence. Despite her brother's death Primrose is haunted by the fear of it being re-opened.

I gave him a shilling and told him that if he was going to be a judge like Grandpa he would have to get used to wearing hot robes.

'Oh, I'm not going to be a judge, Miss Oughterard. I shall go to Merton College in Oxford and then become a slippery art dealer just like Mr Ingaza. He's the one!'

Thanking me profusely for the shilling the metaphor hitched up its robe and scampered off in search of ice cream.

The play over and none the wiser as to its meaning, I was about to leave but was stopped by the headmaster. 'Did you enjoy it?' Winchbrooke asked warily.

'Yes,' I lied, 'very novel.'

He looked startled. 'Really? Ah . . . I see. Well, I'll pass that on to Mr Urquart. I'm sure he'll be most gratified – yes, most gratified.' He hesitated before adding, 'Although, talking of novels, it occurs to me that next year the boys might like to do something based on the Biggles adventures or Bulldog Drummond . . . perhaps more in keeping with the school's stalwart spirit. What do you think?' He regarded me anxiously.

'Oh, *yes*,' I enthused. 'And you could write it yourself, Head-master, and call it *Biggles and the Bulldog Years*. It could be quite a hit – and a money-spinner too, I shouldn't wonder!'

He turned quite pink; and noting an excited gleam in his eye I went away feeling I had improved his evening.

At the car park I thought I should give Bouncer a run before setting off. But we were in a narrow area surrounded by the other cars revving and shunting, so I told him he would have to wait till we came to a quieter spot.

This happened to be opposite the gates of Needham Court, dark and traffic-free; and since the dog was getting restless it seemed a suitable place. Thus, I drew up, decanted him on to the pavement and lit a cigarette. I assumed he would potter about a bit sniffing here and there, then lift a leg and return to the car. I should have known better; for the next time I looked he was nowhere to be seen. I wound down the window and whistled – a fruitless exercise eliciting nothing. Cursing quietly, I got out and went in search.

As the creature had disappeared so quickly I guessed he had slipped into the grounds of Needham Court and was conducting a brisk reconnaissance. The gates were still padlocked as a police precaution against snoopers, but I knew that Bouncer would hardly be deterred by that. And knowing that hedges were his speciality I walked a few yards further on looking for a suitable gap. One appeared, and with determined force I shoved my way through and scanned the lawn. Despite a fitful moon it was fairly dark, and since Bouncer's coat is a delicate shade of mud (unlike the pristine white of the Mountjoys' peculiar bull terrier) he would be difficult to see. The best thing was to listen for low growls and scratchings. This is a sure sign of the dog's presence for he is either interring something or resurrecting it.

I cocked my ears but heard nothing. At the far end of the lawn just by the house there is a small group of bushes, and I suspected that if he was anywhere at all it might be there. Bouncer has a mania for shrubberies and whenever he sees one will gravitate towards it. Apart from burying and excavating bones, I am never quite sure what he does in these shrouded hidey-holes but he certainly seems to like them. Francis used to tell me how at Molehill the dog would often retire to the church crypt and be there for hours on end. Perhaps shrubberies are sort of ersatz crypts and provide similar balm and interest. Who knows – the canine mind, like those of humans, is a total enigma!

Anyway, as I hesitantly approached the house (aware the place was off-limits and slightly nervous in case there was a police presence) I suddenly noticed what looked like a light in one of the upstairs windows, a bedroom presumably. It wasn't a bright light but dim and erratic. I blinked and looked harder, but it had disappeared. I glanced up at the moon, which for a couple of seconds had slid out from the heavy clouds. Had the beam simply been a reflection or a ray glinting on one of the panes? Most likely. I returned my gaze to the bushes hoping to spot the shaggy form of my tiresome quarry, but could see and hear nothing. Blooming dog!

Perhaps the wily creature had pottered off elsewhere; had seen me coming and perversely gone the other way. Typical. But I could have done with him just then, I really could. I wanted to hear his heavy snuffling and pat that tousled head. Why? Because standing in front of that shadowy house whose walls had once sheltered two victims of murder, I suddenly felt afraid . . . Well no, not afraid exactly, but strangely disturbed. I am not a fanciful person and such irrational feelings are alien. Absurd really, but frankly I didn't like it and would have welcomed Bouncer's cheerful presence.

I turned to retrace my steps and exit by the hole in the hedge, but suddenly caught sight of the French window on the terrace, the one which opens into the drawing room. It was ajar. Surely the police wouldn't have left it like that? How very careless. Perhaps the lock was defective. Should I close it? I hesitated, feeling that it was really none of my business and that in any case I was technically a trespasser. But having Ma's tidy mind (Pa's had been bedlam) my instinct was to shut the thing. It was an instinct I followed . . . a course which in retrospect I realize was what novelists call fateful, for it later led to incidents of startling effect. However, I was hardly to know that then, and so approached the large glass door.

I was just putting out my hand to grasp the handle, when I froze. From within the gloom there flickered another light but this time it seemed attached to a shape, the vague outline of a figure: a figure which, with torch in hand, was bending over the writing desk and seemingly rifling its contents. Shocked but riveted, I held my breath.

With his back to me (I assumed it was a man) and clad in a long coat or mac, it was impossible to discern the features, but what I could just make out was the mess of papers scattered on the floor and an upturned ink bottle trickling its contents on to the carpet. As I have remarked before, it is strange the trivial thoughts that strike the mind at such critical moments. But as I glimpsed the dripping ink I couldn't help thinking how annoyed Elspeth would have been. The desk's previous owner had been fastidious to the point of paranoia and to have her possessions besmirched in this way would have grated – though whether her sister had shared those same sensibilities I rather doubted. However, such thoughts vanished in a trice as I continued to peer intently at the scene in the room's far corner.

The rifling continued. But as I watched it suddenly struck me that having obviously entered by the French window the intruder would also leave by it – and possibly at any moment. Swift action was required! Heart in mouth I backed away, thinking I might sneak off and fade quietly into the night. But curiosity – Francis would have called it nosiness – is a potent thing and I was avid to get a proper sighting. Thus, I looked for cover and saw I was only a few feet away from a water butt and a rose trellis, both well in the shadow. I thrust myself behind these, and as a marble statue or Lot's wife, waited. And waited . . .

Stuck there in a state of tension and anti-climax, I became impatient – and chilly for a sharp breeze had got up. 'Chummy' was certainly taking his time. What was he doing – ransacking the rest of the rooms? He had already been upstairs, what more did he want! My left foot was getting pins and needles and I stealthily shifted my weight. As I did so there came a slight sound from around the corner of the house – the faintest click like a latch closing. Imagination? Something creaking in the breeze? I couldn't be sure and in any case was beginning to feel too cold to care. I edged back to the French window, still slightly ajar, and took a cautious peek inside. There was nothing except darkness and silence. Unless he was curled up asleep on the sofa, the intruder had gone . . . and I had missed him, damn it!

Tired by my manoeuvres and in some annoyance, I traipsed back across the lawn and again pushed myself through the gap in the hedge. Once in the road, concern for what I had witnessed was replaced by concern for my dog. Where on earth had he got to? Surely I wouldn't have to spend more time trundling around Lewes whistling and calling his name at this time of night. It was too bad!

I scanned the immediate area but there was no sign. Thus, resigned to patrolling the streets at snail's pace in the hope of a sighting, I returned to where I had left the car. About to insert the key in the lock, I heard a noise from beneath the chassis: a deep, repetitive guttural snore. Admittedly even in these days one does still encounter the odd tramp dozing in the odd corner but, judging from the protruding tail, I took this to be no tramp but the furry fugitive. 'Bouncer!' I exploded. The noise stopped abruptly and like a lazy metronome the tail began to wag.

TWENTY-SEVEN

Emily Bartlett to her sister

My dear Hilda,

    I am so glad to hear that Mother is behaving herself and being more biddable since you last wrote. How wise of you to take my advice and alert Dr Hencroft to the blockage. I am sure that will have done the trick. And talking of such matters, according to Primrose, Bouncer too is restored to rude health – 'rude' being the operative term in my view. That dog is not of the most couth! She brought it to the school play the other night but sensibly left it in the car, so one was spared its boisterous attentions. A great mercy.

    Mind you, had the dog been out of the car and in the school hall we might at least have been distracted from young Mr Urquart's curious production, which was not exactly the gayest of dramas. Doubtless it was all very deep and clever, but I fear it had a soporific effect on some of the parents, which even pride in their offspring's performance did little to dispel. At the time I felt quite sorry for Mr Winchbrooke, who, having to balance evident boredom with a show of rapt understanding, was spending a tense evening engaged in some play-acting of his own.

    However, since then my sympathy has diminished. Apparently Primrose was thoughtless enough to suggest that for next year's event he himself might assume the dramatist's mantle and devise a play based on the Biggles stories and Bulldog Drummond. But isn't that harmless? I hear you ask. Far from it! Mr Winchbrooke has become enraptured with the idea and sees himself as a cross between Shakespeare and Dashiell Hammett and spends hours at his desk imitating the voices of Humphrey Bogart and George Sanders. This wouldn't be quite so bad were I not now required to take endless shorthand notes on the imaginary dialogue between

Biggles and Drummond plus scenes of mayhem and carnage wrought by their enemies. Really, as if one hasn't enough to do without being expected to act the role of amanuensis to a creative genius! It is all very vexing and I blame Primrose entirely. She has the knack of stirring things up, a knack honed to a fine art – not unlike our mother's.

Anyway, on a lighter note, you will be interested to hear that there has been a break-in at Needham Court – the home of poor Mrs Travers and latterly her murdered sister. Yes, quite a little surprise! But I fear rather an embarrassment to the police, who after the appalling fate of Alice Markham had been quick to shut the place up as a deterrent to would-be burglars or trophy hunters. Sergeant Wilding tells me that once word gets about that a house stands empty – for whatever reason – the vultures close in. 'But surely not after a sudden death?' I said. 'You bet,' he replied cheerfully, 'best time for it. People have got other things on their mind, funerals and such.' Well really, it just goes to show how grasping human nature is! And frankly, Hilda, we would do well to remember that danger when Mother eventually passes . . . I mean, one doesn't want any Tom, Dick or Harry bursting in and muddying the carpets; that would be too much!

As to any progress regarding the Markham tragedy itself, I fear there is little to report. Naturally the police play their cards very close to their chest in such matters, but from what the chief superintendent's wife let slip the other day (we were both at the chiropodist's with the same ailment, bunions) I get the impression that Mr MacManus is very morose about it all. When I mentioned this to Primrose she said curtly, 'Serve him right.' Of course, she has never liked him and I have to admit that he is not the most extrovert of our law officers – unlike the new Detective Inspector Ronald Spikesy, who seems very personable and alert. In fact, rumour has it – or at least Sergeant Wilding has it – that Mr MacManus has taken against him, and for that very reason. 'He don't like being upstaged,' Wilding told me indiscreetly . . . Well, I don't know about the chief superintendent being upstaged, but it is quite obvious that poor Mr Urquart will be if the headmaster has his way. It wouldn't be so bad if he were not

so enraptured with his own scribblings – scribblings that I
am supposed to decipher and then tell him what an admirable
dramatist he is!

    Well, Hilda, I must leave off now as Primrose has invited
me to tea. I can't think why. Guilt, probably: she has been
most offhand these last few weeks. I gather we are to have
it in the garden. A nice idea – provided that the table is not
too close to the chinchillas' hutch (I mean, she might unleash
them!) and that I shall not be required to amuse the dog by
playing fetch and carry with its disgusting rubber ring.

    In some trepidation, your devoted sister,
Emily

TWENTY-EIGHT

The Primrose version

N eedless to say, news of the Needham Court break-in soon
got about, and for a brief time fuelled the general excitement about the murder. But both press and police put an
unsporting damper on matters by declaring that such intrusions
were common in houses whose occupant had recently died and
that there had been a similar incident at Seaford only a few weeks
previously. 'It's just an opportunist pushing his luck,' MacManus
was reported as saying, 'it happens all the time.'

'In which case, why hadn't the police been more vigilant?'
Charles Penlow was heard to ask. In the circumstances surely a
fair comment – though I certainly wasn't going to reveal my part
in the event and kept my mouth firmly shut. The pot hardly needed
stirring.

Indeed, this is exactly what I said to Ingaza when, as arranged,
we met by the tennis courts in Eastbourne's Gildredge Park; and
where, idly watching a game of doubles, I told him all about my
bizarre afternoon with Alice Markham, its alarming outcome and
the subsequent incident at Needham Court.

He didn't say anything at first, dragging on his cigarette and eyeing one of the tennis players. 'Legs better than face,' he murmured, 'but nice hips.'

'Oh really, Nicholas,' I expostulated, 'I didn't bring you here to ogle the flanks of cavorting young men. These are vital matters and I should be grateful if you would give me the benefit of your support. I mean to say, I could have been killed!'

'No, you couldn't, the gun was a fake.'

'That's as maybe. But I can assure you that it was all very harrowing and if it hadn't been for the cat anything might have happened!'

'Ah, but anything did, didn't it – she was mown down from the top of your drive. That's the intriguing part. Somebody must have known or guessed she was with you. Or do you think it was just some over-zealous target practice by one of the Erasmus masters? Or maybe that school secretary Emily Bartlett has a pistol and wanted to let off steam.'

If Ingaza was trying to rile me he was certainly succeeding. 'Oh, very funny,' I replied impatiently. 'Besides, Emily has a fear of hedgerows, she thinks they harbour mice.' I paused, and then added ruefully, 'I was rather expecting some congratulations for my unerring instinct re the Travers drowning. You may recall I said all along that—'

'Ah, yes, of course. Remarkable, dear girl. Your nose for trouble never ceases to amaze me. What it is to have such powers of deduction!'

'Oh, be quiet! You could at least give me a cigarette; I've left mine behind.'

He passed me a Sobranie, clicked his lighter and then said thoughtfully, 'This person you saw at the writing desk – how do you know it was a random burglar?'

I told him I was simply echoing 'received opinion', that the police reckoned it was the work of a mere chancer exploiting the situation.

'And is that what you think?'

'What do I think? Well, I suppose—'

'You see from what you have told me about your little tête à tête with crazy Alice you now know a number of things the police don't . . . for example the small matter of she and her friend "X" pulling the plug on Mrs T. Therefore, *you* might conceivably draw conclusions about the identity of this intruder which differ from theirs, especially as there's no news of money or jewellery being taken – something one might expect from a professional thief.' He fell silent and returned his gaze to the tennis court's muscular activity.

Brooding on this I too fell silent, my attention drawn not by the leaping figures a few yards away, but by the one bent over the bureau in Alice's drawing room. What had I seen of that shadowy form? Very little. Although largely obscured by the long coat, it had seemed that the person had been of slimish build and good height, but there was nothing especially distinctive there, it could have been anyone really – Charles Penlow or the Reverend Egge, for instance! And yet, I reflected, that being the case, it could equally have been Alice's accomplice, her 'London friend' searching the house for incriminating material – correspondence between the pair of them perhaps, something rashly penned and thus dangerous . . . notes for a plan of disposal? Or since the desk was likely to have been used by both sisters perhaps it was a family relation, Aston Travers, for example, pursuing a missing will or some valuable he had been hoping to get his hands on before other claimants. It wouldn't surprise me!

I turned to Ingaza. 'Is that what you are thinking, Nicholas? That it wasn't a stranger but someone known to Alice, a confidant or maybe even the nephew?'

'Hmm,' he murmured, 'what I am thinking is that the chap prancing around at the net has remarkably neat ankles . . . Oh, the fool, he's missed it!' The ball thudded into the wire mesh at our end of the court.

'For God's sake, Nicholas, be serious!'

'Oh, I *am*, dear girl, I am.'

Luckily at that moment the players elected to end their session and trooped off. A blessed relief. However, fearful they might be replaced by others equally riveting, I hastily suggested that we stretch our legs and commune with nature, i.e. the frogs in the lily pond. Not a good idea: the pond had been drained and the frogs on holiday. Nevertheless, a leisurely stroll among the park's trees and flowerbeds was not uncongenial and Ingaza seemed more ready for serious debate.

'I suppose it *could* have been Aston,' I said, 'though in the circumstances and being a close relation of the victim, it seems a pretty stupid thing to do. I mean, if the police had caught him sneaking around there in the middle of the night they'd have taken a very dim view. I am sure Sergeant Wilding would have raised a rumpus and been most suspicious! Still, from what I've seen, he's an arrogant young man and I suppose he would take the risk, might even enjoy it.'

'Arrogance and stupidity often go together,' Ingaza remarked. 'It's a common enough blend. Take MacManus, for example. What chief superintendent of any nous is going to chance his arm poncing about in a brothel dressed as a grizzly bear and being prodded by an ostrich with a whip?' He emitted a nasal hoot of laughter.

'I wonder if he still engages,' I mused. 'Unlikely, I should think. It may have been a passing fad, an odd whim which he is now bitterly regretting. I don't suppose the whey-faced wife can be much fun; perhaps it was a novel port in a storm of boredom.'

Ingaza smiled, and then looked grim. 'You could be right. But whether he still practises is neither here nor there: he did once, and *you* have the tangible proof. Any gossip or revelation of that kind would destroy his career. The Topping chap knew what he was doing when he kept those photos and it was a stroke of luck you found them. If Topping had felt threatened by MacManus he wouldn't have hesitated to use them. And if he starts any funny business make sure you do the same. We don't want old Francis's idiocy disinterred, do we? And I certainly don't want my part in the Beachy Head palaver exposed. Bad for business – I've got a couple of lucrative deals on hand and I can't afford to have them scuppered by officious questioning from the boys in blue.'

These were my sentiments exactly, but I couldn't help being amused. Since when had Ingaza not been engaged in some lucrative deal? His art business thrived on such transactions, deals invariably of a delicate nature. I was about to turn back to the Elspeth/Alice topic, but suddenly remembered something and started to giggle. 'By the way,' I said, 'how are you getting on with your admirer?'

He smirked. 'My admirer? You mean a tango fan?'

'No, or at least I don't think so. I mean Judge Ickington's grandson, the little fellow you gave a lift to the other night.' And I reminded him of Sickie-Dickie's avowed ambition to follow in his footsteps and become, to quote the boy's mother, 'the best slippery art dealer on the south coast' – though tactfully I omitted the term slippery and the bit about the ferret.

'Ah yes,' he replied carelessly, 'a bright kid. He was quite appreciative of my voice I seem to remember.'

'But Nicholas, you didn't really sing "*La Mer*" to him, did you?' (I should have known!)

'Why not? You did say he needed to improve his French, and after all it is one of my better pieces. Shall I—'

'No,' I said quickly, 'nature has its own lyricism.' And I gestured vaguely at some roses and a passing duck.

By this time we had reached the park gates and were standing under the arch at the top of the steps. I pressed him again about the recent drama.

'You must admit, Nicholas, it's all fearfully rum. Extraordinary really. Obviously Alice was pretty barmy – though whether before or as a result of the Elspeth project one can't be sure. But who on earth has killed *her*? I know you joked about Emily letting off steam, but maybe that's exactly what it was: some crazy clown fooling about who took a wild pot-shot and is now cursing himself to kingdom come. What do you think?'

He shrugged but regarded me soberly. 'Yes, it could have been – there are such cases and I daresay the police will be looking in that direction. But meanwhile I suggest you continue as you have been: say nothing to anyone and keep your head down. Silence is more than golden, it's platinum. The less one knows the safer one is, that's my motto . . . Oh but I tell you what: make sure you don't keep those bear-suit photographs in your bureau. Shove 'em in a Wellington boot. We don't want any more break-ins, do we?' He grinned, cocked his thumb and sauntered off.

I sighed and walked to my car. What a scintillating ray of sunshine!

In fact, as I drove home to Lewes rays of sunshine were gilding the landscape in the most enchanting way. Enchanting is perhaps an overly romantic adjective, but that evening our Sussex Downs and fields were looking truly magical. The trees of distant Wannock, sleepy Folkington, Wilmington with its Long Man starkly clear, the Berwick levels peppered with placid sheep, the meandering Ouse – all went by in a soothing trail of languid beauty. Indeed, I was so taken by the aesthetics of the hour that my mind was temporarily free of the grisly events we had been discussing.

But the mind is a fickle thing and is readily diverted. And for no reason at all – in fact, just as I was admiring the outline of a church spire – I was suddenly struck by an alien thought. In a trice nature's bright images were replaced by a prospect dark and sinister. The scene of a shrouded Aston rifling through the desk had reappeared. But it was a scene overlaid by another: Aston concealed in bushes, patiently crouching with pistol primed and levelled, alert to every sound and all poised to extinguish his quarry as she came zooming to the top of my drive . . . Possible?

Well, anything is possible – but *probable*? For a few seconds my mind was gripped by the question; so gripped, in fact, that I narrowly missed a squirrel as it leapt headstrong from the kerb. I swerved, hit the brake and hastily collected my senses. Really, what it was to have a dramatic imagination! And yet so vivid was its picture that the landscape – which only a moment ago had held such charm – was now eclipsed and I arrived home in a state of febrile excitement. However, on entering the drawing room and faced by Pa's glaring portrait I was instantly sobered, and his favourite word *balderdash* echoed in my mind.

Yes, the idea was surely absurd. Why should Aston Travers want to murder his aunt? A futile question. How was I to know – or anyone not privy to the exact nature of their relationship? After all, any bland-fronted family could be internally battle-scarred – as Alice Markham had made so graphically clear! But was Alice's resentment of her sister replicated in the nephew's feeling for his aunt? And if so, was it enough to induce the same deadly result?

I remembered his tone when speaking of her in the café – sardonic, snidely dismissive: *no problems with that one, or at least none that can't be handled!* The accompanying laugh had been cold and perfunctory. Of merriment there was none . . . All right, so she irritated him – but did that matter? I thought of our recent encounter after his police interview. He had been civil enough in a provocative way, vaguely human even. At the time I had sensed an air of loss, a loosening of the rigid guard. And yet now as I sat pondering the scene, I remembered he had also called her 'a manipulative old bat' and described her as 'Maddening. Utterly maddening.' Yes, I brooded, despite the somewhat rueful tone the words had betrayed a latent anger, and I wondered in what ways she had been manipulative. And had she become so maddening that despite his boast in the café he could no longer handle her? Had 'Auntie' grown so difficult that she was marked for extinction? Or, I pondered, might there have been a more serious reason to kill her? Revenge. Might Aston have somehow learnt of Auntie's hand in his mother's drowning and elected to mow her down in retaliation? Was that what it had been – a grimly vicious tit for tat? For a few moments I entertained the image, but then dismissed it feeling that from what I had seen of Aston he was not the sort to take up lethal cudgels on another's account (even that of a parent). No, any such cudgels would doubtless be for his own ends: to smooth a personal path . . . and had Auntie been obstructing that path? Quite possibly.

I leant back on the sofa and once more confronted my parent's thunderous brows. From the depths of the past I heard an explosive *Pah! Pure conjecture, Primrose!* 'Yes, yes,' I retorted irritably, 'but conjecture can often contain a strong element of truth. So there!' And on that point I arose and poured myself a liberal glass of his beloved Talisker.

The next day just as I was finishing a late and leisurely breakfast, the telephone rang. It is rare for Ingaza to call me unsolicited, thus when I lifted the receiver I was surprised to hear his reedy tone. 'I've got a little bit of gossip that might just interest you,' he began.

'Oh yes?

'You know your friend we were talking about yesterday, Aston Travers—'

'No friend of mine,' I mumbled digesting a crust of toast, 'a pretty slippery type if you ask me. In fact, Nicholas, I've been doing some thinking and wonder if . . . Er, so what about him?'

Ingaza sighed. 'That's what I am trying to tell you if I am given a chance. Listen, will you!'

I listened and he started to explain. 'Eric has made an interesting discovery via a chum of his, one of his darts pals, Bullseye Bert. He used to be a copper – what you might call of the bent variety, though he's retired now. And that being the case he—'

'Eric knows a bent copper? I find that *very* hard to believe,' I said caustically.

'Well, not bent exactly, what you might call, uhm . . . *flexible.*'

'Oh, all right, so what does flexible Bert have to say about anything?'

'He says that in addition to supplying saucy outfits to that theatre shop in Bognor Travers is also supplying a different form of goods to Mercer's Music Hall, or rather to its backstage sideline.'

'You mean the brothel set-up?'

'That's it.'

'What sort of goods?'

'My dear Primrose, with your sparkling imagination I should have thought you would guess. Ladies of the Night, of course. Tarts.'

'Good lord, you mean he's a pimp?'

'I do. And not just any old pimp, a very accomplished one.'

An accomplished pimp? The term struck me as being an unusual conjunct and I asked him to enlarge.

'He has the trade down to a fine art; it's elaborate, lucrative and smoothly executed. Eric says that according to Bert the inner cognoscenti call it the OTG.' There was a faint chuckle.

'Really – and what's that supposed to mean?'

'Operation Tarts Galore.'

I was startled but couldn't help smiling. Graphic and pithy, the title was not unlike the sort that might grace a military project, and I said as much to Ingaza.

'Nautical would be a closer analogy,' he replied. 'When he's not flogging star-spangled tights to the acting fraternity he is sailing back and forth across the Channel picking up French prostitutes for the British market and transporting ours to the Frogs in Dieppe. He keeps a boat down here. Some of the ladies are regular passengers – one week here, one there. They like to ring the changes and

I gather it improves their language skills no end.' He paused and then added, 'What you might call a way of enhancing the *entente cordial*, I suppose.'

'Oh, *what* a noble enterprise,' I remarked acidly, 'it's just about his level: exploiting foolish women for personal gain. It's odd the way Auntie was so besotted, but then she wasn't the brightest spark in the box, just vain and self-obsessed. He only had to pay a few compliments and he was the blue-eyed boy! . . . But I say, are you sure Eric's got it right – is this Bullseye Bert to be trusted?'

'I am not sure that *trusted* is the word one would choose, but given his contacts and insider knowledge he's as good a source as any. Eric thinks that if that's what he says about Travers and OTG he is probably right.'

'Yes, but—'

'Toodle-oo, dear girl, just thought you might like to know. One always tries to be helpful . . .' He rang off and I was left frowning.

If Bullseye Bert was right about Travers' activities it might explain a lot. I vaguely recalled Charles saying he had heard some rumour about a rift between aunt and nephew. Something Egge or Bewley had said in the pub apparently. At the time I hadn't paid much attention, being too busy preventing Maurice from molesting Duster. But if that indeed had been the case it could certainly account for Travers' less than gallant comments made just recently. Had Alice learnt of the blue-eyed boy's grubby trade and cut up rough, threatening to withdraw support (and funds) for his lingerie business? According to Egge she had pulled levers to secure the latter for him, but was this other venture a sleazy bridge too far? Murdering a sister might be one thing but having a pimp for a nephew quite another – after all, what would those London friends think!

I dwelt once more on Aston's words 'manipulative old bat'. Having procured the deal, had said bat manipulated him into a corner, threatening exposure if he continued in his tawdry trade? Perhaps not – maybe she had just nagged and needled. But then given the woman's increasing instability, could he have counted on her silence? He needed her money, and the worry must surely have cast a bit of a shadow. After all, what smart entrepreneur enjoys having a garrulous albatross clamped to his neck?

Again, my mind went back to our recent encounter and I

wondered where he had gone since driving off in the smart sports car. Needham Court was still temporarily out of bounds so perhaps he was in Brighton or Bognor (was there a flat over the lingerie shop?). I snorted. Hah! No doubt busy ferrying the Dieppe and Bognor belles to their 'language classes' while carefully avoiding Lewes in case its police should require further visits to the interviewing room.

I glanced at Bouncer currently exploring his inner thigh. 'It's a very unsavoury world,' I observed. He thumped his tail and returned to his task.

Breakfast over and despite Maurice's disdainful gaze, I nevertheless buttered another slice of toast and crunched it with relish. It is amazing how greed and inspiration go together!

TWENTY-NINE

The Primrose version

After the upheavals of the last week I felt in need of fresh air and mild exercise. It was a warm, sunny afternoon and I thought that a walk on the Downs would do me good. Normally I would take Bouncer, but not wishing to spend half my time shouting his name fruitlessly, decided against it. Dogs and horses have one thing in common: once up on the high slopes they go mad and become resistant to all command. Thus I set out on my jaunt glad to be alone and equipped with sketchbook should inspiration come for my next picture. I hardly expected this. But one never knows, and as Baden-Powell wisely counselled, it's always wise to be prepared . . . and, alas, as Francis never was.

Striding out from the house, I soon reached the little footpath which leads up to the steep hill and then on to the Downs themselves. It being mid-week and mid-afternoon I met no one, and enjoyed the stillness broken only by the idle buzz of bees and flutter of butterflies – Cabbage Whites mainly, but some Blues and the occasional Red Admiral. Sniffing the summer air, and despite the perplexities of the past weeks, it felt good to be alive!

Nevertheless, though still pretty fit, I have to admit to being some-what puffed as I reached the top, and was looking forward to a rest on the seat thoughtfully placed a good fifty years ago for the benefit of weary hikers.

However, as I approached the seat I was mildly put out to see that it was already occupied. A man was sitting at its far end and, from what I could see, was absorbed in munching sandwiches from a brown paper bag. Oh well, one can't have everything, and if I had to share the splendid vista with someone else then so be it. I sat down and he looked up. And we recognized each other instantly.

'Good afternoon, Councillor Bewley,' I said, 'so this is where you spend your idle moments when free from the hurly-burly of the town hall! A wise choice. Sometimes one needs to get right away from things. As the poet says: "What is life, if full of care/ We have no time to stand and stare?" – though in our case *sit* would be more accurate.'

The smile I gave him was not returned with quite the alacrity I might have expected. But he nodded politely and said something to the effect that he assumed I was doing the same and that it was a lovely day.

This was followed by a silence as he scanned the landscape. And then neatly folding the now-empty paper bag and putting it in his briefcase (yes, these public officials are wedded to their documents), he said, 'As it happens I have been thinking about you, Miss Oughterard.'

'Oh yes?' I said cheerfully. 'Nothing too dreadful, I hope!'

'Well,' he replied slowly, 'that rather depends on one's viewpoint.'

I blinked. It seemed a somewhat cryptic response and I asked him what he meant.

His answer was even more obscure. 'We had differing view-points, didn't we – different angles. You saw me and I saw you.'

By now I was completely in the dark, and somewhat impolitely said I hadn't a clue what he was talking about.

'Oh, I think you have,' he said softly. 'I know you had a good view of me the other night at Needham Court when I was rather officiously "tidying" Mrs Markham's desk, the one that had been her sister's. But I saw you too – had a view of you peering in at

the French window and then later flattening yourself against the
water butt when I slipped out of the side door. I found what I
wanted, thank goodness, but I hadn't expected to have a witness.'
He gave a dry laugh and added, 'It just shows how inept we
amateur burglars are!'

I was stunned. Oh my God! So it had been *him* – Bewley at
the bureau rummaging through the drawers, scattering papers,
upsetting the ink bottle. Bewley sneaking out of the house while
I held my breath fondly imagining I was well concealed; and
presumably Bewley creeping about in that upstairs room. Dazed
yet fascinated, I said the first thing that came into my head, 'But
how did you know it was me? You had your back turned all the
time scrabbling at those pigeonholes.'

'Ah, so you didn't see the mirror, the one above her desk. I
can tell you I had a very nasty shock when I saw your reflection, very nasty indeed. An irony really, I had just found
the thing I was seeking and so in the moment of triumph there
was also the sudden fear. Luckily triumph capped fear which
is why I kept my nerve, left the room and slipped out by the
side door. I saw your shadow still on the terrace but, like you,
stood stock still watching and waiting. And then when it was
clear that you had finished your "researches" I felt free to
move off.' He paused, and then added, 'I noticed you stumble
slightly as you stepped on to the grass – that night dew can be
quite slippery.'

He lapsed into silence, while my eye alighted on the fluttering
gyrations of a Chalkhill Blue and in the far distance I heard a
sheep's petulant bleat. I recall thinking that it must be nice to
be a sheep or a butterfly, munching the turf or winging the air,
doing merely what nature dictated and free from the straits of
human discord. However, such idle musing lasted for roughly
four seconds before I heard myself saying lightly, 'Oh, quite the
stealthy nighthawk, aren't you!'

At first he said nothing but regarded me steadily; and then,
clearing his throat, said, 'It's all been exceedingly worrying and
I've been trying to decide what to do. Meeting you like this has
clarified the problem. Knowing Alice and that garrulous mouth of
hers, I suspect that at your last meeting she doubtless divulged
certain facts unfavourable to me and told you of the rift in our

relations. And with those facts in mind, plus what you clearly saw at Needham Court the other night, I imagine you have drawn certain conclusions.' He raised a quizzical eyebrow.

My immediate instinct was to retort that I had no idea what conclusions I was supposed to have drawn: that when last seen Alice Markham was occupied with matters a trifle more dramatic than her dealings with the town council's chairman – namely the gruesome logistics of how she had disposed of her sister, and that in any case he was wrong to assume I had recognized him as the nocturnal intruder . . . But then in a flash I grasped the significance of what he was saying. It was the words *at your last meeting* which flicked the switch and made me grow cold. There was only one private meeting I had had with Alice and in which she might have 'divulged' something. It had been the one when she had raced up my driveway, crashed the car and was shot. Oh my God, so it was *Bewley* who had killed her, not Aston!

I swallowed hard, gazed into the distance, and as so often in moments of alarm, heard my father's hectoring voice: *Now keep your hat on my girl, no need to make a grand kerfuffle. Easy does it!*

'Ah,' I said coolly (fear wrestling with curiosity), 'so it was you after all, I had rather wondered. But I am not quite clear why.'

He hesitated, and then said smoothly, 'Alice was what one might call a loose cannon, or as some might put it crudely, a pain in the arse. She was an encumbrance, a blight on my plans; and as such had to be expunged. I took my chance, followed her and hid. I had seen her go down your drive and obviously at some point she would come up again. Patience was all that was required. I'm a good marksman – my one sporting skill, I fear. My intention had been to shoot her through the windscreen as she passed the laurels. But typically she crashed the car.' Bewley shrugged. 'Still, I was able to pick her off when she opened the door and floundered off.'

Pick her off? Had she been a partridge? *Expunged?* He spoke as if editing a council report. I regarded him bleakly, collecting my thoughts and recalling another 'pain in the arse', the tiresome Mrs Fotherington, Francis's bane. There seemed a mild similarity of motive. But my brother's reaction had been one of impulse – a sudden intemperate flurry of terror of which he was barely aware

until, within seconds, and to his appalled consternation, the deed
was done. There had been no preamble, no cool calculation but a
heady, spur-of-the moment thing, and whose nightmare grip had
held him captive to the end of his days. But Bewley's act – this had
been considered, prepared for and adroitly executed. And judging
from the perpetrator's present manner there seemed not one jot of
regret or shock. Francis had sought relief from coy pursuit, a sudden
crazy bid for peace and quiet. What had this man sought?

Such were the thoughts crowding my mind as I studied the
impassive features and pale eyes – studied not so much in disquiet
as in puzzlement.

'You look bemused, Miss Oughterard,' he observed.

'I should jolly well think I do!' I exclaimed. 'It's all very well
you complaining that Alice Markham was an encumbrance and a
pain in the butt – something I heartily agree with, as it happens
– but I really can't see the rationale for mowing her down with a
Luger or whatever, and on the edge of my property. It's all been
very embarrassing.'

'Hmm,' he murmured, 'embarrassing for you perhaps, problematic
for me . . . Oh, and incidentally it wasn't a Luger – what on earth
would I have been doing with one of those! No, it was a Mauser,
a friend gave it to me as a keepsake from the previous war.'

'Immaterial,' I snapped. 'What I want to know is *why* did you
do it?'

He sighed. 'It's a rather complex saga, and one I suspect you
wouldn't really understand.'

'Try me,' I demanded indignantly. Really, why did he think I
wouldn't understand? Did he assume I was defective in some way?
I fixed him with one of my better glares, which on occasions has
quelled the town clerk – but not evidently the council's chairman,
for he leant back against the seat and lit a cigarette. (Nothing
proffered in my direction, I noted.)

'Well, you see, it is all a question of background,' he said with
a smile.

'What do you mean – what sort of background?'

'Social,' he replied.

I must have looked puzzled, for he gave a rueful laugh and said,
'You see, Miss Oughterard, you and I have rather different experiences. You come from a family well ensconced in the upper

echelons of the English hierarchy – solidly respectable, moderately moneyed, safely schooled, brother a clergyman and father of officer rank. My own esteemed parent was a lesser NCO, with little money and little education. In the twenties we lived on the outskirts of Wigan in a far from salubrious part. Life was hard, or so I felt. And as a boy of twelve I vowed to better myself – to achieve rank and status, and the respect not only of my peers but of my so-called betters. To this end I have worked assiduously and effectively. My accent is now refined, my clothes modest, my manners decent and I have acquired a little money. However, I am not without intelligence and I propose to go further than being a mere Gauleiter of the local council. That might be sufficient for some but not for me; I have other plans. The county is the next step and then—'

'And then?' I asked in wonderment.

He gave a modest smirk. 'You may think this is unduly ambitious. But I am forty-five now, and in another ten years I fully expect to be the lord lieutenant – with all the bells and whistles that that entails.'

I stared at him, dumbfounded, amused and appalled at the same time. 'You mean to say,' I exploded, 'that you murdered Alice Markham merely to strut about in a smart uniform chatting up dowagers and having your photograph in the *Tatler*? You must be mad!'

For a moment the bland smile faltered, and an irritable frown took its place. 'No, it is not I who is mad, but the tedious Mrs Markham *was*, or at least severely unhinged: hence her removal from my path. The unhappy fate of her sister had clearly played on her mind: she lost her grip – went peculiar, drank too much and began to open that foolish mouth in a way unhelpful to my career. Indeed, at the point when she came to your house I believe she had reached the stage of total breakdown.'

He could say that again! I thought. I was about to make some scathing comment but didn't have the chance, my words checked by his own.

'But you see,' he continued, 'the breakdown per se was of little account – what mattered were the likely consequences. She was already dangerous and her mental state increased the threat.'

'What threat?'

'I mean that while staying at her sister's house and sorting her effects she had found two items belonging to me. Items which could have proved very damaging: a letter and a cufflink. The former in the writing desk, the latter in Elspeth's bedroom – among her underclothes apparently.'

'Oh tut,' I said caustically, 'how careless! Still,' I added more lightly, 'less obvious than a sock suspender, I suppose . . . But in any case, why should Alice have assumed the thing was yours? And would it matter?'

He cleared his throat and frowned. 'She assumed it was mine because it had my initials engraved on the back – R.C.B. The links had been a present from my wife in the early months of our marriage. In those days she had enjoyed little absurdities like that. Personally I didn't care for the design but would wear them now and again. Unfortunately one such time was when I was visiting Elspeth. We had become exceedingly good friends.'

I shrugged. 'Well, it's hardly the first time that a personal posses-sion has been dropped in a lady's bedroom. Why, I remember when I was at the Courtauld—'

'Yes, yes,' he said impatiently, 'but there was the letter as well, the one in her bureau. That was the real problem. I said a moment ago that it could have been damaging; that was putting it mildly. In the wrong hands it could have blown my career and future plans to smithereens.'

'And those wrong hands being Alice's, I presume.'

'Exactly.' He paused and gazed out over the distant Ouse and its basking meadows, his brow furrowed as if deep in thought, perhaps envisaging the dire scenario had the letter been found.

'Er . . . I take it that this letter was one you had written to Elspeth, one she had kept.'

'What? . . . Oh no, not from me, from my wife.'

'But I thought you were estranged.'

'We are,' he said dryly, 'but that doesn't stop her writing letters. Somehow she had learnt of my friendship with Elspeth and being of a *helpful* nature thought it her duty to acquaint the lady with certain facts.'

'Ah, a sort of jealous warning-off, you mean.'

He shook his head. 'Nothing to do with jealousy, at least I don't think so. It was what some would call a kindly hint – but others a crass and twisted altruism!' The modulated tone flared into biting anger, and I was reminded that I was seated barely two feet away from the man who by his own admission had shot Alice Markham. I shifted uneasily, trying to increase the distance.

However, just as quickly as it had flared the anger subsided, or seemed to. He sighed and for a few moments regarded me sombrely, before murmuring, 'You see, Miss Oughterard, the problem is I am one of those who, I have recently discovered, bats for the other side – well, more or less – and my witless wife thought it was something Elspeth should be aware of. I take it you get my meaning?'

'Of course I get your meaning,' I replied briskly, 'I wasn't born yesterday, you know. You share the proclivities of half of London's thespian fraternity and many of our distinguished aristocracy. Given your social aspirations, I should say you are in quite good company. Why, it could probably come in handy – assuming of course the ice isn't *too* thin as in the novel we were recently discussing.'

A flippant response and I could see he didn't like it. He pursed his lips and scowled. 'You know perfectly well that in my position I could not run the risk of exposure. The cufflink was tricky and could have made mischief, but this was potential dynamite. At best I would become the butt of scandal and snide mockery and at worst, given our archaic laws, there would always be the fear of police prosecution. Still, coming from your sheltered background I suppose such dangers are beyond your ken.' He gave a sardonic laugh.

Inwardly I also laughed sardonically, thinking of Ingaza's gaol sentence after his Turkish Bath caper and of Francis's moment of madness in a Surrey wood . . . No, one was not without imagination in such matters.

'Yes, I can see that,' I conceded, 'a bit of a knife edge. Still, it seems a trifle extreme to shoot her just on the off-chance that she might blazon it abroad. I mean to say, she could have been sympathetic as many of us are, or was she intending to use it for blackmail of some sort?'

'Hah! It was some sort all right! And can you guess what her price for silence was?'

I shrugged. 'The usual I presume: money.'

'No,' he said tightly, 'it was marriage. If I became her husband she would keep her trap shut and with her wealth we would live a life of style and bliss . . . Have you heard of anything more outlandish, Miss Oughterard?'

The colourful panorama of my own life danced before my eyes, and I had to admit that it was difficult to recall anything quite so bizarre. I then ventured to say that considering what he had just told me about his personal bias, marriage was rather an odd bargaining chip.

'Oh, she was going to reform me, of course,' he said with heavy sarcasm. 'I did not *wish* to be reformed, least of all by Alice Markham. The prospect of being married to her was horrific and I told her it was out of the question. And besides, it was a most intolerable intrusion – the killing of all my hopes. I mean what lord lieutenant could be taken seriously with someone like that on his arm? Far too loud and vulgar!' He shuddered.

Somehow I managed not to gape. Yet given the image he had just presented I have to admit to experiencing the merest twinge of sympathy. I tried to think of some useful response. None came, so I said lamely, 'Oh dear, Alice or exposure: quite a facer.'

'You bet it was a facer,' he barked, 'and as such she had to be removed – and quickly! You can understand that, I assume?' The voice had taken on a hard edge.

'Oh absolutely,' I assured him, staring fixedly at a mess of sheep droppings by my foot.

It passed through my mind that I should be doing something dramatic – calling the police, screaming for help, standing up and threatening him with my walking stick. Except that there were no police, my throat had turned strangely dry and I carried no walking stick. Should I just run away? Pathetic. He was bound to catch me, and in any case, where to? I certainly couldn't see any convenient farmhouse or friendly shepherd's hut beckoning. I wondered what Ingaza would do. Try to flog him a dud painting, no doubt. But then I reasoned that so far the man had shown no actual aggression. He had simply sat talking – quietly, bitterly – but with no suggestion of physical malice. Perhaps like mad Alice he too had a need to 'unburden' himself. And perhaps the more he talked the more malleable he might become.

With luck he would tire and become docile. For a moment I entertained a touching image of me taking his hand, murmuring gently and leading him back to Lewes to meet MacManus and his just deserts . . .

Fool! With a quick movement Bewley snapped open his briefcase and withdrew an object. I gazed transfixed by what was in his hand. This time it was no plaything but the genuine article: an only too real revolver. I have scant knowledge of guns but this I recognized, having often been shown Pa's old Mauser, a relic from his days in the trenches. But the hand gripping this weapon was not my father's, gnarled and a bit shaky, but one smooth and nerveless. And this time the muzzle was pointing not at the ground, but straight at me.

'They will hear the shot,' I mumbled.

'Who – the sheep? There's no one anywhere. Look around.'

Look around – with that aimed at my heart? No fear! I took his word for it and continued to stare warily at the gun.

'You are not really going to do this, are you?' I croaked. 'It will only mess things up even more.'

'I think I probably am,' he replied in a tone drained of all feeling. 'You are too dangerous: you saw me that night ransacking her desk. I can't afford the risk, you see.' His index finger stayed curled round the trigger and, glancing at the expressionless face, I realized he meant it. I was about to bluster that actually I had not recognized the intruder as being him, but such denial was far too late. The man had already accused himself of something far worse.

'How about making a deal,' I said in quiet desperation, thinking of Ingaza and trying to look business like.

Not surprisingly, the suggestion was ignored. I could see the tightening mouth and the vein twitching in his temple, and knew I was for it.

I took a deep breath, and shifting my eyes away from the weapon scanned the wide blue skies, the slumbering line of Kipling's 'whale-backed' downs, the familiar curve of Firle Beacon, the ring of beeches at far-off Chanctonbury, clusters of yellow gorse and purple willow herb . . . a sweeping vista of rural peace and silent beauty. Were these images to be my last sight on earth, my final vision? One could have worse, far worse. I rested my eyes upon ancient Firle . . . and waited.

THIRTY

The Primrose version

N othing happened. Instead of the gun's explosion, the stillness was rent by an unholy whine, a throaty roar and the sound of frenzied revving. Noise bludgeoned the air.

As if yanked by a puppeteer's string, Bewley thrust the gun aside and leapt up exclaiming, 'Those bloody motorbikes! I've told them before – this isn't a dirt track, it's council land! They've no right to—'

On pure instinct and like an automaton myself, I too leapt up, seized the discarded pistol, and turning, hurled it as far as I could into a gulley of prickly gorse bushes. *Let him crawl for that!* I thought with satisfaction. At the sound of screeching brakes I turned back, and to my astonishment saw Bewley flat on the ground, face down and arms flung wide. Not crawling but sprawled and motionless.

'Christ!' a voice yelped. 'It weren't my fault – he tripped and fell.'

I gazed at the muffled figure on the solitary motorbike, the heavy boots and leather gauntlets, and experienced a spasm of déjà vu. The rider dismounted, cautiously approached the recumbent figure, and squatting down turned him over and looked long and hard.

'He's a gonner,' Phyllis announced.

'No!' I gasped.

'Oh yes,' she said firmly, a finger on his pulse, 'there's no doubt. There's blood everywhere – it's that big flint he's hit. Pierced his brain it looks like. He won't be going nowhere.' She paused, and then muttered, 'Poor sod.'

'Yes,' I whispered faintly, 'poor sod.' And then looking at Phyllis, who by now had removed her helmet, I said, 'Er, I think we may have met before. You kindly delivered my cat and dog from—'

'Oh yeah, those crazy loons! You're Miss Oughterard; I'd know you anywhere.'

Quite why she thought she would know me anywhere I wasn't sure. But I shelved the question, there being more urgent matters to consider. One of those matters was that I felt suddenly faint and had to sit down quickly on the bench.

Phyllis regarded me sympathetically. 'You look awful,' she said. 'But I've got just the thing that'll put you right. It never fails, or so my Uncle Eric says. He gave it me for my birthday.' She went to a pannier and returned with a hip flask. ''Ere, this'll put the roses in yer cheeks again. I could do with a nip myself. Not used to blokes running out in front of me and falling flat on their faces – especially when they turns out dead!'

For about a minute we sat in ruminative silence, sharing the hip flask and contemplating the placid downland and now and again the figure collapsed on the turf in front of us. It occurred to me that it might be seemly to cover his face. I removed my cardigan, performed the ritual, and then despite the sun's warmth felt freezing cold. A small penance in view of what might have been.

'A friend of yours, was he?' Phyllis asked.

I said he was not exactly a friend but an acquaintance and that we had met quite by chance while taking afternoon strolls. 'Actually, he is fairly important locally; he is Mr Reginald Bewley, chairman of the town council – though living in Brighton I don't suppose you would know him.'

'No,' she said slowly, 'I don't know him but some of my mates do. They used to call him Bastard Bewley. He had a thing about motorbikes, couldn't stand them and was always making complaints about our lot using this area for practice rides. Said it was an appalling desecration, or some such. But they reckoned it was a really good bit of ground, which is why I came up to give it a trial run. It's my first time here and, Sod's Law, look what's happened!' She gave a puzzled frown. 'But what was he doing running out like that?'

Omitting to mention he had been about to kill me, I explained that he had been sitting on the bench but when he heard the noise of the engine he had leapt up, bounded forward and then slipped and fell.

'I see,' she said slowly. 'So what you are saying is that it was my fault he came a cropper, that if he hadn't heard my bike he would never of got up and would be here on this bench now. So I suppose that indirectly I was the cause of his death.' She looked at me glumly.

'No!' I cried aghast. 'Certainly not! In no way were you responsible, Phyllis. It was his own fault, he was chasing a rabbit.'

'But you just said that—'

'Yes, but he didn't like rabbits either – rabbits and motorbikes, he had an aversion to both. The rabbit appeared just before the noise of your bike. I assure you he was already on his feet.'

It always amazes me how fertile my imagination can be in moments of crisis. Nevertheless, Phyllis gave me what is known as an old-fashioned look. Actually, I have never been entirely sure what that term means but assume it to be a look of steely scepticism. If so, that is exactly what her face registered. But she took the point well enough, and said, 'Ah, so that's what we tell the cops is it when we make our report? That he snuffed it seeing off a rabbit.'

'Our report?' I said vaguely.

'Oh yes, we'll have to do that pronto. Otherwise they'll have us up for harbouring a stiff. Cor, Uncle Eric would go bananas!'

The reference to Eric Tredwell naturally brought Ingaza to mind and I winced. Barely six weeks ago he and I had been involved in just such a subterfuge, and to learn that I had been now similarly engaged was unlikely to give him joy. I closed my eyes, hearing only too vividly the nasal stream of mordant invective.

''Ere, it's no use shutting your eyes, Miss Oughterard,' the girl broke in. 'We've got to get weaving! I mean we don't want the old sheep getting at him, do we?'

'No,' I agreed firmly, 'we don't.'

Thus replacing her helmet and snapping down its visor, Phyllis ushered me to the bike which, after some hesitation and awkwardness, I managed to straddle.

A varied life I may have had, but those variations did not include riding pillion on a motorbike whose driver clearly saw the machine as some sort of medieval war horse. With snorts of equine power we set off at an alarming rate, scattering turf and flints in all directions and – although I dared not turn my head – doubtless leaving hordes of disaffected rabbits in our wake.

I will draw a veil over the course of that ride. Suffice it to say that we reached our destination unscathed, and that despite shattered nerves and sinews I mustered dignity, and with Phyllis bringing up the rear entered the police station and announced we had left a dead body unattended on the Downs.

'Is that so?' said Sergeant Wilding.

'It most certainly is so,' I replied, adopting my most authoritative tone. 'And if officers don't go up there forthwith it will be eaten by the sheep.'

THIRTY-ONE

The Primrose version

The events of the last two hours had left me doubly dazed: physically in that I was barely recovered from the trauma of that nightmarish bike ride (and thankful to be now firmly seated in the safety of the police station), and mentally in that I was still reeling from Bewley's personal threat and extraordinary revelations – the latter in particular leaving me in a state of bewildered shock. It just goes to show what risks people will take to secure their ends – even if those ends be risible. Really, lord lieutenant, if you please!

However, as I faced Sergeant Wilding across the table my most pressing concern was Phyllis Tredwell and her fear that she might be thought responsible for Bewley's fall. In a time of jeopardy she had been a veritable *dea ex machina* and had proved a stalwart comforter. Clearly ethics dictated a white lie and I would honour our tacit pact.

Answering my query regarding the beleaguered Bewley and the threat of ovine interest, Wilding assured me that even as we spoke officers were 'proceeding hot-foot to commandeer the corpse'. (What it is to have a natural eloquence!) We then got down to business, he with his notebook and me with some sickly sweet tea.

'So what you are saying,' he said, 'is that, having consumed his sandwiches, the deceased was admiring the scenery when his attention was diverted by the appearance of a rabbit thus causing him to vacate his seat at an alarming rate.'

'Yes, it was a very large rabbit,' I emphasized, 'and Mr Bewley was exceedingly perturbed.'

Sergeant Wilding nodded and wrote something in his notebook. And then, looking up, he said slowly, 'And this rabbit – was its name Harvey by any chance?'

I stared at him. 'Harvey? Whatever do you mean, Sergeant!'

'Well, if memory serves me right Harvey was a pretty big fellow, wasn't he?'

I had always considered Sergeant Wilding an officer of sound common sense and thus could only assume the man was ill or had been drinking.

'I don't follow you,' I replied coldly. 'As far as I am aware South Down rabbits, large or small, do not have names. Now if you don't mind—'

I was about to suggest that Inspector Spikesy should take over the interview but was forestalled by a sudden snort of mirth. 'My apologies, Miss Oughterard,' he spluttered, 'I know this is not a time for levity, but when you said Councillor Bewley was perturbed by a large rabbit I couldn't help thinking of that James Stewart film *Harvey*, all about an imaginary rabbit that followed him about. Very droll, it was. I expect you know the one?'

I sighed. Really, what one has to put up with! However, I told him politely that I was indeed familiar with the film but that I hoped he wasn't suggesting that my tale of the rabbit had been an hallucination. (I spoke firmly, for by this time I was beginning to believe in it myself and was already visualizing the creature's twitching nose and popping eyes.)

'Anyway,' he continued more sombrely, 'in his haste to repel this rabbit he tripped and fell, bashing his head on a flint. Is that so?'

'Exactly.'

'So you actually saw him trip, did you?'

I hesitated, before saying that my eye had been momentarily

distracted by a flight of birds but that when I next looked, there he was sprawled on the ground. (I could hardly say I had been otherwise engaged hurling the wretched Mauser into the gorse.)

'Hmm. And then Miss Tredwell turned up on her motorbike?'

'Yes, and it was such a relief as I was shocked to the core!' (True enough.) 'But you know, Sergeant, life is so unfair . . . I mean to say if only Phyllis had arrived just a minute earlier the noise of the engine would have frightened the rabbits and poor Councillor Bewley would have remained sitting on the bench and been with us now. As it is . . .' My voice trailed off with a wistful sigh.

Wilding shut his notebook, and with a sympathetic smile said sagely, 'Ah well, that's the way of things, isn't it? Things that we *do* want to happen don't, and things we *don't* want do. Take your gates, for instance . . .'

As I climbed into the police car, which they had again been kind enough to provide, I was pleased to think that only one major fact had been invented: the role of the rabbit. The rest of the narrative had been broadly true with little omitted – except of course for the piece in the middle. This was a piece I needed to brood upon over a stiff libation – anything to take away the taste of that outlandish tea!

Riding pillion on Phyllis's infernal machine had banished all thoughts from my head except how to stay on. And at the police station, too, my mind had been focused on only one thing: how to answer Wilding's questions while keeping silent about the dead man's confession and his fatal reaction to Phyllis's motorbike.

Both experiences had been exhausting, but now home at last and mercifully alone I could relax, straighten my mind and reflect upon Bewley's incredible account. In doing this I was aided by Maurice and Bouncer, both of whom seemed to have an uncanny sense that I was in a state of some *bouleversement*. The dog trotted over and laid his filthy rubber ring at my feet. He then laid an equally filthy paw on my knee – which I could hardly dislodge for fear of causing offence. However, tribute paid, he then settled to sleep with his head on my foot. Maurice too expressed a rare matiness by draping himself on my shoulder and emitting a grating purr. Soothed by their solace and a pink gin, I closed my eyes and reviewed events.

I contemplated my mistake about Bewley and Travers. What a gaffe! The latter had clearly been elsewhere when Alice was being gunned down. It just goes to show that despite its value conjecture can also lead one badly astray! Evidently for all his faults, Aston was no murderer. Yes, I had taken a couple of wrong paths all right – for example, believing in that rift between Alice and Aston as mentioned by Charles. Hadn't he said he had heard it from Egge or Bewley? Probably the latter trying to divert suspicion away from himself. And I had certainly been mistaken in thinking Alice's amatory intentions had escaped Bewley's notice – that fishing net had obviously been giving him nightmares!

And then as I continued to mull over Bewley's account I was struck by a piquant irony: he had been ignorant of Alice's killing of Elspeth – or so it would certainly seem. He had made no mention of it, talking only of the danger to himself had she opened her mouth re his 'proclivities' i.e. had the thin ice cracked and his sexual bias revealed. So dear were those grandiose plans for status and high office that he would have done anything to protect them. It was the threat of failure that had caused him to 'expunge' Alice, nothing to do with Elspeth at all. And judging from his words in the tea shop he had been quite fond of the latter and had genuinely felt her loss. Ironic therefore that in a bid to preserve his own ambitions he had been the unwitting agent of her sister's nemesis . . . But what really struck me was the moral irony. After murdering her sister, Alice had in turn been destroyed by Bewley, whose own retribution had come in the form of a motorbike engine. Neither killer could be brought to legal justice, each having paid the requisite price; a resolution which, while not ideal, would at least save the taxpayer some money. I gave a grim smile.

I stared into space contemplating life's strange perversity, but also thanking my lucky stars that I had miraculously escaped that particular turn in Fortune's flighty wheel. 'Damn close shave,' I muttered to nothing in particular.

So the decision made, and shifting Maurice, I went to forage in the kitchen. I was ravenous!

THIRTY-TWO

The dog's view

You know these humans don't half get themselves in a right old lather – huffing and puffing, effing and blinding, moaning and groaning! I mean even Maurice when he's in one of his tantrums doesn't go quite so doolally, and that's saying something! When we were in Molehill with our old master the vicar, we saw a lot of that kind of PAL-AV-ER – him in a muck sweat rushing all over the shop tearing his hair and his dog collar, throwing down pills and crunching gobstoppers. Oh yes, he was generally in some sort of stew . . . but that was because he had done something BAD like getting rid of that silly Fotherington lady or like me when I rattle the cage of those stupid chinchillas. And after that he got into a lot more scrapes, so you can see why he was always so het up. The cat says that some humans can cope with being BAD but others can't, it sort of churns them up. Well F.O. was often in a state of CHURN, which for a lively fellow like me made things quite interesting.

I mention this because when we came to live here I thought life might be a bit flat and *pi-ahn-o* (as Maurice says) because P.O. is very different from her brother – just as tall and thin but sort of cooler, more in charge, if you see what I mean. And at first I thought she wouldn't get ruffled about things. I'm a pretty smart dog, you know, but for once I was wrong. The Prim *does* get ruffled but it's a different kind of ruffle from her brother's. His ruffle would be the blue funk sort; hers is the stroppy-poppy type. She gets in bates – like when she's tearing strips off her friend Enema or cursing that galumphing Manus person. I quite like that because it 'pro-vides a die-vart-ing KABARAY', to quote the cat again. (Phew! It's taken me weeks to learn that lot!)

So, as our mistress is usually bossy and tough, we were quite worried when she came back the other evening all white and windy.

I mean, if she was a cat her fur would have been stuck up like bristles on a yard brush; and I bet if she was a dog the old tail would have gone all droopy just like mine does when I've been given a clip round the ear or can't find my bone.

Anyway, I had a word with Maurice. 'What's up with the Prim, then? She looks like something the cat's brought in.'

'Or the dog's spat out,' he replied.

We watched her as she poured a whopping glass of pink stuff and then slumped into the chair looking glazed and twitchy. 'You know what,' I said, 'she needs cheering up. I'll lend her my rubber ring.'

'Must you?' Maurice muttered. He's not keen on the thing – don't ask me why.

Anyway, I went to my basket in the kitchen, rummaged about for it and then came back and dropped it on the floor next to her chair. She didn't seem specially keen to play with it, but I think she was pleased all the same because she pulled my ear; then I put a friendly paw on her knee and she closed her eyes. Mind you, it's tricky keeping a paw on a human's lap because after a bit your leg goes numb. So I put it down again and went to sleep – though not before I had seen Maurice jump up and start to purr down her neck. He's not always that chummy and I thought it was pretty decent.

When I woke up, I could see that she was her old self again and looking all sharp and thoughtful . . . too thoughtful, because by this time I was dead keen for some nosh and she didn't seem to notice my helpful hints. Typical of humans, they get wrapped up in themselves and take their eye off the ball – in this case Bouncer's grub!

As things turned out, when supper did come it was JOLLY GOOD. The Prim started to eat like a horse, wolfing it down at the rate of knots. And then when she'd had enough fodder and I had finished mine she scraped the rest into my bowl. Cor, what a feast! The cat was hoity-toity, picked at its pilchards and said that being with the two of us was not unlike feeding time at the zoo. Still, after she had gone off early to bed and I had pulled his tail (which he quite likes) we put our heads together and had a big bow-wow.

'I think things are frort,' Maurice said.

'Frort? What's that?' I asked.

He explained that it meant things were heating up and reaching a stage of threat and ten-shun.

'What?' I said. 'Like when I'm stalking some bastard bunnies or when you are about to be hosed down by the doctor's wife for frightening her budgerigar?'

He seemed to think for a moment, and then said, 'Yes, Bouncer, on the whole I think you could say that.'

Well, of course I could. I had just said it, hadn't I? (Sometimes talking to Maurice can be a bit like one of those crossword things humans are always doing; a dog doesn't half have to keep his wits about him!) Anyway, I asked him if it was to do with the CONTRITOMPS with the mad woman and did he think the Prim was in danger.

'Indubitably,' he said. Now that's one of the cat's favourite words so I often hear it and know just what it means. It means: *Yes, you are damn right, Bouncer.*

'Hmm. But she's dead,' I said, 'and you have to sit on the other gatepost and—'

'Yes, Bouncer, I am aware of my discomfort, thank you, and I also know that its cause is dead. But there are other humans just as troublesome who need to be quelled – and I don't just mean the Brighton Type, vexing though he is. We must keep our eye on the distasteful policeman, the big MacManus with the rumbling voice. You may recall he has crossed our mistress's path before. She doesn't like him and if he stirs up trouble for her it will rebound on us. He must be kept under close observation and—'

'Shall I duff him up?' I barked eagerly.

Maurice flattened his ears and hissed. 'Be patient, Bouncer! On no account bite his backside unless I tell you to, otherwise we shall all be in the can!'

When he wants to the cat can speak quite clearly, so I got the message pronto. 'Right-o,' I said, 'but meantime you want me to be the crafty hound and sniff about a bit, taking mental notes while looking gormless.'

He blinked and studied his left paw, the white one. 'Ye-es,' he said slowly, 'you have a natural flair and could do that exceedingly well.'

'You bet I could,' I roared, 'no fleas on Bouncer!' And, giving him a friendly shove, dashed off to chivvy the chinchillas.

THIRTY-THREE

The Primrose version

I f I thought that Sergeant Wilding's questioning at the police station was going to be the last of things then I could think again! That was just the warm-up, for at twelve o'clock the following morning MacManus himself rolled up (no warning of course – they do it deliberately) and lugubriously asked if I had a few minutes to spare. Well, naturally I hadn't, though not that that would have bothered him. He started by telling me that Mrs MacManus sent her regards (which I doubted) and then said piously that Councillor Bewley's sudden death was all very distressing. He didn't sound in the least distressed, just tedious.

Anyway, realizing that I had got him for at least half an hour I took him into the drawing room and enquired politely if he might like a small sherry. Grave-faced, he replied that he never indulged in the daytime but could do with a weak tea. (Typical.) I had the satisfaction of informing him that there wasn't a tea leaf in the house but he might like some soda water. This he accepted; and I wondered if, to assuage the boredom of the water, I should offer an Abdulla cigarette. But something about pearls and pigs came to mind and I decided against it. He cleared his throat and I braced myself for the inevitable questions.

Out of the corner of my eye I saw that Bouncer had trundled in and was sitting a few yards off, paws splayed and head tilted on one side – gawping mode. And then suddenly there was Maurice perched on the window seat looking particularly malevolent. He must have slipped in through the open window. I wondered if I should shoo them away, but as MacManus seemed oblivious of their presence it seemed easier not to. I smiled engagingly at the superintendent and adjusted my features to appear attentive.

'You will have realized, Miss Oughterard,' he began, 'that Sergeant Wilding's interview with you yesterday was just to get the immediate gist of things, the general picture. But naturally there are a number of aspects that need to be confirmed, to be considered a little more closely.'

'Oh, naturally,' I murmured, but then couldn't help adding unctuously, 'but, Chief Superintendent, I am rather surprised that you yourself are here and not one of your subordinates – Inspector Spikesy, for example. It's quite an honour!'

'He is engaged elsewhere,' he replied abruptly. 'And sometimes it is useful to get the full story oneself and not indirectly from those new to the area or less practised in these matters.'

Full story? He would be lucky! And why less practised – Spikesy had struck me as being perfectly competent. Besides, what 'matters' – sudden deaths in open spaces? Surely the police were always having to deal with such incidents. So why should MacManus assume that his own skills in this respect were superior to Spikesy's; there had been few recent successes. Perhaps that was it: keen to redeem himself with the chief constable and make his mark, he had started to sniff at anything he could. Well, I determined, the mark wouldn't be made via Primrose Oughterard!

He began by summarizing my account to Sergeant Wilding the previous day and asked me to confirm the details. I nodded and waited for a more searching enquiry. It came.

'Were you often in the habit of meeting Councillor Bewley on the Downs, Miss Oughterard?'

I was enraged! *Often in the habit of* . . . What on earth was the man suggesting? 'Certainly not,' I replied coldly, 'I barely knew him.'

'Hmm – that's not what I've heard.'

Well, that pulled me up sharp all right, and I stared at him in bemused indignation. However, retaining my poise (just) I said that I had no idea what he was talking about and would he kindly explain. 'Oh, really?' I asked. 'And from where exactly have you obtained this information – or is that perhaps hush-hush? One gathers that policemen rarely reveal their vital sources.' My voice had assumed an acid note, reminding me of Mother's when dealing with Francis caught plundering the pantry or apple store.

'Oh, this wasn't a vital source,' he replied casually, 'it was my wife. She happened to mention that she had seen you and the deceased together on a few occasions, so . . .' He shrugged vaguely.

His *wife*? One might have known! It's often the mousiest types who are the most lethal, and this was a fine example. But having no base, Mrs M's tittle-tattle was irrelevant. What a fool the woman was, and her husband an even greater fool for listening! Yet I was puzzled to think just where she may have made her observations. Certainly I had happened to sit next to Bewley in church one Sunday (and owing to Egge's parsimony been forced to share a hymn book), but apart from our encounter by the town hall and the earlier meeting in the new café Hearts & Flowers – an absurd name – there had been only fleeting contact. But presumably those three occasions were the bases of her gossip. I thought of the café and made a mental note never to cross its threshold again. Far too many spies! Perhaps the watchful Alice had had a companion: the two women sitting together, their eyes magnetized by the occupants of the corner table; one insanely jealous, the other plain nosy. At the time I had been unaware of either presence – but I could envisage the scene well enough: the pair huddled over tea cakes, casting covert glances and exchanging meaningful looks.

'So I take it you weren't on close terms,' MacManus's ponderous voice broke in. I told him most certainly not. 'But, nevertheless, you may have had a view about the gentleman,' he said.

'A view?'

'Yes. You must have formed an opinion. What was your impression of him . . . did you find him congenial, for example?'

Oddly enough, considerably more so than present company, I thought angrily.

'Or perhaps you found him a bit annoying. Don't be afraid to say so, *nil nisi bonum* and all that – but I gather he wasn't everybody's cup of tea!' He produced one of those gratingly false laughs but seemed to regard me intently.

I was puzzled. What was he getting at – what sort of question was that, for goodness' sake? How did my opinion of Bewley have anything to do with his demise? And then, of course, it dawned . . . He was hoping I might say something hostile, something that would betray a buried dislike – a dislike so intense that, who knows, I might just have been minded to take up a piece of flint and bash the man's head in. My God, the bastard was hoping to pin Bewley's death on me. The cheek of it!

Just as the penny dropped I sensed a movement across the room: Bouncer. Half crouched, the dog seemed to be edging towards the visitor's chair, quietly, purposefully, and through the maze of fur round his snout I glimpsed the upper lip beginning to curl. A scene from the past flooded my mind, and I froze. I had seen such a display before with Topping. He must be stopped! But then from the window seat came a shriek like a banshee: Maurice venting his spleen, something he does in times of maximum vexation.

The dog halted immediately; and then rather sheepishly slunk back towards the door. Exclaiming that the animal needed to go out, I leaped up and hustled him from the room. Halfway into the hall, Bouncer turned to stare at MacManus and gave a short bark, and for an instant I thought I saw a look of baleful regret. (It's amazing how fanciful one can get over the behaviour of pets!)

I returned to see MacManus eying the cat with some distaste. 'He's certainly got a good pair of lungs,' he remarked. 'Now, where was I?'

'We were just discussing the way Mr Bewley was regarded,' I said lightly. 'Personally, I always found him the model of common sense and courtesy. It's a shame more public officials aren't like him. Wouldn't you agree?' I smiled sweetly and he grunted.

There followed a silence as he took a gulp of the rather flat soda water. And then with what passed for sympathy, he said, 'Can't have been much fun for you, Miss Oughterard, seeing the deceased sprawled at your feet on the grass like that. Quite a shock, I imagine . . . just as it must have been having Mrs Markham shot down on your property, or near enough. Not nice. Still, I suppose some people just happen to be in the way of Fate when these things strike. Take your brother, for instance.'

The wretch! I might have known he would come to that. 'My brother?' I asked in my most dulcet tone. 'I am not quite sure I follow you, Chief Superintendent.' My hackles were up but I had no intention that he should see them.

He hesitated fractionally, and then said he meant that from all accounts (i.e. doubtless Sidney Samson's) Mrs Fotherington's body had been discovered very close to the vicarage and that her being his parishioner it must have been a harrowing business for the reverend.

Harrowing? Too right it had! However, I nodded gravely, and then, more than tired of my visitor and wanting to get my own back, said, 'Yes, such incidents are always so disturbing, not least for the wider community. For example, as I was saying to Sir Robert only the other day, I fear that Lewes is terribly concerned about this shocking Markham affair and will be *so* relieved when it's all cleared up. May one enquire if any progress is being made in that direction? The local rag is being ridiculously critical in its reports, so cynical . . . But I am sure you and your officers are doing their utmost to bring the scoundrel to book and doubtless we shall all soon be resting easy in our beds!'

It was satisfying to see a mottled flush come to his cheeks as he muttered curtly that the matter was well in hand. And with that convincing assurance he stood up, thanked me for my time and brusquely took his leave. Whether he had prepared any more questions about my part in the 'incident on the Downs' I do not know, but at the mention of Sir Robert Hacking, the chief constable and my occasional bridge partner, he seemed to lose interest. Odd really.

THIRTY-FOUR

Charles Penlow's account

'Well, I must say,' my wife remarked, handing me the local paper, 'Primrose Oughterard is having a busy time – first Alice Markham and then poor Councillor Bewley. Rather bad luck, I should think.' Her meaning escaped me, but then it sometimes does and I asked her to enlarge.

'It's in the paper,' she said, 'on the inside page. Apparently Primrose was the one who was there when he had the fatal accident up on the Downs. It was she who alerted the police, she and some girl on a motorbike. It must have been frightful for her, especially coming so soon after the Markham business. Very dispiriting, I should think.'

Applied to Primrose, I think the term dispiriting was not the most apt. I have seen our friend in a number of moods – furious, indignant, disdainful, belligerent, exultant, genial, jocular, and indeed grim – but never, I think, dispirited. However, wisely I did not query Agnes's description and instead asked if she had seen her lately.

She shook her head. 'Not since church last week when she was berating the Reverend Egge for the length of his sermon. I heard her saying that her late brother had been streets ahead in the brevity stakes and would he like one or two tips.'

I grinned. 'Really? And what did Egge have to say?'

'He said that doubtless the clergy in Molehill had always had its fair share of speed merchants but here in Lewes the congregation was possibly more thoughtful and thus preferred a slower pace.'

'That was rash – how did she react?'

'Took it in good part and went off to boss Emily Bartlett about her stall at the school fête.'

Later that morning, having consulted with the chief bricklayer about the coving in the west wing, I took Duster into Lewes to buy a new collar and lead. Being of a conservative bent, the cairn is sceptical of anything unfamiliar and I had some trouble in persuading him to cooperate. However, flattery prevailed and he emerged from the shop looking stern and smart in matching tartan. Jenkins the proprietor had been eager to add a plaid coat to our purchase but I thought that might strain Duster's tolerance; he is not the most malleable of creatures.

We were just pottering along to the fishing tackle shop when I was met by Sergeant Wilding pushing his bike up the hill and looking distinctly puffed. I asked what felon he had been pursuing, to which he replied that it was wasn't a felon but an 'f' something else, i.e. a springer spaniel called Lionheart who, left in its owner's car outside the sweet shop, had contrived to scramble out of the window to plunder the chocolates and challenge the proprietor's cat to fisticuffs. Cat and chocolates had been left in a state of disarray – as had the dog which had been resolutely sick over the sergeant's boots.

'A policeman's lot is not a happy one,' I commiserated cheerfully, glancing at Wilding's ochre-coloured footwear. I asked what he thought of Duster's smart tartan collar and lead, to which he replied that he had seen worse and that presumably the little tyke would be wearing a kilt next.

At that moment we were passed by a police car driven by Inspector Spikesy, my interviewer after the Markham shooting.

'He seems quite a bright cove,' I remarked, 'and no doubt a useful addition to the local force.'

Wilding explained that he had been seconded here from London and wasn't permanent, and then added, 'But oh yes, he's on the ball all right. Vice, that's his real thing, and by all accounts he's very good at it too.'

'Good at vice, Sergeant?' I exclaimed. 'Whatever do you mean? Does Lewes really need such expertise?' I have to admit to being slightly bemused.

He gave a slow grin. 'Ah, got you there, sir, didn't I!'

He had indeed, and I asked if he meant that Spikesy was attached to Scotland Yard's vice squad.

'One of their best operators, or so the chief constable reckons. Very slick is Inspector Spikesy, got a nose like a pointer . . . Mind you, apart from nailing the illegal bad boys, one hears he is quite an embarrassment to the Mayfair punters; they get windy, especially the big-wigs.' He chuckled.

I was intrigued. 'But surely,' I said, 'there is not much call for his services around here. I should think the denizens of Lewes are far too staid for such high jinks.' I laughed.

'Don't you believe it,' he assured me, 'a lot of it gets about.' And then, looking more serious, he said, 'But there's a difference between high jinks and the plain nasty, and that's the stuff Spikesy deals with – trafficking, often with youngsters, and the supplying of London vice rings. It's big business and dangerous too.'

'So are you really saying that sleepy Lewes is the hub of such activity? You do surprise me, Sergeant. I'd better keep my eyes skinned . . . or watch my step!'

'Oh, not here, Mr Penlow, but there *could* be other places in Sussex, which of course I am not at liberty to mention.' He cleared his throat. 'Still, I've mentioned too much as it is – so I'd better give over and be on my way. There's a vital matter to attend to: that new postmistress says the dynamo on her bike has been tampered with, and we can't have that, can we? What our friend Miss Oughterard might call outlandish.' He closed one eye.

He was about to mount his own bicycle when a thought struck me. 'But tell me, Sergeant, if Inspector Spikesy is so hot on vice why was he conducting the interviews of Miss Oughterard and myself over the Markham murder? I take it that poor Mrs Markham was not the arch-controller of some call-girl outfit!'

Wilding smiled. 'Not as far as we know she wasn't. But' – and he lowered his voice – 'the reason you were interviewed by Spikesy and not another officer was that Mr MacManus had specifically selected him. He had been scheduled to knock off early that evening but MacManus decided otherwise. Between you and me, the chief isn't too keen on Mr Spikesy – says he's too clever by half and that the sex business is greatly exaggerated and we are perfectly capable of making our own investigations without the help of London coppers. So he gives old Spikesy any job that's going – to show that he is no different from the rest of the team and to ensure that he doesn't have a cushy number.'

'And is pursuing sex traffickers "cushy"?'

Wilding shrugged. 'According to the chief superintendent, it is.' He winked and thrust his boots on to the pedals.

I walked on down the hill feeling faintly puzzled. From what Sergeant Wilding had been saying it sounded as if sleepy Sussex had become a hotbed of vice of the kind to rival Tangiers or the sleazier parts of Chicago! I thought of that mysterious dewpond murder not so long ago, and indeed of the yet unsolved case of Alice Markham. Thus it passed through my mind that Primrose might have grounds for her obsession with the Elspeth Travers accident. Life here did seem to be getting a trifle murky . . . perhaps Agnes and I would have done better to remain in London after all!

Such brooding was interrupted by a loud shout, and a familiar name sliced the air. 'Bouncer!' Primrose's voice commanded. 'Come here at once, you wretched boy!' Tightening my hold on Duster's lead, I sidestepped smartly as the shaggy mongrel shot into view. He was holding something in his mouth, which at first I thought was alive, but which fortunately was nothing more than a drooping toy rabbit. He dropped the thing at my feet and gave a friendly growl to Duster. The latter made his usual response: turned away as if he hadn't heard and stared into the distance.

'Hello, Primrose,' I exclaimed. 'How's life? Haven't seen you for ages.'

'Life?' she replied, '*My* life is perfectly reasonable, it's just the insanity of other people. Take MacManus, for instance: he came sniffing around yesterday asking impertinent questions about my so-called relations with Councillor Bewley. I suspect he thinks I did him in!' She gave a mirthless laugh. 'Honestly, you play the upright citizen and report a death – and what do you get? Nothing but sly questions and innuendos . . . But I can tell you, I settled his hash all right – sent him off with a flea in his ear. Actually, he was lucky that was all he got; the dog was ready to tear his hide off!' The angry frown gave way to a snort of mirth.

I glanced down at the ravening hound, sprawled docilely on the pavement licking the eviscerated rabbit with kindly concern. 'I suppose he's a sort of Jekyll and Hyde figure,' I observed, 'and when—'

'What, MacManus? Hardly. He has neither the wit nor the teeth. But I tell you one thing, if he continues poking into my affairs he'll regret it. I have something up my sleeve that he won't like at all!' She looked very grim and I almost felt sorry for our esteemed chief superintendent. When I enquired what it was, she flushed and clammed up and muttered something about it being top secret.

Clearly nothing further was forthcoming, so I told her of my conversation with Sergeant Wilding. 'He implied that MacManus isn't too keen on Inspector Spikesy; apparently there is some kind of local vice racket afoot which the latter has been detailed to investigate. According to Wilding MacManus resents the intrusion and is giving him a hard time. It just goes to show, you can never escape the tyranny of internal politics . . . Why, I remember when I was in Whitehall—'

'Vice racket!' she echoed excitedly. 'In Bognor?'

I was startled by her sudden outburst, and replied that I had no idea but that genteel Bognor seemed a most unlikely place for such goings-on. 'Why there?' I asked.

She shrugged, muttered something vague like 'as good as any,' and promptly turned her attention to Duster and his new accoutrements – which, I am glad to say, met with her approval.

With a few more pleasantries and her promise to come to supper one evening, we parted and went our separate ways. I am fond of Primrose but occasionally find her manner baffling. I rather wish I had known her brother.

THIRTY-FIVE

The Primrose version

'You will go, won't you?' Melinda asked as we sat on a bench in the Castle gardens. 'Everyone will be there and Peggy Mountjoy is making up a party – sherry first at her house.'

'Including the daughter?' I enquired warily.

Melinda shook her head. 'No, she can't dance. Besides, I gather there is a clash with some deeply meaningful lecture by the Bakeshaft woman. Some things take priority: serious mind over frivolous matter, as it were.' She grinned and added, 'But you must come, it'll be a hoot!'

I doubted that a ball hosted by the Winchbrookes would be a hoot exactly. But not wishing to appear curmudgeonly (and fearing my absence might be ascribed to a preference for the Bakeshaft lecture) I told Melinda that it would doubtless be just what the doctor ordered . . . or at least surely a sweeter pill than that awful school play!

Thus a week later and suitably clad in best bib and tucker, i.e. green taffeta gown, mink wrap and elbow-length gloves dug from some murky recess in the spare room, I sallied forth to trip the light fantastic among the best of Sussex stalwarts.

Rather to my surprise the Erasmus school hall, normally bare and austere, looked almost inviting. The lights had been adjusted to cast a mellow glow, swathes of flowers (plastic?) decorated the walls and the central dance space was lined with pink-clothed tables bearing candles in Chianti bottles. On the platform – normally kept for prayers and stern announcements – a rather raffish quartet was playing jaunty show tunes. I relaxed and began to mingle, but was immediately accosted by the Reverend Egge resplendent in tails – though incongruously retaining the dog collar. He made a deep bow and asked if he could 'have the pleasure' to which a little uncertainly I agreed.

Unexpectedly the Reverend Egge proved himself to be quite a nifty dancer – not of course with Ingaza's gyrating hips, but a neat little mover all the same. His forte was the quickstep and I have to admit that I rather enjoyed the process of being smoothly steered. It doesn't happen often – least of all with Freddy Balfour who, while commencing with a lavish waltz, whatever the rhythm, invariably switches to a lumbering foxtrot halfway through. This is manageable provided you are prepared for the sudden change. Not all his partners are and suffer accordingly.

To my amazement the Winchbrookes, whose foxtrot might be termed resolutely turgid, put on an extraordinary display of jitterbug! I wondered if it was their secret vice – honed and practised in private and then produced for stunned acclaim on special occasions. In fact, rather cynically I suspected that the event's whole *raison d'etre* had been to serve this very purpose. Rather disappointingly we were treated to only one such bout – which was just as well, for once the music ceased both looked totally shattered. Like many of the middle-aged their physiques are not built for such antics. But it was a valiant show and certainly broke any residual ice.

After such encouragement the evening proceeded with gay abandon: that is to say that the wine – of undistinguished quality – was consumed in remarkable quantity, the saxophonist and drummer who had begun with muted subtlety became progressively assertive (i.e. violent) and the dancing, while not of the Winchbrooke style, was indulged with a decorous frenzy. Clearly those trustees who had stoically endured Mr Urquart's less than riveting school play were now being aptly rewarded.

'It's all going very well, isn't it?' Emily said breathlessly. She had been engaged in a stumbling quickstep with Blenkinsop the maths master. Neither was especially fleet of foot, but perhaps inspired by the Winchbrookes' startling display had been attempting some rather wobbly crossovers. Emily is not normally so game, and I mentally applauded her efforts. In fact, I was about to say so when she plucked my sleeve and exclaimed, 'Oh look, there's the chief superintendent. I didn't realize they were coming – there was no reply to the invitation. Too busy with other matters, I suppose.'

I followed her gaze to where MacManus was standing just inside the doorway (no sign of the wife – early bed with cocoa?). Like a number of those present he was wearing tails rather than a dinner jacket, and with his height and broad shoulders cut quite a distinctive figure albeit of the lumberjack variety. (No elegance there!) But whatever good features he may have had were suddenly displaced in my mind by the image of that cavorting pantomime bear, and I gave a snort of laughter. In fact, so potent was the image that I laughed again and nearly upset my drink.

'Oh really, what a noise, Primrose!' Emily protested. 'And what on earth are you laughing at?' Recovered from her exertions on the dance floor, Emily had resumed her frequent air of vague disapproval.

I retorted that my trilling laugh was nothing as compared to the saxophonist's racket and didn't she think that Mr MacManus looked like a lone lemon in a bowl of cherries.

'No,' she said shortly, 'he looks very manly. I must get him some canapés.'

'Ah, *animal* magnetism!' I spluttered.

Emily tossed her head and stalked off in search of fodder to present to the manly hero.

I was just about to procure an addition to my glass, when I was tapped on the shoulder by the Reverend Egge. 'May I have the pleasure again?' He beamed. 'I think we make rather a good pair.'

Actually, I think we did, and we twirled with brio. I complimented him on his expertise and asked how he had become so accomplished.

'Ah, my missionary days,' he replied, 'dancing with the natives. They taught me their steps and I taught them mine. They took to the western style like ducks to water and were very discerning especially with the waltz double-reverse. That kept me on my toes all right!' A wistful look came into his eyes, and I said that he must find Lewes rather dull in comparison.

'Oh, not dull, just different. Less lively perhaps, but intriguing nevertheless. I mean to say, what could be more intriguing than the fate of poor Mrs Markham? *Very* peculiar, I consider . . . and between you and me there is more to that business than meets the eye. Though whether the chief superintendent's eye has alighted on anything I rather doubt – I fear he is out of his depth. Still, I am sure the good man means well – as do we all in our stumbling way.' So saying, he executed a particularly deft manoeuvre which I was only just able to follow.

A little later I slipped out to powder my nose. The long passage was ill-lit and shadowy (a miser at heart, Winchbrooke rarely permits bulbs above a forty watt), and to reach the Ladies one has to pass the back stairs. To my slight alarm I saw a small figure huddled on the bottom step. At my approach it leaped up and squeaked, 'Oh, hello, Miss Oughterard! Are you having a nice time?' Needless to say, it was the pyjama-clad Sickie-Dickie.

'Yes, very nice, thank you, Dickie,' I said. 'But whatever are you doing down here – shouldn't you be in your dormitory?'

He put his finger to his nose, asked me not to tell and whispered he was on a mission to nab some leftovers for a midnight feast. 'Stokes Major bet me a bob I wouldn't find any as the grown-ups were sure to have guzzled the lot. But I think he's wrong; he generally is.'

'So where do you propose putting it all?' I whispered back. He gestured to something slung on the banister which I saw was his satchel.

'You see,' he confided, 'when the music starts up again and they are all dancing, I can sneak along and raid the trollies by the kitchen door. I bet I win my bet!'

'Not if the chief superintendent of police sees you. Purloining discarded pastries is considered theft, you know,' I said in mock reproof.

He shrugged. 'Oh, I don't think Mr MacManus will notice anything. He had to give evidence once in one of Grandpa's court cases. I heard Grandpa say to Mummy that he had been promoted above his station . . . I don't know what that means really. But they both laughed so I don't suppose he'll be a danger.' Oh, the confidence of youth!

At that moment the door to the Gents banged and out walked the subject of our conversation. Seeing me he stopped, wished me good evening and muttered something about there being a good turn-out. And then, noticing Dickie, he frowned. 'Hmm. Shouldn't you be in bed, young man? Rather late to be roaming about, I should have thought.'

'Oh yes, sir,' Dickie agreed earnestly, 'but you see I couldn't sleep because I was worried about my satchel. I had left it downstairs and it's got all my Latin prep in it, and it would be awful if I couldn't find it. So I came down on a *rescue* mission.' The blue eyes stared up guilelessly at MacManus's looming figure.

MacManus nodded curtly and was about to return to the main hall when the boy stopped him. 'I say,' he piped, 'I've seen your picture, the one Mr Topping had on the desk in his study. It was jolly good!'

My heart lurched. Oh my God, the child was going to mention the bearskin! For reasons which I won't now recap Dickie had once seen that insalubrious photograph and had happily swallowed my explanation of it being a pantomime rehearsal. Since then he has never mentioned the incident and I assumed he had forgotten the whole thing. But children, like dogs, have buried memories and can regurgitate matter at the most embarrassing moments.

'Er, my picture?' MacManus asked. 'Do you mean the one in my dress uniform, the one that was in the *Lewes Tribune*? Yes, that was quite—'

'Oh no, sir, the one where you were in—'

'Oh, come on Dickie,' I said hastily, 'Mr MacManus is right. It's high time you were in bed, otherwise Matron will be after you and then we shall all be in the soup!' I gave a gay laugh and hustled him up the stairs certain that he would pursue his foraging once the fogies were gone and the coast clear.

After this little interlude I retreated to spend a well-earned penny, and then rejoined the mêlée in the hall. Here I was buttonholed by Freddie Balfour and inveigled into a dance of no known steps or rhythm, after which I felt it was time to leave. However, before I could pursue the idea I was approached by MacManus . . . approached a mite unsteadily, it would seem. Had he abandoned his customary sobriety?

'Oh, are you going to ask me to dance?' I asked with fake gaiety. 'I'm afraid I am just about to—'

'No,' he said woodenly, 'I want to speak to you.'

I raised an eyebrow. 'Here?'

'It'll do.'

'Very well, but as I said, I am about to go.' Pointedly I picked up my wrap and handbag.

'I have some more questions about the Markham case,' he said abruptly. 'I want you down at the station by ten o'clock tomorrow morning.' He paused and then added roughly, 'Doubtless you can manage that.'

The cheek of the man! I stared at him coldly. 'I am afraid that is out of the question, Chief Superintendent. I have an important engagement in London. I shall not be here.' As it happens, I had half promised Ingaza I might go over to Brighton to be dazzled by his tango technique in the Latino Cup.

He regarded me with glassy eye. 'In that case I will get Sergeant Wilding to make an appointment.'

I shrugged and turned, but he had the gall to tap me on the shoulder. 'By the way,' he said in a tone distinctly slurred, 'your brother, the Reverend Canon Oughterard – he was a funny cove, wasn't he? Very funny, by all accounts. My colleague at the Yard, Inspector Samson, says they never did solve that murder near his vicarage in Surrey.'

In a tone of such steel that I barely recognized it, I replied, 'We are all funny coves, Mr MacManus – present company not excluded.'

Hands clamped to the steering wheel and muttering, *'Bastard! Bastard!'* I made my resolution: no more delay. I would send him the blooming photographs – and to the press as well! I rammed my foot on the accelerator and careered off into the night.

The following morning, I was slightly surprised to see my car still unscathed and the ruined gates with no additional damage. Relieved and with breakfast over, I seized the telephone and told Ingaza of my intention.

'Calm down and hold your horses,' he muttered. 'If you send the things to MacManus, he will tear them up and nobody will be any the wiser. And how can you send copies to the press unless you have duplicates? You haven't, have you – and there are no negatives.'

Yes, well, that sobered me, and so I asked what he advised.

'I happen to know someone who might be useful. He's a keen amateur photographer, bit of a whizz-kid really. He'll probably be able to make copies – for a fee, naturally.' But naturally. After all, what self-respecting friend of Ingaza's wouldn't charge a fee? 'He's away at the moment but will be back in a couple of days or so. Leave it with me and I'll see what he says.' I accepted his kind suggestion and said I would bring the snaps pronto when his contact returned.

Calmed by Ingaza's handy advice and relishing the prospect of trouncing MacManus, I went up to the studio to begin a fresh canvas. As a posthumous nod to Councillor Bewley, I thought that perhaps my usual theme of munching sheep could be enhanced by a few bounding rabbits. Or maybe just one big one. As a memento it would be more in keeping with the rural scene than a motorbike.

THIRTY-SIX

The Primrose version

My labours at the easel were proving most productive and certainly made a change from my more recent pursuits. As decided, I had eschewed the motorbike in favour of a couple of cavorting rabbits and for quite a while was absorbed with these and also with the possibility of including some distant pigs. But inevitably my thoughts abandoned the rustic scene and wandered back to the raw reality of death and homicide. I put down my brush and, knowing that little more would be achieved that morning, returned downstairs to indulge in a coffee and cigarette. I sat at the kitchen table and was immediately assaulted by Maurice leaping on to my lap. Occasionally when feeling gracious he will do that. Thus to the sound of quietly sinister purring I sipped my coffee and brooded.

Extraordinary though Bewley's revelation had been, in some ways it afforded mild relief: at least now the mystery was clarified and I knew for certain what had happened. Knowledge is always reassuring however strange or distasteful. It meant too that I could fully banish the annoying Aston Travers from my mind – trading in call girls being mild in comparison to murdering an aunt. Why, he was virtually an injured innocent! And now that both his relations were dead and out of the way it was unlikely I would see him again.

My thoughts returned to the aunt and her dastardly disposal of Elspeth. Bewley's method had been so much simpler than Alice's elaborate scheme! I reflected on that scheme and its gruesome mechanics – the rabbit punch to the sister's neck and the forcing of the dead head into the bathing hat. Ugh! But even as I flinched, I was assailed by another image: Alice's companion on that fatal voyage. Who the hell had it been? Who was it that had administered the punch and assisted in the struggles with the cap? An obvious question – but so hectic and disturbing had been recent events that that particular concern had vanished from my mind. It now returned with vivid force.

Thus, suddenly stirred, I discarded the cat and bounded to the window to stare out at the somnolent Downs. They yielded nothing except the ghost of Councillor Bewley spreadeagled at my feet. 'No, not you,' I whispered, 'the other person – the one on the boat with Alice. Who *was* it?' I turned to go back to my chair, but it was occupied: Maurice lay curled there, tail twitching and eyes defiant. Rather than risk a fracas I ignored him and sat dutifully on the harder one.

Settled once more, I began to review matters, beginning naturally with Alice's bizarre visit and her intemperate confession. I recalled the vulgar hat and the grating truculent voice and, concentrating on the latter, tried to dredge up her exact words. She had referred to them as a loyal helpmate, implied they lived in London and said they were close and she had known them for years. She had also firmly stated that they shared her vehement dislike of Elspeth as the latter had once upset them financially – 'she let them down appallingly' had been the words.

I racked my brain for more useful clues. None came. And then just as I was deciding that Alice's co-murderer was indeed some faceless London crony and thus any speculation futile, something hit me. Oh, of course! Why on earth hadn't I thought of it? It was the bloody boat itself, the boat that had been moored at Newhaven! When I had asked Alice where her friend was, she had replied curtly, 'They have gone away on their boat.' So that was it – at last, a tangible lead!

Thus, it would seem that 'X' was somebody who lived in London and yet kept a boat nearby, and would therefore be familiar with this area. Alice had called me a nasty piece of work, adding that the friend thought so too. Charming! But why should they think that unless we had met? Actually, as far as I was aware there was only one person who had a rooted dislike of me (other than MacManus) and that was Purvis the town clerk. But I couldn't imagine that little creep being matey with the Markham woman. Still, her comment did suggest I was not unknown to the friend. So, I mused, it was somebody with a boat, with local knowledge and who knew Elspeth sufficiently well to have been mistreated but yet ostensibly was still on friendly terms (why otherwise would she have consented to go on that birthday jaunt?).

But again my mind went blank and I gazed round the room uselessly scanning its wallpaper, dresser and untidy sink. It's absurd, I thought angrily – by her own admission she had an accomplice and I *must* discover who it was. I *must* get to the bottom of it! I fixed my eye on the cat, demanding inspiration. Blank wall.

And then slowly, very slowly a picture began to emerge . . . I took a deep breath as the name Bullseye Bert came to mind and I was reminded of his disclosure to Ingaza of Operation Tarts Galore: the ladies' little boat trips across the Channel between Dieppe and the Sussex coast. Trips chartered by their arch-pimp and navigator – Aston Travers.

'It fits!' I yelled to Maurice. 'Oh, crikey, it fits – it was *his* damn boat and he was the accomplice!'

My eruption had no effect on the cat, who merely wafted his tail and closed his eyes.

I closed my eyes, once again hearing Austin's caustic reference to his mother in the café: *I don't imagine she would have approved.* Was that what it was about? Had she balked him financially in some way, withheld what he considered rightfully his or tampered with his father's will, leaving him to rely on his aunt for help? Such things were not unknown in families and caused rifts of chasmic proportion. Had this been such a case? Alice's words about Elspeth having treated him badly might well suggest so.

And yes, if aunt and nephew were indeed co-murderers in revenge for a shared injustice it would explain the meaning of Dickie's note – nothing to do with the lingerie deal but all to do with Elspeth Travers' successful disposal and the necessity to lie low. I thought grimly of the '*Il faut fêter ça*' and shuddered. Hmm. Sex and money, the most potent causes of greed and anger, and also of revenge – and yes sometimes of celebration.

And so, what was I supposed to do with this brilliant deduction – go to the police? No fear. I'd had enough of MacManus's boorish innuendos. He could do without the help of Primrose Oughterard and follow his own blundering nose! Besides I had to admit – albeit reluctantly – that like the earlier ones my conclusions were of the conjectural variety. There was no hard evidence to offer. *I* might believe I was right but would anyone else? And after all, I thought soberly, there was always the Francis factor to consider . . . there always would be. Yes, Ingaza was right to trust in the platinum value of silence; and I remembered my mother's weary injunction when I was a child: *Be quiet Primrose. Sit still and wait and see. Just sit still!* For the time being, at least, I would abide by that.

THIRTY-SEVEN

The Primrose version

Thus to quiet my thoughts of Aston, that afternoon I had another go in the studio but it wasn't terribly effective and, tired of ruminant sheep and playful rabbits, I went downstairs to look for the evening paper. To my irritation it wasn't the *Lewes Tribune*, the usual one, but the *Sussex Rattler*, a publication I wasn't enamoured of. How tiresome, presumably the paper boy was new. I glanced at it idly, not bothering to sit down, assuming

it would be quickly discarded. In this I was wrong, for the head-
lines leapt at me and I read with rapt attention:

Police Raid on Mercers' Music Hall

Following an unexpected police visit yesterday, the doors
of Bognor's historic vaudeville theatre have closed for the
last time. According to Detective Inspector Spikesy, liaising
with the Bognor police, the theatre has been under special
surveillance and it has now been established that the
premises have long been the hub of prostitution and other
illicit activities.

Patrons of the hall's legitimate programmes will be
shocked at this revelation and sad to see it go. However,
they will recognize that public standards must be maintained
and that seemly pleasure must bow to the extinction of the
gross and unsavoury. To this end the *Sussex Rattler* has
always been dedicated and will continue in its pursuit of
such matters.

An unconfirmed report reveals that a photographic record
of those clients availing themselves of its dubious offerings
has been kept by the theatre's management. If such exists
doubtless the data will be invaluable to the police in their
continuing enquiries which we trust will be successful. As
yet Lewes's chief superintendent, Alastair MacManus, has
been unavailable for comment – but our reporter did have a
brief glimpse of the chief constable looking particularly
cheerful. Meanwhile the *Rattler* will endeavour to keep its
readers abreast of any fresh revelations.

Well, I gasped, here's a turn-up for the books! What do you know!
The *Sussex Rattler* is a frightful rag full of drivel and unctuous
prurience. Normally I would have cursed the paper boy for his
mistake, but this time I was grateful. I re-read the article, especially the bit about the photographic records. Interesting. Had they
been the source of Topping's snapshots now in my possession?
It seemed likely. And if so, were there others of similar style?
But either way, assuming that MacManus (and fellow punters)
had been ignorant of such graphic records no wonder he was

unavailable for comment! Perhaps, after all, my own data would
be surplus to requirements and save me both postage and other
costs! I grinned at the dog, who naturally took that to be an
invitation for a walk and began to prance accordingly.

As Bouncer tugged me towards the field where he knew I would
unleash him, I grappled with the new development as outlined
by the *Rattler*. If indeed Spikesy had closed the place down, how
would that affect Aston Travers – assuming he was still plying
his cross-Channel trade, Operation Tarts Galore? Would he simply
call it a day as arch-pimp and navigator and melt into the ether?
Or was Spikesy already on to him and sharpening his sword for
an imminent arrest? If the latter, would the charge be confined
to his pimping activity of supplying goods other than bizarre
underwear? Or in the course of interrogation might suspicions
be aroused in another direction, i.e. to the murder of his mother?
And should that be the case, where did that leave me? Silent or
ready to play the upright citizen and report my 'conversation'
with Alice?

Thinking of Francis and other complications I still inclined
to the former, but it was a delicate problem and not helped by
Bouncer's bellicose roars as he confronted a thunderstruck
heifer. In turn I yelled at him to come to heel. Stuck between the
two of us Bouncer hesitated, looking from right to left as if torn
between war and peace . . . Yes, we all have our moments of
indecision. And exploiting the hiatus the heifer calmly walked
away, an act of studied indifference which left the dog looking
foolish.

As we regained the road I saw Sergeant Wilding trundling
towards us on his bike. Hmm, presumably this was when he would
stop me and try to fix that interview MacManus had so rudely
threatened. I braced myself to be politely agreeable and wondered
if I could persuade the sergeant to give a clue regarding the questions. I gave a friendly wave but felt rather tense.

He dismounted immediately, and with a broad grin exclaimed,
'Well, Miss Oughterard, you had a fine time last night, I should
say! Erasmus House lit up like a Christmas tree and you all in
your fine togs shrieking and laughing, and I don't know what.
What you might call a night on the flipping tiles!'

I was taken aback, not only because his account seemed a trifle florid but because I had expected a sterner tone and the brandishing of a notebook.

'Er, yes,' I conceded, 'I suppose it was rather merry. But still it's nice for people to relax a little and I suppose it shows the Erasmus boys that we're not all starchy has-beens.' I gave a diffident smile wondering when the notebook would appear.

'Starchy? No, I should think not.' He laughed. 'As it happens, I picked up two starched collars from outside the school gates only half an hour ago. Cor, things must have gone well! Why, even the chief looked under the weather this morning, very grim and silent he was. Didn't want to speak to no one and just locked himself away in his office. Not like old Speakeasy – grinning like a Cheshire cat, he is.' Wilding lowered his voice. 'Between you and me, he's had a coup: buggered up that Bognor brothel and is on the heels of their chief supplier – and I *don't* mean of hymn books!' So saying, he mounted his bicycle and with a matey wave rode off.

I gazed after him relieved and perplexed. Were the effects of last night's revels really the cause of MacManus's morose silence (he had certainly been squiffy when he ordered the interview). Or was there another reason for his bleak manner: Spikesy's raid on the brothel, for example? And if so, was his silence due to fear of being exposed as the lolloping bear or pique at his subordinate's triumph and his own lacklustre record? But professionally links with the brothel would be the more shaming, and thus the more damaging . . . And what about Aston, for goodness' sake? Was Spikesy really on his trail? It would be nice to think so, the nasty little creep! Yanking Bouncer's lead, I started to stride back along the lane suddenly eager to resume my painting.

However, we were again detained, though this time by Louis Lionheart, Bouncer's friend, and who last heard of had been ravaging the sweetshop and being sick over PC Wilding's boots. But now the springer looked on sparkling form, as did its owners (well, moderately) and I was glad to pat the dog and chat with the latter.

I said I was sorry not to have seen them at the Erasmus ball, at which they flinched and explained that having endured the rigours of Urquart's play they had lacked the strength for another function quite so soon. One saw their point. We turned to other things, and I suppose that because it had been on my mind I nearly asked if they had read about the Bognor business and the raid on the music hall. But I stopped short, suspecting that they took only the national newspapers and certainly nothing as virtuously grubby as the *Rattler*.

As we talked, the two dogs spent a sniffy time chatting each other up and vying as to which could wag its tail the fastest. It was a cheering sight, and not for the first time I wondered what on earth went on in those furry minds and what it was that animals said to each other.

Despite Bouncer's liveliness with the springer, on our way home I thought he was looking a bit disgruntled and not showing his usual zest when I spoke or tossed his ball. Oh well, presumably a fresh bone would soon fix that.

I was right: the bone improved his mood straightway, as did Maurice who greeted him affably and for once seemed resigned to his growly attentions.

THIRTY-EIGHT

The dog's view

'**D**o you know what that friend of the Prim's said to me?' I roared at the cat when I got home from my walk.

Maurice said he couldn't imagine and would I kindly lower my voice.

'She *said*,' I told him, thumping my paw, 'that I was a funny bunny. So what about that!'

'Very nice,' the cat said vaguely.

'Very nice! What do you mean, Maurice? It was . . .' I paused, trying to remember the word. 'It was OUTRAJUS!'

The cat looked startled and flattened his ears. 'But what's wrong with that?' he asked.

'Wrong?' I growled. 'What would you think if some human called you a "funny mousey"?'

Maurice sneezed and gazed at his white paw (the mouse-catching one). 'Disgraceful,' he said.

'EGGSACTLY,' I snorted. 'It's a bit much. There I was being all chummy with my pal Lionheart, when his mistress stoops down, pulls my tail and says that to me!'

The cat gave a sort of splutter, which could have meant anything, and then said that one had to be *fillo*something and that humans were not known for their tact and often put their feet in the manure when meaning to be kind. 'You see,' he explained, 'she probably thought you were being rather charming.'

Well, that gave me paws for thought, all right! 'Hmm. Do you think so?' I asked with interest.

'Oh, indubitably,' he replied, and closed his eyes.

Now when the cat uses *that* word I know he is being serious. So I felt a bit better then and got on with the new bone that P.O. had given me.

As I chewed and spat and rattled it against my bowl, I had some BIG thoughts, such as A: the Prim is in trouble again. B: I wish Maurice had let me bite that policeman's backside when I had the chance. C: that I've still got the mad Markham's hat stored in my basket (P.O. put it in the dustbin but I took it out to keep as a trophy), and D: if I ever see that blithering heifer again I'll chase it to buggery!

I went on chewing. And then something else struck me. It was what Lionheart had said this afternoon when we were sniffing each other up or making *lively banter* as Maurice would say. I had just been telling him what I would do to that heifer if it tried mooing at me again, when he gave an extra wag to his tail and said, 'Yippee, that sounds good sport! You're a brave one, Bouncer, and it just shows there's life in the old dog yet!' At the time I was quite chuffed as it's nice to have one's PROW-ESS saluted . . . But thinking it over, I am none too pleased. I mean, what did the springer mean by 'old dog'? Bouncer is NOT OLD, he's tough and full of woof & *yoof*! Just because I'm not a pup like L.L. doesn't mean I'm on the slippery path to the Dogs' Paradise. Not yet I'm blooming not! It's a bit much and I shall go and tell Maurice about it.

*   *   *

It's nearly bedtime now but I was able to catch the cat before he set off on his nightly prowl. He was just climbing out of the pantry window, but I yanked his tail and he fell back into the rice pudding. Ho! Ho! That gave him a jolt! Still, it meant I would have to be extra diplo in my approach. No fleas on Bouncer! 'Oh dear,' I said, 'you are covered in all that white gunge. But a nice bit of haddock will soon cure that!'

The cat looked flummoxed (or poleaxed) and asked what the flea's something frog's leg I was talking about. (Just occasionally – about once a year – Maurice's lingo can hit the roof.) I told him that I had just happened to observe our mistress hiding some fresh haddock fillets behind the tinned pilchards and would he like me to fetch him one.

Still sprawled in the rice pudding, the cat *mewsed*, and then said that on the whole this was a good idea and would I kindly be quick about it. So I got the stuff, shoved it at him and waited.

It didn't take long. And when he had finished he was actually smiling. 'So what was it you wanted?' he asked in one of his chummier tones.

'What I want,' I growled, 'is for you to tell me I am not *old*!' And I told him all about my afternoon and Lionheart's words.

Quite clearly the haddock had done the trick as Maurice was really decent. 'Old, Bouncer? You? Certainly not. Why no one with lungs, fangs and a gullet like yours could be termed old . . . a veritable Puck of the canine world!'

'A what of the canine world?' I asked with interest.

'Puck, Bouncer, *Puck*!' the cat replied, brushing some rice pudding from his front.

Well, that was very nice of Maurice and I began to feel quite pleased. But then I said that I thought it was time I did something amazing, something that only a young dog or one in his prime could do: something bold and daring and which would make everyone SIT UP.

I gave a brisk bark and told Maurice this but he didn't seem too keen. 'Must you?' he said.

'Yes,' I barked again, 'this is a challenge to my wit and my doghood!'

'Good Cod!' the cat muttered, and started to scramble out of the window again – this time with his tail tucked in.

After he had gone I settled down in my basket and tried to work out a crafty scheme. This was quite tricky as I kept dozing off. But I knew that if I kept gnawing away, like with a bone, I would get there in the end. Bouncer always does!

THIRTY-NINE

The cat's memoir

R eally, that dog! Not content with barring my exit from the pantry window for my nightly stroll (and thereby landing me in the rice pudding) he now has some hare-brained scheme to prove his 'doghood'! Apparently the Lionheart springer had foolishly referred to him as being old – a friendly term and not meant to be taken literally. Or not by anyone of sense. Alas, sense is not one of Bouncer's better traits and he has applied a rigid interpretation. Thus, furious at being thought less than young he is hell-bent on cutting a dash and doing something youthful and daring. I shudder to think what – his normal rampages are bad enough. Nevertheless, the prospect is intriguing. Might he trash the chinchillas' hutch? Vandalize the church vestry? Urinate on the Bartlett woman's suede shoes? Hurl himself into the head-master's lily pond and terrorize the newts? Who knows,with that hound it might be anything! I await events with some nervousness – for whatever he does the thing could rebound and have unfortunate results for *all* of us!

Having kept a low profile by skulking in the shrubbery, I can now report that Bouncer's plan has been revealed. It is, thank goodness, less crude than you might expect – in fact, if properly executed it could be mildly amusing.

Bored with worms and insects, I felt it time to look for some fresh diversion, and was just wandering off to see what I could find when Bouncer appeared. Before I could take evasive action, he tweaked my tail and in a throaty whisper said, 'I say, Maurice, I've got a good wheeze. Want to hear about it?'

To have indicated otherwise would have been imprudent and likely to cause general uproar. Thus, marshalling supreme tact, I told him that I could hardly wait.

Plonking himself down and grinning from ear to ear he announced, 'I am going to interfere with MacManus's marrows.'

'*Interfere* with his *marrows*?' I exclaimed. 'In what way – savage them, do you mean? I cannot see that tearing chunks out of vegetable marrows is going to enhance your image in the canine fraternity . . . it's the sort of thing that an elderly Pekinese minus half its teeth might do, but not a fine fellow like you!' I gave an indulgent laugh.

The dog thumped his tail impatiently. '*No* Maurice, you've got it wrong. My plan is much better than that.'

'Glad to hear it,' I said drily. And so he told me.

Apparently, according to Tootles (the gossipy tabby who lives opposite the MacManus house), one of the policeman's few interests is cultivating giant marrows which he exhibits at local shows. Tootles says the things are without smell or taste and serve no discernible purpose. But evidently their owner thinks otherwise. So Bouncer's plan is to sneak into MacManus's garden late at night, wrench the marrows from their stalks, drag them into the middle of the front lawn and then scratch rude words across their skins. Thus, the marrows would be rendered unfit for exhibition, MacManus would go berserk and Bouncer would have struck a blow in revenge for his pestering of the Prim. Tootles would pass the word around that Bouncer was responsible for the bold sabotage, and since MacManus was known to dislike both cats and dogs, he would be applauded by all.

The account finished, its exponent sat back, panting. 'So what do you think, Maurice?'

I cogitated for a moment, and then enquired what sort of words he had in mind.

'Oh, easy ones,' he said, 'you know the sort: *twerp, berk, ass, prat, dumbo, stoopidimberceel.*'

I pointed out that the last term, having five syllables, was hardly easy.

'Oh yes, but you can do that one,' the dog replied carelessly.

'*Me!*' I hissed. 'Surely you do not imagine I am going to get embroiled in this piece of braggadocio!'

'Piece of what?'

'Piece of . . . oh, never mind.' I sighed.

The dog moved away, padded over to leer at Boris and Karloff in their cage, lifted his leg and then returned. 'So how about it, Maurice? You'll come, won't you?' He gave a falsetto yelp which he fondly imagines can charm. 'It'll be good sport!'

I was silent considering the pros and cons. If caught, we would surely suffer for it and be thought fools by neighbouring colleagues . . . and my chance of winning the CFE (Companion of the Feline Empire) would be scuppered. However, if successful Bouncer would win kudus; *and* assuming that Sir Perivale Puss-Coley was informed, I should be a step closer to gaining that noble award. Thus, I took a deep breath and a mad punt. 'All right, Bouncer, I will come to oversee your antics.' The cod was cast.

Thus, two nights later, we set out on our mission. Conditions could not have been better: warm, dry and moonless – and our mistress snoring her head off in bed. We sneaked out of the house via the broken panel in the basement door (typically P.O. has never had it fixed), and raced up the drive into the road before taking the shortcut across fields to MacManus's back garden. Here everything was still and shrouded in darkness: excellent for an intrepid cat and dog, but less so for humans whose senses are defective.

I was slightly irritated to find Tootles lurking behind a watering can. Tabbies are notoriously nosy and he was obviously hoping to have a front seat at our activities. However, I told him that his presence was surplus to requirements but that if he wanted to be useful he could stand sentinel at the front gate. This seemed to appeal and he scampered off.

We soon located the marrow patch and I selected the sort Bouncer should deal with – the biggest ones and whose size would best accommodate the rude words. These we decided to inscribe once the marrows had been detached from their stalks and placed on the lawn. As a matter of fact, I was quite impressed with the dog's dexterity in cutting the marrows' moorings. I had expected frantic wrenching and twisting with much snorting and dribble. But to give him his due the job was done with relative

ease. I suppose practice on his bones and the Prim's insistence
that he attends the dentist (F.O. never bothered) has kept those
teeth in sharp condition.

'First stage over.' He grinned. 'Now for the hard stuff.' By this
he meant dragging the things onto the front lawn where they
could be observed in all their mangled glory. But fortunately the
distance was only a few yards and the path uncluttered by plants
or other obstacles. The marrows were too big for Bouncer's jaws
but he could roll them with his snout, while I could tug at the
severed stalk ends. It was an arduous process but we got there in
the end. After taking breath we then started to arrange them in a
small circle, with the dog using his snout again and me doing
some head-butting.

When we had finished Tootles came sloping over and said he
thought they looked very pretty.

'Pretty?' Bouncer snorted. 'They won't be pretty when the
words are on 'em!' He lifted his paw and tried to scratch *twerp*.
It wasn't very successful: much scrabbling with little result.
'Hmm. Perhaps I should try with my teeth,' he muttered.

'No, Bouncer,' I commanded quickly. 'I will do it.' Unsheathing
my claws I incised the words *berk*, *prat* and *dumbo* in impeccable
calligraphy. Not for nothing had I been top of the kitten class all
those years ago.

'That's pretty good,' the dog grunted, 'but you've got the long
word now, *stoopidimberceel*.'

I selected the largest marrow and was just sharpening my claw
for this last assault, when there came a sudden howl from Tootles
back at his post by the front gate. 'He's coming!' he screeched.
'Take cover!'

We dived to the hedge and took up commando positions to
watch the road. A large car was driving very slowly in our direction, and as it reached the turn into MacManus's entrance it
braked, and then stalled. (I know about stalling because when we
lived with the vicar he was always doing it.) We heard the starter
turning . . . And then we heard and saw something else. Another
vehicle came hurtling along at breakneck speed, hit the rear of
the first car, tipping it into the ditch, and with thunderous noise
careered on into the night. We could hear the faint whine of its

engine, followed suddenly by a screeching of brakes and then a most stupendous crash.

'I wonder what that was,' said Tootles conversationally as Bouncer and I scrambled out from the hedge.

'Dunno,' Bouncer said, 'but I can tell you who's in the ditch – it's old Manus. We had better take a look.'

We scurried into the road and then down into the ditch where the car was half on its side. I leapt on top of the bonnet and, pressing my face against the glass, saw the policeman's form slumped across the front seats. As I gazed he began to stir and then lifted his head. The tilted bonnet made perching tricky but I clung on and pushed my face closer against the glass to inspect the damage. MacManus seemed to start, and then, putting his hand over his eyes, cried, 'Oh my Christ!' The side window was slightly open so I heard this quite distinctly.

By this time Bouncer had come snuffling up. 'I suppose we ought to let the blighter out,' he growled. 'Mind you, after those marrows I'm not sure my gnashers can stand any more biting and pulling. What do you think we should do?' He stood on his hind legs and peered in at the driver's window. Again, MacManus moved – to remove his hand from his eyes. But seeing the dog's furry face, he replaced it instantly and groaned, 'Oh, dear God, help me!' I have to admit that I have had that reaction myself when the dog has broken my slumber, but why my own friendly face should have prompted such a response I cannot imagine. Humans are funny creatures.

'Shall I try to bite the handle to make it open?' Bouncer asked.

I said that on no account should he attempt such a thing, as if he broke his teeth there would be an interminable fuss. (I winced at the thought.) 'I have a far better idea,' I said, 'which will release MacManus, save your teeth and bring much credit to both of us. Why, we could become heroes!'

The dog pricked up his ears. 'Hmm, that sounds a bit of all right,' he growled, 'what is it?'

I told him that it was perfectly simple: that we should rush into the gardens of the adjacent houses barking and caterwauling for all we were worth until people came out to investigate and hurl abuse and bedroom slippers. Once they were alerted we could lead them to MacManus and the wreckage of his car.

'Right-o,' Bouncer barked, 'I like that.' Well he would, wouldn't he? Anything that involves noise and drama. But before we commenced the alarums he asked where Tootles was.

'Still admiring the marrows,' I replied.

FORTY

The Primrose version

U nwisely I had gone to bed early, and as a result awoke some hours later fully alert and restless. So I went down into the kitchen intending to nibble a biscuit and complete the crossword. My movements were stealthy for fear of waking the dog normally snoring in his basket. But there was no snoring and no dog. How strange . . . I called his name and listened for a bark or flurry of paws but there wasn't a sound. Odd. I recalled letting him in from the garden before going to bed. Had I perhaps carelessly left the back door open and he had slipped out again? Or maybe Maurice had permitted him entry to his own hidey-hole in the airing cupboard. I went to look. But not only was there no Bouncer, but no cat either. This was absurd – and worrying. Certainly the cat goes on a nightly prowl through the cat flap or kitchen window if I've forgotten to close it, but invariably returns by the small hours – normally around two o'clock. It was now nearly half-past three.

There was nothing for it but to dress and go and search for them. Little beasts, they had sneaked out and 'gone a-roving' or on a dustbin raid . . . Unless of course some crazed animal lover had broken in and whisked them off. But I suspected not: the mayhem would have been excruciating!

Equipped with torch and Bouncer's lead I had just opened the front door, when to my shock the telephone rang. Shrill and insistent it cut the silence like a knife, and I froze. Who on earth at this hour! Wrong number? A hoax? I put down the torch and tentatively lifted the receiver.

'Ah,' a voice said, 'we've got your dog [Oh my God, so he *had* been kidnapped!] and were hoping that—'

'Who's that?' I said sharply, 'and what are you doing with my Bouncer!'

'It's not what we're doing with him, but what *he*'s doing with us. You see he keeps getting in the way and it distracts the medics. He's already knocked over the stretcher and—'

'What stretcher?' I demanded of Sergeant Wilding (for it was he).

'The one that's taking the chief superintendent to hospital.'

I went cold. Oh, surely the dog hadn't attacked MacManus! He might have him destroyed!

'So could you come immediately, Miss Oughterard? That would be very helpful,' the sergeant continued.

'Yes,' I said faintly, wondering what frightful thing I was going to face now.

As I approached the town's outskirts and drew level with MacManus's house further progress was abruptly halted, for in the middle of the road was a makeshift barrier, an ambulance and a crowd of police and pyjama-clad onlookers. In the ditch lay a car with its headlamps still blazing. I stared in consternation . . . Oh my God, had Bouncer caused the accident?

I parked my own car and with some nervousness got out and looked around for the dog. He was not in evidence but Wilding was. 'Where is Bouncer?' I said tightly.

He gestured to a couple of onlookers. 'Over there. They're feeding him biscuits.'

'Biscuits – why?'

Wilding chuckled. 'Oh, he's been the little hero – except when he knocked Mr MacManus off his stretcher. Bounded over, put his paws up and – whoops! – the whole thing toppled in the mud. Still, no bones broken and they are about to take him off now.' As he spoke the ambulance engine started and it began to move away.

In some bewilderment, I cleared my throat. 'Uhm . . . you say Bouncer is a hero, Sergeant. Er, may I ask in what way exactly?'

I shot a sceptical glance at where the dog was being patted and fed and clearly enjoying itself.

Wilding explained that MacManus had been pranged by a speeding car and tipped into the ditch. Apparently no one would have known had it not been for Bouncer and some 'yowling mog' rampaging around and waking everyone up. And then when one of the householders appeared in his dressing gown Bouncer had grabbed the cord and pulled him towards the car where MacManus was trapped. The latter was unconscious when they pulled him out but it was no more than temporary concussion.

Well, naturally I was glad to hear that but even more glad that Bouncer was off the hook. What a relief! 'The yowling cat,' I said, 'was it that tabby who lives close by and is always mooching about?'

'Tootles? No fear, dim as they come, he is. They say it was a black fellow with a white leg, but he seems to have sloped off now.'

Yes, I thought wryly, sloped off home and dozing in the airing cupboard no doubt . . . or raiding the pantry! I thanked Wilding for the telephone call and said I would retrieve Bouncer from his attentive admirers and take him home. But the sergeant stopped me and asked which route I intended taking. I shrugged, and told him the way I had come.

'Oh, that's all right then, because if you had wanted to take the shortcut down the old lane you wouldn't have been able. It's blocked.'

'Oh yes? Roadworks?'

He shook his head. 'No, another accident. A real nasty one too. It's obviously the same chap that knocked Mr MacManus sideways. Must have been going at one hell of a lick. Smashed through a farm gate and landed halfway up a tree. A terrible mess.'

It sounded horrific and I shuddered. 'So what about the driver – is he all right?'

Wilding hesitated, and then said, 'Well no. Not so as you'd notice . . . poor bugger is hanging off a branch. Dead. They are cutting him down now.'

I closed my eyes trying to blot out the image. 'Poor young

man,' I murmured, 'or at least I assume he was young going at that speed. A joyrider presumably – hardly some pensioner in an Austin Seven.' Pride in Bouncer's exploit was suddenly eclipsed by the thought of the youth's awful end and I felt quite shaken.

Wilding shook his head sadly. 'We see a lot of that, I'm afraid, and the vehicle has certainly lost its oomph now; ready for the scrap heap, I should say! Ah well, these speed merchants – they never learn, do they?'

I agreed that they didn't. And on that bleak note I went over to collect Bouncer and to drive us soberly home.

During that somewhat pensive journey I had permitted Bouncer to sit on the passenger seat, his favourite place. I told him that he was a very good dog and deserved a whole bar of chocolate. (He loves chocolate but normally is only allowed it at Christmas.) He emitted what I took to be a grateful grunt and then struck an erect pose gazing straight ahead at the car bonnet. I think he thought he was looking noble.

As guessed, when we arrived it was to find Maurice out for the count in the airing cupboard. By this time it was nearly morning but Bouncer made a beeline for his basket and I too managed to snatch a couple of hours back in bed.

Later that morning there was an excited telephone call from Emily avid to hear of the night's drama and the antics of the animals. 'Everyone's talking about it!' she twittered. She asked me to join her for coffee in the Hearts & Flowers, but for reasons already explained I declined that particular venue and suggested another.

I cannot say that I was unduly curious nor moved by the spirit of altruism, but on passing the cottage hospital on my way to meet Emily, I thought I might call in to enquire after MacManus. I didn't wish to *see* him, merely to show polite interest at the reception desk.

As I approached the desk I encountered Nurse Roberts, as always looking spruce and competent in her white uniform and black stockings. On seeing me she said, 'Ah, I expect you've come to have a word with Mr MacManus. I daresay he'll want

to thank you for your sweet doggie rescuing him like that. The
ambulance men told me all about it!'

'Oh no,' I said hastily, 'I wouldn't dream of disturbing him. I
just thought I'd check to see how things were going, that's all.'
I flashed a concerned smile.

'Oh yes, he's all right. Nothing that a couple of days' bed rest
won't cure. But they say his wife is very worried.'

I remarked that given what had happened to her husband I
supposed she would be.

'Yes, but it's not him that she's bothered about so much as the
car. They were going to drive up to Clacton for their holiday, but
the thing can't be repaired in time and they will have to go by
train. Mrs MacManus doesn't like trains – says they give her
palpitations. So she's very put out about it . . . Mind you, he's
being quite gloomy too. Last night when they brought him in
he said he was convinced he had suffered a near-death experience – something to do with fiends and mad bears, I think it was.'
She laughed. 'Oh yes, that's it: he said that as he lay in the car
he saw a malevolent succubus at one window and a ravening
grizzly at the other. "You've been reading too many horror
stories," I said, and offered him a sleeping pill. "No fear," he
replied, "they may come again!"'

'Goodness,' I said with a smile, 'that can't have been much fun,
stuck in a ditch with a great bear trying to get in . . . Er, I don't
suppose he mentioned an ostrich by any chance?' Odd the way
our vices come back to haunt us.

Nurse Roberts shook her head. 'An ostrich? Not yet he hasn't
– but you never know with some of these crash victims. They
may be all right physically but mentally they are all churned up.
It's the shock, you see. But it doesn't last long. He'll soon be
his old self again.' She glanced at her watch. 'Oops, it's time
for Mr Purbright's injection. He'll complain if I'm late. Says his
nerves can't cope.' She bustled off, shoes squeaking and syringe
at the ready.

Left alone, I reflected uncharitably on the likelihood of the
superintendent regaining his old self: did one really want that?
Hmm, not specially . . . But I did not pursue the question for
at that moment the Reverend Egge appeared equipped with
invalid fodder (grapes and chocolates) and a kindly smile. Unless

destined for the nervous Purbright, I assumed such offerings were for MacManus. His beaming benevolence made me feel mildly guilty – a state of mind which, like the latter's near-death vision, was unlikely to last.

FORTY-ONE

The Primrose version

E mily was in a very garrulous mood and showed a surprisingly warm interest in Bouncer's escapade. I say surprisingly because I know very well she is not enamoured of the dog. But actually I think her plaudits were just a prelude to the subject of MacManus in the ditch.

'I daresay he was driving erratically,' she said tartly. 'I am told there has been quite a bit of that recently. For example, after the ball the other night Mr Winchbrooke was very puzzled to see him trying to advance the car sideways out of the school gates. And Jones Minor swore he had had a . . .' Emily paused and tittered, 'a *skin full*!'

'Hmm. Perhaps he had,' I said cheerfully, 'but in this case I gather he had been hit by another car.' I refrained from mentioning the fate of its driver as I was enjoying my cream bun too much. I had the impression that Emily was unaware of the second accident for she went prattling on about MacManus languishing in hospital. I detected a note of satisfaction in her voice which surprised me slightly. 'The other night I thought you said he was rather manly,' I reminded her slyly.

She sniffed. 'I was mistaken. When I suggested he might like to give me a twirl on the dance floor, he declined and said that life was too short to take chances. Quite what he meant by that I am not clear, but whatever he meant I was *not* impressed. Most ungallant!' Emily frowned and pursed her lips.

Yes, I thought wryly, Alastair MacManus certainly had one sterling trait: the power to alienate people. And I thought fleetingly of his snide hints about Francis and the Fotherington case. We turned to other matters, namely Emily's ailing mother and her 'quaint little habits' and the outlandish plot that Mr Winchbrooke was eagerly devising for next year's school play *Biggles and the Bulldog Years*. (Oh yes, evidently my title had been approved!)

No sooner had I left Emily and was about to return to my car, when I was grabbed by Melinda Balfour emerging from the draper's. 'My dear,' she gasped breathlessly, 'have you heard the latest? It's poor Mrs Travers, it's her—'

'But Elspeth Travers is dead,' I interrupted.

'Yes, yes, of course. But not her: her son Aston Travers. *He* is dead now. In a car crash and stuck up a tree. Would you believe it!'

Not for a couple of seconds I didn't, but then of course I did. My God, so *he* had been the one. Aston hoisted by his own Aston! And doubtless the sports car had been bought with his aunt's money or his pimping enterprise. 'Good lord,' I muttered. 'How do you know?'

She said that Freddie had told her. Apparently he had gone to the police station to renew his shotgun licence but had had to wait ages as the Travers accident was claiming everyone's attention. Eventually he got a junior constable to do the job. The youth kept repeating that Inspector Spikesy was very peeved. Typically Freddie had said that if he didn't hurry up and sign the certificate Spikesy wouldn't be the only one peeved, and would he kindly put pen to paper.

'Yes,' I replied faintly, still inwardly reeling, 'with two crashes, one of them fatal and the other the chief superintendent's, I suppose the inspector would be peeved. Quite a drama.'

'Ah, but Freddie thinks it may be something more than that. He happened to see Spikesy in a huddle with other officers, looking very sour indeed, and he heard him mutter to Sergeant Wilding, "The bastard's pulled a fast one. Just when I'd got it all tied up." He thought he heard Wilding reply, "You can say that again, sir – too damn fast!"' Melinda paused, and then said, 'You know, Primrose, just occasionally my Freddie can be quite astute and he was sure they were referring to Travers. He's convinced that there was more to their dismay than just the crash itself and that Travers' death had ruined some project . . . Frankly, if you ask me there was something not quite nice about that young man. I mean to say, what sort of person chews toffee at his mother's funeral, keeps checking his watch and then disappears before the final hymn? It's just not on.'

'How do you know it was toffee?' I asked with interest.

'Because Peggy Mountjoy was sitting next to him and a piece fell into her open handbag – she had been rummaging for collection money. Anyway, she was most put out as it stuck to her best lipstick. She's never forgiven him.'

'Well, it's too late now,' I replied. And making a hurried excuse I departed, pondering and intrigued.

When I reached home I was greeted effusively by Bouncer doubtless hoping for more chocolate. 'Two squares and that's your lot till Christmas,' I told him sternly. 'Just because you rescued the big policeman doesn't mean you'll get any more.'

He gobbled the chocolate and retired to his basket where he started to scrabble about. A moment later just as I was making a sandwich to take up to the studio, he jumped out and deposited something at my feet . . . No, not his usual offering of the grimy rubber ring, but a grimy mangled hat: Alice Markham's hat which I had scornfully thrown in the dustbin after our last encounter. I stared at the beastly thing and then at the dog who gave a roguish wag of his tail.

'It's no use, Bouncer,' I said crossly, 'if you think I am going to trade chocolate for that absurdity you can think again,' and shoved him into the garden to chivvy the cat. Before returning to the smell of paint and turpentine I hovered by the chinchillas' cage to address its occupants and to admire the jasmine bush. The day being warm I stood for a few moments savouring the jasmine scent and reviewing my conversation with Melinda.

Travers' fate was certainly a shock and I couldn't help dwelling (albeit briefly) on the awful details of his death. But I was also curious about Spikesy's words as overheard by Freddie. The former's testy comment did rather suggest that Travers was being investigated and his arrest imminent. This would certainly fit with Wilding's earlier remarks about Spikesy being on the trail of the sex traffickers' ringleader. And assuming Bullseye Bert had been right about Travers' part in Operation Tarts Galore then he could indeed have been the police target. No wonder the inspector had been looking sour! Death had snatched the glittering prize.

Later that evening I had a phone call from Charles Penlow wanting to chew the cud about Bouncer and MacManus. 'So he's not as daft as he looks,' Charles observed.

'Who, MacManus?' I asked.

Charles laughed and said that of the two he would back Bouncer any day. 'Puts Duster in the shade,' he said. 'My little chap would have sniffed the car, cocked his leg and walked away. Very dour is our Duster. He's not made for theatricals . . . But returning to the other dour one, have you heard about MacManus?'

I told him that as far as I was aware he was still bed-resting in the cottage hospital.

'Oh yes, he's doing that all right, but rumour has it that he may put in for early retirement – well, when I say rumour, I mean his wife. Agnes met the lady this afternoon and she was told, in strictest confidence, of course, that once they had taken their holiday in Clacton he was going to apply for "gardening leave" and take a long break. Apparently he feels he has been overdoing things . . . not that one would have noticed.' Charles gave a dry chuckle. 'Anyway, when Agnes asked if that would be difficult to arrange, Mrs M. said no, not at all and that the chief constable is all in favour. If you ask me I don't think we shall be seeing much more of our stalwart chief superintendent, he'll be too busy with his stamp album and tending those misshapen marrows. Oh, and incidentally, talking of which, I gather some prankster had nipped into his garden while he was otherwise engaged in the ditch and scratched unflattering words across their skins. Inspector Spikesy, I daresay. I gather there's a mutual antipathy!' Charles laughed again and wishing me a good evening, rang off.

For a few moments I stayed where I was, gazing thoughtfully at the now silent telephone, studying its dial as if it were some contraption from Bletchley. *Intriguing intelligence*, I mused . . . And then suddenly galvanized, I mounted the stairs to the studio where with renewed vigour did a pretty good job on a church spire and a sheep's hindquarters.

*   *   *

The next day, although not needing to, I went into Lewes to sniff the waters about Travers and to buy a newspaper less discreet than my usual *Lewes Tribune*, i.e. the *Sussex Rattler*. It was displayed prominently in the newsagent's and even from afar I could see that its front page had an article on the car crash. I bought two Mars bars and a box of matches, and casually included the *Rattler* which I stuffed into the bottom of my shopping basket. After all one didn't want to be *seen* with the thing! Thus equipped, I returned to the car, unwrapped the Mars bar and withdrew the newspaper. As I had hoped, the article was long and accompanied by a smudged photograph of the victim Aston Travers. SYCAMORE OF DEATH! its headline helpfully informed us. (Tree might have been snappier, but perhaps the writer was a keen arborist.)

'Aston Travers, son of the late Mrs Arthur Travers of Needham Court, Lewes, was the victim of a fatal motor accident in the early hours of Tuesday morning,' the item began. It went on to provide distasteful details of the deceased's exact position when found, and emphasized that his vehicle – 'an opulent sports car' – had been 'smashed to smithereens'. The writer observed that it was a tragic irony that the victim should have been killed in the vehicle bearing his own name. 'Such is fate's cruel levity,' he ponderously declared. However, less ponderous and with speculative relish, the article went on to query the reason for the driver's inordinate speed.

Was this simply the case of a reckless young man testing his nerve – youth at the wheel and pleasure at the helm? Alas, probably not. The *Rattler* believes there was a more sinister reason. We have it from a most reliable source [Bullseye Bert?] that the victim had been engaged in certain nefarious activities linked to the Bognor brothel, now thankfully closed down. Could it have been that in order to escape the long arm of the law (and with £3,000 stashed in the car boot – perhaps gains from his unseemly trade), Mr Travers had been bent on making a desperate getaway? This would explain why his car had collided with the chief superintendent's only half a mile distant – a collision which, had it not been for the valiant efforts of a raucous hound of impenetrable pedigree, could so easily have brought further tragedy. [No

mention of the hound's brilliant owner, I noted.] Another
source has confirmed that Mr Travers had a boat at Newhaven,
and could well have been on his way to the harbour, intending
to flee across the Channel. Currently recovering from his
ordeal, Chief Superintendent MacManus remains silent on
the matter. We send him our warmest sympathy. However,
keenly aware of our duty to alert readers to events of grave
public concern, the *Sussex Rattler* will leave no stone unturned
in exploring this strange and unfortunate matter.

I discarded the remains of the Mars bar, lit a cigarette and expelled
a whoosh of smoke. 'Pompous piffle,' I muttered. I glanced at
the article again. Yes, pompous certainly, but piffle? Not necessarily. Assuming Freddie Balfour wasn't deaf and that Bullseye
Bert (*pace* Ingaza) really did have insider knowledge, then the
article was spot on. But the writer seemed to assume that
MacManus had been involved in the chase. This I doubted as
according to his wife Tuesday was Rotary night, something he
rarely missed. He had probably been returning from there when
hit by the speeding Travers.

I was just collecting my thoughts and hoping that Charles had
been right about the man's retirement, when there was a sharp tap
on the window. I jumped. And then nearly jumped again when I
saw who it was: Inspector Spikesy. Oh my God, not another parking
offence – or was it worse, the delayed order to attend the police
station for more questions re the Markham case? With MacManus
indisposed perhaps Spikesy had been assigned the task. Mustering
a nervous smile, I wound down the window.

'Glad I've caught you, Miss Oughterard,' he began. 'I have a
request.' (Oh, here we go, I thought wearily, my smile wavering;
and waited for him to make some official pleasantry such as
asking me to kindly accompany him down to the station.) 'You
see,' he went on, 'my sister-in-law keeps sheep, Jacobs actually,
and she was wondering whether you might . . .'

I listened in dazed relief as he outlined his proposal. For that's
what it was: a proposal for me to paint the sheep as they wandered
about in the lee of a nearby church. The sister-in-law, who lived
locally, was fond of both sheep and church and was eager to
commission a large canvas to be hung in the bedroom. Apparently

she and her husband were insomniacs and felt that contemplating the rustic scene while quaffing Horlicks might induce slumber. (Personally I thought that a stiff brandy was a better bet, but it was hardly in my interests to say so.)

Well, compared with parrying tricky questions about the Markham woman's fateful visit, painting a few old sheep was a piece of cake – especially if the price was right. Thus I smiled brightly at the inspector and said it was a charming idea and that of course I would oblige. I added that as I had never painted little black Jacobs before it might be quite a challenge. 'Still,' I laughed gaily, 'one is always ready to learn!'

'As it happens, I have some snapshots,' he replied eagerly. 'Perhaps I could come and show you them and then we could also discuss terms.' (Oh yes, I am always happy to discuss terms!) Thus it was agreed that he should call on me the following evening, – 'Unless a burglary forbids.' He laughed.

When I got home I told Maurice and Bouncer that we had the prospect of another policeman's visit and that they should be on their best behaviour. Bouncer gave a genial bark but Maurice stared expressionlessly. I don't think he was impressed.

FORTY-TWO

The Primrose version

The inspector arrived promptly at six o'clock still in uniform and looking cheerful and dapper. When I asked if I could offer him an aperitif, to my relief he said that a small whisky would be most welcome. (Unlike MacManus who, despite later manifestations, would soberly request tea or water.) Not wishing to risk any disturbance, I had taken the precaution of putting both pets in the kitchen, thus ensuring I could attend to my visitor without fear of noise or feline rebuke.

He produced the sheep photographs and we got down to business – that is to say he informed me of the creatures' names e.g. Barnabus, Beatrice, Roxana and Robert. There were others too, including a Baloney, but frankly they all looked the same to me and it would only be when I applied the 'artist's eye' to the live animals that I would discern some difference. The church looked easy enough and vaguely familiar. I suspect I had painted it before – there are few in this part of Sussex that I haven't. For a Londoner Spikesy seemed to have an unusual interest in the sheep and I felt that if I played my cards right he too might commission a picture. Never pass up an opportunity for lolly, as Pa would counsel.

In fact, lolly was the next subject. And after a brisk negotiation we came to a most agreeable arrangement and it was decided that I should inspect the subjects on a date of mutual convenience. 'Hetty will be delighted,' Spikesy said, 'she hasn't slept properly for ages.' I found this a trifle unsettling – after all, one's reputation rests on being a painter not a sleep therapist. And besides, supposing it didn't work!

Given the recent Travers furore it seemed reasonable to make delicate enquiry. 'The press seems to have some notion that he had been involved in that Bognor business,' I said casually. 'It just goes to show how appearances can deceive: he seemed a rather nice young man . . .'

'No, he wasn't,' Spikesy said shortly, 'a very dodgy specimen.'

'Oh dear, and yet his mother was charming!' Well, mildly so.

Spikesy made no answer for a moment, contemplating his whisky. And then he murmured, 'Hmm. A funny business that – her death, I mean. Odd circumstances.'

I looked at him sharply. 'In what way?'

'Well, for one thing I gather the woman couldn't stand the cold and hated swimming. Seems an odd thing for a lady to do who doesn't like either – to go bathing all alone on that dangerous part of the coast. Strange when you come to think of it. I am surprised it wasn't checked out. Still, too late now.'

I seized my moment (after all, we all have to have one). '*Exactly*,' I said with barely concealed triumph while topping up his glass, 'just what I had thought. And she couldn't stand floral bathing caps either.'

He looked startled. 'What?'

I explained her aversion to such headgear.

He raised an eyebrow. 'That's quite a detective's nose you have, Miss Oughterard. Ever thought of joining the force? You could be useful!'

As it happens my nose *is* rather distinguished. And, inwardly preening, I gave a modest shrug and said it was just common sense, adding that I had mentioned my suspicions to the chief superintendent but he hadn't seemed interested.

In the middle of munching a Bath Oliver, Spikesy's response was indistinct but I thought I heard him mutter, 'That follows.'

Now that we were on the subject of MacManus I thought I would check if Charles Penlow was right about his long leave and the likelihood of retirement. So I asked if there was any truth in the rumour.

At this he looked slightly shifty and cleared his throat. 'Ah well, I'm not sure about a full retirement, but he will certainly be taking some long leave and that can sometimes be a prelude. I believe HQ are planning to reduce the quota of chief superintendents in this area. In fact . . .' He hesitated toying with a bit of biscuit and spilling crumbs on the carpet. 'In fact, as it happens, they have appointed me to take over in his absence.' He paused again and I saw a faint flush. 'Actually, Miss Oughterard, I have just been promoted. The news came through this afternoon . . . my rank is now chief inspector.'

'Oh, how splendid,' I cried, genuinely pleased. 'That is excellent news for Lewes, new brooms, etc. We must celebrate! Here, have some more whisky.'

'No, no,' he said hastily. 'Better not or I shall be demoted again!'

Despite being cheered by his news, I also felt nervous. Would this mean a sharper handling of the unsolved Markham murder? A more probing enquiry? Perhaps I should be asked to accompany him to the police station after all. Cautiously, I tried to sound him out on the matter, saying that I feared he would have an awful lot on his plate, not least the mysterious affair of the unfortunate Mrs Markham.

He replied that the case had been MacManus's pigeon not his, but obviously he would have to take a look at it. 'We can't let it go, of course, but temporarily at any rate it'll have to be shelved.

There's something very murky going on at Alfriston – a body in the Old Clergy House and the Eastbourne police are baffled. So that'll take immediate precedence . . . Mind you, by all accounts she was a strange woman and it's my belief the nephew did it – our friend Aston. She was probably cutting up rough about his prostitute racket and threatening to blow the gaff. You know the sort of thing – desperate straits need desperate remedies.' He gave a dry laugh.

I nodded. Yes, I knew exactly the sort of thing – as would my poor brother had he been alive. Or for that matter foolish Reginald Bewley.

Thrusting the sheep photos back in his briefcase, the chief inspector stood up to leave. But as I escorted him to the front door he paused, his eye fixed on something lying behind a vase on the hall table. I followed his gaze. Oh my God, it was the fake revolver Alice Markham had brandished! I recalled leaving it there after her eruptive exit and for some reason had never noticed or thought of it again.

'I say,' he exclaimed, 'fancy you having a toy gun like that. It's a very old make – quite a rarity, in fact. It's the sort of thing my small nephew would love. He's gun-mad at the moment.'

I emitted a silvery laugh. 'Er, yes, I won it in one of those absurd raffles ages ago. Can't think what it's doing there – it's no use to me. I tell you what, *Chief* Inspector, why don't you take it and give it to your little nephew. He might trade his sweets in return!'

'Well, if you are absolutely sure, Miss Oughterard, that would be most kind. It's always good to keep in with the young!' He gave a hearty laugh which I echoed. It's always good to keep in with the police.

I waved him goodbye from the drawing room window thinking of the gun in his pocket – doubtless smeared liberally with Alice Markham's fingerprints. Ah well, the child could add a few more for good measure.

After he had gone I sat a long time on the sofa staring into space. Honestly, the things one was put through! The silence was broken by an almighty thud against the kitchen door: the natives were getting restless.

*   *   *

Following a rather thoughtful supper I telephoned Nicholas Ingaza.

'I think the coast is clear,' I breathed.

'What?'

'We are off the hook!'

'Hmm, I don't know what hook you are hanging from, dear girl, but I am perfectly comfortable here, thank you,' the thin voice informed me.

'Oh, don't be so obtuse, Nicholas,' I said impatiently, 'you know perfectly well what I am talking about. We shan't have to worry about MacManus nosing into the Topping affair and resurrecting that whole Beachy Head business. He's in hospital and is going to apply for—'

'Early retirement.'

'You mean you *know*?' I felt deflated, indignant really. 'But how?' I barked.

He explained that Eric had had it from Bullseye Bert – 'such a handy snout,' he enthused – and who had also relayed news of Travers' death. Ingaza sighed and declared piously that good never came to those who transgressed.

'Oh, I don't know, you've always done all right,' I replied briskly.

'Haven't we *all*,' came the quick response.

I took a breath and, changing my tone into one of plaintive charm, said, 'As a matter of fact, Nicholas, in view of what I have been through recently I feel in need of a rest cure – I might take myself off to Baden-Baden, it could be most therapeutic.'

'Oh yes – back playing up again, is it?' he asked cynically.

'My back? Er no, just my nerves. I need to be soothed.'

'I seem to recall that the last time that necessity arose the cure was Sidecars in Nice at the Negresco . . . or was it Martinis in Menton? Something like that.'

'Yes, well, this time it's going to be bloody anything in Baden-Baden. So there!'

There was a pause, and then he said mildly, 'So I suppose you won't be around for my superlative lecture on art attribution? It's not far off now. Still, probably just as well – one less tiresome questioner to put in their place.'

I ignored that and instead suggested sweetly that once his talk was over he might like to join me in Baden-Baden. 'I

daresay you too could do with a rest, after all one doesn't get
any younger.'

'Join you in Baden-Baden? No fear, far too dangerous. With
your suspicious nose anything could happen!'

'In that case, I wonder if you could possibly accommodate—'

'The wild animals? I am sure Eric will be delighted, he's very
fond of . . . Oh, here he is now. I'll hand you over.'

A voice totally at odds with Ingaza's – loud, raucous and cheerful
– bellowed down the line. 'Wotcha, Prim! Long time, no hear!
How isya?'

I flinched, said I was very well and then asked diffidently if he
would like to take charge of Maurice and Bouncer for a brief spell
as he had once kindly done before.

'You bet! And so would Phyllis. She thinks a lot of you, Prim.
Says you'd done 'er a good turn the ovver day and she owes you
one. She'll come on her motorbike and fetch 'em. Leave it wiv
me. Toodle pip for now! His Nibs wants to speak again.'

It was quite a relief to be returned to Ingaza's reedy drawl.
'Such a stalwart chap,' he murmured. 'Now seriously, Primrose,
when you return from your *fortifying* rest cure we'll celebrate – go
on the razzle to the Old Schooner, toast the end of MacManus
and raise a glass to foolish Francis.' He chuckled and added,
'Probably turning in his grave, the dear boy!'

After he rang off I looked around the room and smiled. Yes,
turning in his grave and still chewing those awful humbugs, no
doubt . . . I looked up at Pa's portrait, and then at myself in the
mirror. What a pair he had produced!

FORTY-THREE

The Primrose version

I was just making a list of the clothes I would need for Baden-
Baden when the back doorbell rang. I went to answer, assuming
it was the butcher boy with the weekly lamb chops. Not at all.
To my surprise it was the diminutive figure of Mrs MacManus.

'I do apologize for not using the front door,' she twittered, 'but your cat was in the porch and I thought he looked a bit – well, you know – uhm, *threatening*. I'm afraid I am not too good with animals so thought it safer to come to the side. I hope you don't mind.'

'No, of course not,' I said in some puzzlement, and noting the slightly windswept appearance enquired if she had walked all the way from the town. She explained that she had – partly because she enjoyed a 'little constitutional' but also because her husband's car was being repaired and that in any case he was still recovering and thus incapable of driving anywhere.

'So tiresome!' she tutted. 'I mean, the other evening I could have missed my sewing class in Bognor. But I was determined to be there and took the bus – *not* a pleasant experience! And so you see,' she continued brightly, 'I've had to bring you these myself.' A large carrier bag was thrust at me and my spirits drooped for I could guess its contents.

Naturally I had to invite her in and my fears were confirmed as I looked glumly at the first title of the pile of books, *A Posy of Pictures*. I offered coffee and thanked her for the kind thought, and then nervously enquired if she had any more at home. To my relief she explained this was no longer the case as the Reverend Egge had just accepted the last few for the church fête. 'I did take them to that art gallery in Brighton near the sea front but the owner didn't seem very keen. In fact, it was he who suggested that you might like them. Naturally I told him you had already had the pick of the best, but he seemed to think you would be glad to have one or two more.'

'How thoughtful of Mr Ingaza,' I said with feeling. *Oh, the bastard!* And then an uneasy thought struck: supposing she expected to see 'the pick of the best' displayed on my bookshelves or lying idly on a coffee table (instead of languishing in the local rubbish dump)? Hmm, tricky. Oh well, if pressed I could always say they were in my studio at the top of the house. And, quickly changing the subject, I asked after her husband, murmuring sympathy about his accident.

'Oh, he's all right. You know what men are like – such babies at times!' She smiled sweetly but I thought I detected a note of irritation. Well, little wonder living with the tedious MacManus!

But then, still smiling, she added, 'Although as a matter of fact I rather doubt if it was an accident.'

I blinked. 'Really? But I thought he was hit by the speeding Travers man and knocked sideways – literally.'

'Yes, but that doesn't make it an accident. A mistake perhaps but not necessarily an accident.'

Oh, honestly! Was the woman a verbal pedant? I cleared my throat. 'Er, I'm sorry if I appear dense but I can't quite see the difference. I'm afraid I don't—'

'The crash itself was unlikely to have been accidental; the *mistake* was in not killing him . . . I fear Mr Travers was not as clever as he thought – or as deft. Probably took his foot off the throttle at the last moment.' To emphasize her point, Mrs MacManus gave a brisk nod, and then folding her hands in her lap, gazed out of the window – while I stared at her in shocked surprise.

'Do you mean to say that Aston Travers had deliberately tried to mow down your husband?'

She withdrew her gaze from the window. 'Well, yes, on the whole I think he did,' she said simply.

'Goodness! But why?'

She frowned and looked thoughtful. 'Because he hated him.' She paused fractionally. and then in a tone of mild apology murmured, 'And between you and me, Miss Oughterard, I fear that I may have been the cause of his action.' My shock must have shown for she added, 'Well, yes. You see, I think it was something I had said – about Alastair, I mean – and this may have put the idea in his head.'

I blinked, and then more than a little intrigued asked her to explain.

She gave a delicate cough. 'As a matter of fact, I said I could murder him.'

Even in my astonishment I could see her point, but other than lifting a quizzical eyebrow made no response.

'Naturally,' she went on, 'my words were a mere *façon de parler* and a little jest – Alastair can be so exasperating! – but I fear the remark may have set Travers thinking. Still, it's all over now and one will never know . . . And anyway, he missed.'

It may just have been my imagination, but I thought those

last words held a faint note of regret. Mechanically I offered her some more coffee, curious to learn how she had known Aston Travers. As I returned her cup, I suddenly recalled doing the same with my last unheralded visitor, Alice Markham. The present one occupied the same chair. But now no gun was in evidence, toy or otherwise, and at least the lack of car would spare any further assault on my driveway and gateposts. And besides, in contrast to the previous lady this one seemed marginally sane.

'Ah – so how was it you knew Mr Travers?' I enquired politely.

'It was his silver ostrich costume; some of the feathers had come off. I am a good seamstress and it didn't take a jiffy to fix.'

I closed my eyes, wondering if my hearing was defective. 'You see,' she continued, 'Alastair has always had a love of theatricals, particularly romping around as a pantomime bear. I think it gave relief from his police work. Personally it didn't appeal to me, but anything to wean him off those dreary Mongolian stamps. So for a little while I complied and played the part of Goldilocks. But you know I did get rather bored and then when my bunions started to play up I thought enough is enough and I told him he would have to find another partner.' She paused, and then lowering her voice, added, 'Besides, things started to become a trifle unsavoury – you know what men are – and I really felt I had nicer things to do of an evening.'

Vaguely I wondered what those nicer things were – carding wool? – but was too engrossed to enquire. Instead I asked how the problem had been resolved.

The small voice became quite animated as she explained that at first he had been shirty and accused her of being a killjoy, but that one day he had returned home all smiles and announced he had found the very person: a young man of similar thespian bent and who, having exceedingly long legs, specialized in dressing up as an ostrich.

'And this was Aston Travers?' I asked faintly.

She nodded and said she had first encountered Travers when she and MacManus had called at Needham Court some months previously to thank Elspeth for her large donation to the Police Benevolent Fund. They had been passing and stopped on the off-chance that the lady would be there. She was not, but the son was. 'Apparently he was down for the weekend and invited us in and offered sherry. I can't say I liked him particularly – rather condescending, if you know what I mean – but Alastair seemed to approve. Anyway, a few weeks later Alastair indicated that I could forget my role as Goldilocks as this Aston was keen on ostriches and in his spare moments found it amusing to dress up and engage in tomfoolery.'

I tried to keep a straight face and enquired soberly where such tomfoolery took place.

'Well, at first they used the spare bedroom, as we had used to, but I complained because the noise was too much – nothing but deafening thuds and loud growls. It was really annoying!' She pursed her lips in recollection. 'But fortunately Aston said he had found a better place – somewhere outside Lewes, I think, though I couldn't say where. Alastair muttered something about a drama group in one of the coastal towns – Worthing or Bognor or some such. I didn't bother to enquire. To be perfectly honest it was quite a relief to have some time to myself of an evening and not have to be constantly searching for his lost stamps or cooking those interminable marrows.'

As I listened to that whey-faced, grey, little woman I was reminded of the extraordinary ways in which some people choose to conduct their lives! However, what really intrigued me was her allusion to Aston's first crash not being an accident. Other than the lady's jocular *façon de parler*, what had prompted him to make an attack on MacManus? After all, it was Spikesy who had been on the case, not MacManus. In fact, MacManus had appeared quite indifferent, even hostile to the investigations – which given his brothel high jinks was hardly surprising.

'But why—' I began.

'Why do I think he wanted to kill Alastair? Because I believe he saw my husband as a threat. Alastair had begun to get bored with the bear antics and felt increasingly that such nonsense might reflect badly on him should it ever get about – people have such suspicious minds, don't you agree? – and so he started to distance himself from the young man, indeed began to show an active dislike. I fear he is not the most tactful.'

She could say that again! I thought acidly.

'And then when Mr Spikesy arrived and started to investigate that disgraceful place in Bognor and implicating Aston in all manner of dubious goings-on, Aston wrongly assumed that the whole thing was being directed by my husband. He was furious and actually had the nerve to telephone and told him to lay off – or else. Quite what that was supposed to mean I am not sure – doubtless the spreading of distasteful rumours or perhaps even a violent attack.' Mrs MacManus sniffed loudly, and in a tone of righteous satisfaction added, 'Well, the *or else* didn't work, did it? And as I always say, pride comes before a fall!' The smug face almost lit up.

I reflected on that last comment, thinking that in Travers' case it had been not so much a fall as an *elevation*. And in Francis's case – well while there had certainly been a spectacular *fall*, of pride there had been little evidence . . . However, such musings were interrupted by her next words.

'I expect you would like to know why I have so many art books,' she said brightly. Having seen the samples I didn't, but smiled obligingly. *Oh lord, when would she go?* 'You see, when I was a girl at school I was awfully good at drawing and was sure that one day I would become a famous artist. Silly really, but when you're young you have these fancies. So I started to collect helpful manuals, and what with one thing and another never bothered to get rid of them. Anyway, that fad was replaced by another – the combustion engine.'

She must have seen my startled expression, for she continued, 'Oh yes, it was motor cars that took my fancy, not the driving but their insides. I dearly wanted to become a lady mechanic and started to practise.' She tittered. 'Rather racy, really. I mean, can you imagine me flat on my back under a car chassis or bent double tinkering with its sparking plugs?'

'Er, no, not really,' I said, trying hard to conjure the vision.

She tittered again. 'But yes, that's what I used to do until I met Alastair. Gearboxes were my speciality. But brakes too – oh yes, I was a dab hand at those . . .' She smiled in happy reminiscence. And then the face clouded and she said something about never knowing what lay round the corner and that life was full of surprises. Yes, well, if MacManus had been the surprise round the corner then I could understand the rueful look.

*   *   *

When she had gone, which did eventually happen, I made some more coffee and sipped thoughtfully. From what she had been saying it seemed that Mrs MacManus had no idea of her husband's visits to the brothel and still assumed that his relationship with Travers had simply been a sort of quirky game enjoyed by over-grown schoolboys. Well, for her own sake one hoped the gullible woman would remain in ignorance . . .

But then as I continued to brood on our conversation and her surprising interest in car mechanics, my mind suddenly jolted and I began to wonder if she was as gullible as all that . . . or as innocent. It seemed that, unless the police diverted their interest in Operation Tarts Galore to the more anodyne antics of apple-scrumping schoolboys, Aston Travers had threat-ened to expose MacManus's ursine dalliance and penchant for whip-wielding ostriches – games which even without the brothel link would have made him a laughing stock and hardly helped his career. While his wife may not have suspected the whole truth, her view of Travers was less than positive: she had never liked him and latterly she had reason to fear him. He was dangerous: perhaps physically but definitely socially. Had the 'or else' preyed on her mind and had she done something about it? 'Brakes too, I was a dab hand at those,' she had laughed. The words chimed with others – Sergeant Wilding's comment as overheard by Freddie Balfour. 'And I don't suppose the dicey brakes helped,' he had said.

Oh lord! Surely the woman couldn't have tampered with them, could she? But if so, when, where? She had twittered something about having to go to Bognor on the bus for a sewing class. Was it likely that Aston had been in the habit of keeping his car there? In that car park belonging to the theatrical costumier's, perhaps? I thought of the nosy way she had reported seeing me and Bewley together a couple of times. Sharp eyes, sharp mind – did the woman know more than she was letting on?

I was gripped with a sudden excitement and, discarding my packing list, bounded to the telephone.

'Nicholas,' I gasped, 'I have it on good authority that the frightful Travers was the ostrich in the brothel photographs, and what's more I think that MacManus's wife may have screwed him up, i.e. fixed his brakes! The woman may seem all meek and mealy but I think she is dangerous. This needs pursuing, don't you agree?'

There was a sigh and a long pause. And then he said, 'Do you want my advice?'

'Yes,' I cried eagerly.

'Have a large gin and paint another sheep, you'll feel better.'

'But I—'

'Listen, Primrose – just because the Spikesy chap has endorsed your views of the Travers' drowning and you were spot on about Hubert Topping does not confer bloodhound status. Forget the MacManuses – he's dead wood anyway. Look after Number One, keep in with Spikesy and go to Baden-Baden tout suite! The change will do you good. Now there's a good girl . . . Oh, and if you come back too soon I'll charge you extra for dog food. Bysie-bye.'

The line went dead and I was left staring into space, or rather into the querulous eyes of Maurice. He emitted a tired mew not unlike Ingaza's sigh. I took the hint, picked up my list and dutifully went upstairs to pack.

EPILOGUE

The cat's view

B eing a self-effacing cat, I hardly like to mention my own part in Bouncer's madcap enterprise – but it has to be said that without my involvement and shrewd direction it would not have achieved the success it undoubtedly did. I suspect that lacking my presence it would have remained merely an amusing *divertissement* giving pleasure to the dog and annoyance to the policeman. As it is, due to my quick thinking the dog is now a local hero . . . and I have achieved that coveted distinction of CFE, Companion of the Feline Empire.

Yes, in this latter respect that rather inane tabby, Tootles, has been quite useful. An inveterate gossip, he quickly spread the word not only regarding my part in the marrow jaunt but also in the masterly rescue of the tiresome MacManus. Naturally such intelligence reached the ears of Sir Perivale Puss-Coley, who, after swift consultation with fellow big-wigs, conferred the distinguished honour.

The inaugural ceremony was conducted at midnight with all due pomp and caterwauling on the rooftops of the Anne of Cleeves house – a building much respected by Lewes humans. I was required to wear a cape of fish scales and mouse fur (rather smelly actually) but I am told I looked suitably patrician. After the ceremony Sir Perivale took me aside and said that although my rallying of Bouncer and the householders had been excellent, he rather wished that the object of our rescue had been less obnoxious. I explained that its aim had been to bring honour to my friend the shaggy dog, and that to this end MacManus had been a mere cypher. 'Ah most noble, most noble,' Sir P. purred, and urged me to share his haddock and cream – which naturally I did.

I have just learned that we are about to be guests in the Ingaza household again while our mistress swans off to foreign parts. My feelings are ambivalent. On the one paw I shall be subjected to the Brighton Type's tasteless jokes and his companion's bawling bonhomie. But on the other there will be the benefit of fresh fish, the whiff of catmint and ozone (as opposed to the scent of turpentine and wilting lilies), and long periods snoozing in the sun while the dog gallivants on the beach. Yes despite the drawbacks, on the whole it could be mildly congenial – and of course has the added bonus of being ferried to and fro on that *exhilarating* motorbike! A fur-raising experience, but which I have to admit I shall thoroughly enjoy. Bouncer is less keen as he says that last time it gave him a funny tummy. However, I have told him that since he has proved himself to be a dog of such valour he can easily weather a mere motorbike ride. 'Do you think so?' he asked anxiously. 'Indubitably,' I replied. That seemed to reassure him and he thumped his tail.

After all the praise that has been heaped on him, I was afraid it might go to his head and he would become insufferable. But I am glad to say that he is behaving well – irritating and boisterous of course but manageable. Well, moderately. In fact we have spent some merry times together baiting the chinchillas and playing tag in the garden of that big house where Bouncer went one night with P.O. – the night when he said he had been 'cat-knackered' and slept under the car leaving her to blunder about in the dark doing Cod knows what!

And regarding our mistress and her questionable life, from what I can discern things seem to have calmed down somewhat. (Though as with her late brother F.O. it doesn't do to be complacent.) I like to think that on our return from Brighton there may be a period of tranquillity . . . And let us hope the gatepost will be mended by then so I can return to my preferred place. In many ways, also like her brother, the Prim is dilatory in getting things done – except when she is pursuing some pet obsession, when she can become deadly! However, there are far worse owners around (I can think of several but being a CFE one is naturally discreet). Louis Lionheart's people seem couth and civilized – but one's judgements should not be hasty. Time will tell.

And talking of time, it is also time for me to make preparation for the rigours of Brighton and the Type's dubious company. Ah well, as I told Bouncer regarding the motorbike, increased status

confers strength. Armed with my CFE I am sure I shall take stoical
pleasure in our visit, and like our mistress return well braced to
keep a watchful eye on things.

The dog's view

Cor! It hasn't half been fun – lots of noise and racing about in
the town the other night and now everybody saying what a brave
boy I am! And I didn't even get the boot when I knocked the
big policeman's stretcher into the mud – and with him on it. Ho!
Ho! And it's not just our mistress and her cronies who have been
nice but all the local dogs and cats too. 'Bouncer's a JOLLY
GOOD fellow,' they cry. Mind you, Maurice was very handy
with the marrows and it was him who said we should make a
din and wake the humans. The cat is good at working behind
the scenes, it's his FOR TEA. But Bouncer was the BIG ONE
and who made the most noise.

'Smatter of fact, the cat is pretty chuffed as well because he
has been given some medal or other. It's called CFE. I think that
means Cod For Ever though I could be wrong. Anyway, he's very
pleased with it and goes about purring his head off – and that
doesn't happen often! I thought at first it might make him go all
hoity-toity (more than usually, I mean) but he is being very decent
and we've played some good games. And NOW we are off to the
seaside where old Gaza and Erk live. I liked it there last time but
the only snag is the motor thing that the girl brought us back on.
Sort of churns you up. But Maurice says it's all a question of head
over gut and that with my stout nerve I'll rise above it. Not quite
sure what he means by that . . . Will I fly through the air doing
the dog paddle? ON VERA as Maurice says, leastways I think
that's what he says. (Can't think who Vera's supposed to be.)

The Prim's off to la-la land again. I wonder if her legs will be
all brown when she gets back like last time. Ah well, we'll on
vera that as well. But meantime I must sort out my best bones for
Brighton. No fleas on old Bouncer!

Lightning Source UK Ltd.
Milton Keynes UK
UKHW010752081220
374816UK00001B/81